This Space Between Us

Rebecca Carenzo

Copyright © 2013 Rebecca Carenzo
All rights reserved.
ISBN: 1492165883
ISBN-13: 978-1492165880

DEDICATION

To God, who created my spark.
To Nick, who fanned the flame.
And to Ryan, who set me ablaze.

CONTENTS

Acknowledgments	I
Chapter 1	1
Chapter 2	10
Chapter 3	21
Chapter 4	32
Chapter 5	43
Chapter 6	56
Chapter 7	68
Chapter 8	83
Chapter 9	95
Chapter 10	102
Chapter 11	112
Chapter 12	123
Chapter 13	139
Chapter 14	153

CONTENTS

Chapter 15	162
Chapter 16	175
Chapter 17	187
Chapter 18	193
Chapter 19	199
Chapter 20	208
Chapter 21	224
Chapter 22	235
Chapter 23	240

ACKNOWLEDGMENTS

Writing a novel is a marathon, not a sprint. Especially for me. This book was many years in the making from concept (which came to me when I awoke from a dream) to completion (which was done with a sleeping baby in the next room and the letter 'o' missing from my keyboard). There were times, for months on end, when I did not pen a single stroke and my husband Nick would casually ask, "What's going on with your book?" Hint taken. He was my first reader and often a sounding board for my "next move" in the story. His tremendous listening skills and honest perspective gave me an ear for my thoughts which at times, desperately needed to leave my head. Thank you.

When I was nine I wrote my first poem and declared that I wanted to be a writer. Evidently my grandmother, Ruth DeLuca, took me seriously because she promptly signed me up for a writing class and bought me journals in every color imaginable. Luckily she is not only a wonderful encourager but also a cheap and thorough proofreader. Without her, this book would be full of misspellings, omissions, and nonsense of every kind. Thank you.

My dad and stepmom, Ralph and Vicki DeLuca, have supported me emotionally, physically and financially in every decision of my life and taught me that a dream mixed with talent should never be wasted. Here is my dream, thank you for helping me realize it.

Those who also deserve special thanks are: my aunt, Amy DeLuca, who fostered my love of reading and imagination from a young age; my sister, Stacey DeLuca, who provided childhood memories that inspired some of the situations in this story; my fellow writer, Cheryl DeLuca, whose constant cheerleading spurred me on and helped me know I wasn't alone in my manuscript madness; my grampa and great gram, Ralph DeLuca and Barbara Metivier, whose passing got me to thinking about what-lies-after; my cousin and lifelong friend, Heather Vail; The DeLucas who are the best family anyone could ever hope for; The Carenzos, my in-laws who never make me dread a holiday; Jean Lawler, Janet Powers, Conall Ryan, Gene Molter, and Dianne Morr, thank you all for the knowledge that you freely and generously gave to guide me in the publishing process; and finally to my son, Ryan, I finished this book so that someday you could be proud of me and hopefully fulfill a dream of your own. I love you.

"Life is full of missed opportunities."
~L.M. Montgomery

CHAPTER 1

"I need to tell you something," I said, gulping hard.

My heart's beating a thousand times a minute in the space between my lungs and my flesh. The deafening sound of the pounding is all I can hear; it sounds like the march of a protest, a protest against being trapped within its possessor while desperately wanting to escape to its complement. I am aware now that my heart is simultaneously emotion and substance. My mind whirls thoughts around my brain at the speed of a racehorse who is desperate to beat a rival. Every breath within me threatens suffocation but won't escape my mouth. My tongue feels chalky and my face is stiff as I try to form the words I've wanted to speak for so long.

"What is it? What do you need to tell me?" Sara asks.

I was trying to tell her the very thing that I hadn't been able to for the past seven years. I was trying to tell her that I purposely lingered my hand while opening doors for her so that I could feel a brush of her fingers on mine. I was trying to tell her that since the moment I knew she existed, nothing else did. I was trying to tell her that our close contact over the years had tortured my body and mind. I had tried so many times to say all of this and more to the girl I love, but the words never seemed to come when I needed them. Now today, when I finally had the words poised to speak on the edge of my tongue, fear was holding me back; fear of being rebuked for waiting until now, the night before her wedding, to tell her that Christian, my best friend, is not the one she is meant to spend her life with. She is meant to spend her life with me.

She sinks her olive toned hands deep into her jean pockets, rocking up and down on her tiptoes, like she is expecting to hear an exciting and juicy secret from me, her trusted friend.

"Is it about tomorrow? The wedding?" she asks.

"Um...yes, it is. You see," I begin to say.

I take a deep, cautious breath before going any further. Darting my dark brown eyes up and sideways, I try to avoid direct contact with hers. Desire and consequence wrestle fiercely within me. I am starting to wonder if I am being sensible. Could it be that fate has just deemed us never to be together and I should leave it at that? She flicks her chestnut hair, which is wavy and soft tonight, and I am distracted from my thoughts. The strands tickle the tops of her shoulders as she tucks the left side behind her ear.

"So, what is it? Come on Sam you're killing me here."

Her toothy smile overpowers every other feature on her sun-kissed face as she waits on my words. I think about the time she confessed to me that her perfect teeth were the result of two years of torturous braces when she was in middle school. I felt like we knew everything about each other, except for the one thing she didn't know about me: how much I still loved her.

"Are you really, really sure you want to know?" I ask.

"I'm really, really one-hundred-percent-triple-sure," she says.

Fighting through the fear of what I have to say, I try to think hard on memories of her that I treasure, hoping they will be a spark of hope to summon forth my bravery. Right away, I easily recall the summer afternoon we met and the weeks that followed, when every possible life path was laid out before us; the time in life when it would have been easy to choose each other, with no complication or heartache involved for anyone else. But that was the problem, there *was* someone else and that someone else was the one person, besides Sara, who I never wanted to hurt. Almost all the memories I shared with her, seemed to be tied up with memories of Christian as well; memories which pushed themselves forward to be recognized before I dared to speak another word.

∞

I was only sixteen the summer I met her. At the time, I felt I knew a great deal about the world around me; looking back, I now know otherwise. I was still sharing a bedroom with my brother Mark that sizzling New Hampshire summer in 1986 and the close quarters were becoming increasingly bothersome. Three years age difference had never seemed like much before I turned sixteen. Now two teenagers, who were practically worlds apart, were forced to co-exist behind the same closed door. I attended Merrimack Valley High, land of endless hallways, double-stacked lockers and debate clubs, while Mark remained on the bottom rung of the pre-teen food chain at East Peak Middle School. Since there wasn't a single nook under our parents' roof where I could achieve privacy, I spent most of my time over at Christian's house.

Christian and I were constant companions since the day in first grade when we had raced side by side on the monkey bars the entire recess period. We were almost too alike as children, differing only in the degree of our recklessness. Christian always had to push the rules as far as they would bend, and when they snapped, I was there to bail him out with a believable alibi. Like Hamlet and Laertes, we were a perfect foil to the other's folly; it was an equal relationship in every part. No matter what faults Christian displayed, he could be counted on to give me as much self-esteem as I needed at any given moment. As it turned out, the summer I was sixteen, self-esteem was what I needed a lot of.

Having been demoted to "friend" status by my then-girlfriend, I had lacked a date for every outing that school year. By the time summer started I had already stood on the sidelines at two parties and played as a single instead of a team on Saturday nights, much to the detriment of my bowling average. Any prospect of a new girlfriend looked doubtful, as I watched the pimples on my face spreading into crop circle like patterns. Nevertheless, Christian vowed to have me on the cover of every teen magazine by the time summer was over, with the headline, "No One's Finer than Christian Fine, except Sam Davs!". Ok, so maybe that was an unattainable goal, but at that point I was more than willing to put my love life in his hands. After all, he had three girlfriends his sophomore year alone. Christian's last steady girl Emily had been the victim of the "I-want-to-be-free-for-the-summer" speech. Definitely not Oscar-worthy parting words but it seemed to suit his purpose just fine, and my purpose for that matter, since now I would have the full attention of my best friend for the next three months. The girls at school had given him the reputation of being an easy-going, yet non-committal type of guy. Of the last nine girls he dated, none had lasted longer than six months. But even that didn't stop them from pursuing him, probably hoping to hold his attention a little longer than the last girl had.

Of course, that was all part of the magnetism that was Christian; he just seemed to attract all the right people. Black tousled locks and shockingly green peepers aside, Christian gave off an air of confidence that most people could not resist. On many occasions, I felt grateful to be his pal. I even let it slip out-loud once that I thought so. We had both been invited to go with our classmate Justin and his parents on their boat for the weekend. I knew I had only been extended an invitation because I was attached at the hip with Christian, who knew Justin from our school's golf team.

"Wow, I didn't realize one of the perks of being your best friend was weekend getaways on a yacht! I'm a lucky guy to know you!" I said, giving Christian a hearty slap on his shoulder when he told me about the planned excursion.

Contrary to what I expected, my kind words hadn't exactly been accepted with gusto.

"Oh, *you're* the lucky one, are ya? HA!" Christian belted in his most colorful tone. "Who was it then that saved my life when I was nine? I need to meet *that* guy; wouldn't it be lucky to be his best friend?"

Christian always exaggerated that story. I hadn't actually saved his life. But I guess when I think about it, I did come pretty close. We had been the only two left on the playground while camping one weekend with Christian's father. We stayed at this campground near Mt. Washington a few times a season and knew our way around the fishing ponds and pine trails there well. So, we were given a reasonable amount of freedom to ramble around on our bikes all day on the dirt roads. The playground was situated at one end of an expansive safari field where there were three or four campers speckled about on the lawn. We made frequent stops there to jump on the old pillar stones which were lined up by size, tall to short, and run in and out of the tractor tires which wobbled from being forced halfway into the soft ground. Mr. Stanley Fine's 1973 orange and white striped RV with matching canopy was parked on the other end of the trodden grass field which was barely within our eye sight, and certainly not within earshot of Christian's old man.

Our current amusement had been *Godzilla Attacks*, a game we invented which required a lot of imagination and fabricated fear to play. We fantasized that the slimy, overgrown reptile was walking above our heads trying to sniff out our presence with his long, rapid-firing tongue. The solid concrete tunnels in the play area, which were just big enough for young kids to hide in, really added a realistic atmosphere to our game.

"I can hear his footsteps! Put your ear to the ground Christian, listen!" I yelled out to my pal.

"Oh yeah, I can hear it too!" he said, kneeling on the bare grass. "We better take cover before it's too late. Ahhhh!" Christian screamed. He took off running into the aged tunnel at top speed, then suddenly his yell stopped. I wondered if he was trying to pretend that he had been captured by the bad guy.

"Christian! No! Don't let him take you!"
There was no reply.
"Christian? Did Godzilla get you?!" I called out.
Still nothing.

I walked over to the entrance of the tunnel expecting to see a dramatic Christian huddled in the corner in fright. Instead, my eyes saw my friend's motionless figure on the ground, blood trickling down his face. I bolted to the spot where his unresponsive body lay. Directly above the ground where Christian had fallen was broken cement which had chipped away from its solid frame. I deduced from the evidence that he must have run head first into the cracked area.

"Christian?" I whispered.

Although I was trying to stay calm, my shaking voice gave away the fact that I was in total panic mode. I gently shook his left arm in hopes that some action might stir him to awaken, but it didn't help. He was out cold. Time was passing quickly while I tried to figure out what to do next. I wanted to run across the field and get Mr. Fine, but I worried that Christian would wake up disoriented and I wouldn't be around. He might be scared and even cry if he found himself alone in a tunnel with blood on his face. No, I realized I couldn't leave him like that. Finally, I settled on what I should do.

"Chris, if you can hear me, I'm taking you to Pop, everything will be ok." I said it so bravely, I almost convinced myself.

At that moment, it was a very fortunate thing that Christian was only slightly taller and heavier than me because I hoisted his limp arms in a lock with mine and proceeded to drag my unconscious friend out of the tunnel and into the already dimming light of the fading day. The distance between me and the RV seemed much longer now, as I was exiting the tunnel, than when I had gone in it.

"HELP...Anybody!" I called. My small voice was carried away by the mountain wind.

Realizing there was no one who could hear me, I continued my arduous journey across the field. I made a habit of stopping every few steps to reposition my arms and check on my still-quiet friend. The few trailers I passed must have been unoccupied since no one emerged to check on the strange scene outside their door.

"Is anyone here? My friend is hurt, please help us!" I yelled, as I trudged along, stooped over and walking backwards toward campsite B-11 where we had left Christian's dad earlier in the day.

About halfway across the field, I felt movement in the once lifeless arms of my friend and at that same moment I noticed a male figure coming at us from the direction of our campsite.

"Uhhhh," Christian moaned, barely audible; it was the first sound that he had made in five minutes.

"Kids? What's going on?"

I looked up and the man across the field was getting closer now and picking up speed as he ran toward us. His face came into view and I realized it was Mr. Fine; Christian turned his wounded head to see his father, whose expression quickly turned from confusion to worry as the blood came into sight.

"Sam, what the heck happened? Is he ok?" he demanded at me.

"I don't know, we were just playing and he ran into the tunnel and then I found him lying there like this," I said, pointing first to the play area and then down at Christian's defeated looking body.

"Let's get him back to the campsite first, to assess the damage. Don't worry boys, blood doesn't always mean it's bad," said a stoic Mr. Fine, effortlessly swooping down and picking up Christian into his arms like a bear cub being scooped up by the scruff. He was obviously trying to keep the mood calm.

The adrenaline I just felt was starting to subside as I realized that there was now a grownup in control of the daunting situation. I replaced the look of fright that I felt on my face with a can-do expression and an attitude to match. We all hurried back to the camper. Upon wiping away the dirt and blood from his face, the source of the wound became known. Unfortunately it wasn't just the bump or scrape that we were hoping it would be; on the top front of Christian's head was a two inch long by one inch wide hanging flap of skin that resembled the beginning of a tribal scalping. Mr. Fine's eye widened and he gulped hard as he realized the extent of his son's injury.

"Sam, hold this bandage on here, just like this." He demonstrated with an uneven hand.

I nodded quickly and took over the unpleasant duty. Even with the bandage in place, there was a lot of blood coming fast and too much loose skin to ignore.

"I'm going to run down to the main office - you hear me Sam?" he asked. "I am going to run. I will be right back. I'm going to have them call an ambulance and take him to the hospital. You have two important jobs, hold the bandage were it is and don't let him fall asleep. OK?"

I was listening intently and gave a quick nod in recognition.

"Do not let him fall asleep," he said slowly so that I would remember. And with that, Mr. Fine bolted out of the camper, staying true to his word that he would run.

My arm was tingling as I held the white cotton gauze in place just as I had been instructed to do. Christian's eyes were already starting to close and his father had only been gone two minutes. I jolted him back awake.

"You have to stay awake. Your dad will be back really soon. He doesn't want you to fall asleep."

"Huh? Yeah...alright," he muttered.

"At least Godzilla didn't get you," I half-laughed. I didn't feel like joking at all but I had to think of a way to keep him awake until an adult arrived.

"Yeah, I heard he has nasty breath," Christian whispered. His voice sounded weak and lazy but at least he was talking.

I was able to keep Christian entertained, with rude body humor and a recounting of the giant fish he had seen leaping in the frog pond, for the next five minutes or so until his father returned. However, by then Christian was looking very pale and slurring his words.

"The ambulance will be here in no time now," his father assured, as he applied a cool cloth to the nape of his son's neck and rubbed his back while we waited for what seemed like an eternity for the ambulance to arrive.

Hearing the blaring sound of the sirens and the crunching tires over the gravel road, we ran out to discover that every person in the lower half of the campground was out there as well. Everyone watched with concerned eyes as Christian was carried into the vehicle on a stretcher.

When we got to Saint Mary's Hospital, we were rushed right into the ER, past the rows of waiting room seats, into a private space where the doctors could assess him. Twelve stitches, four hours and some extra strength Tylenol later, Christian was able to walk on his own. The stitches hadn't taken very long but the doctors wanted him to stay for a couple hours for observation to check for signs of a concussion. Mr. Fine was told to wake him every hour to make sure that he didn't drift into a potentially dangerous deep sleep.

By the time we started our journey back to the campground, all our eyes were drooping in Huckleberry Hound fashion as we struggled to fend off sleep until we reached our soft bunks. I laid down next to Christian and woke up every hour with his dad to make sure that he was ok.

"I wish I had such a true friend," Mr. Fine commented as he watched me get up for the third time.

Listening to Christian tell this story (and he told it to any willing-body he could find), you would think I had pulled him out of a burning high rise building, given him CPR, and performed a field tracheotomy, all without breaking a sweat. I had heard the recollection so many times now that I barely noticed the dramatics and variations Christian had attached to it over the years. I think the only thing that remained consistent each time it was told was the shade of bashful red that my cheeks turned when Christian concluded with, "...there's no one else who could've saved my life that day, only my Sammy."

CHAPTER 2

At the start of the summer of 1986, the weather was all anyone could talk about in my small town. As New Hampshirites we were accustomed to refreshing breezes and cool mountain air, so the arrival of ninety degree days in early June took everyone off guard. By the end of the month, when school finally let out, I was more than happy to be freed from the sweaty, stifling classrooms.

Christian and I already had our learner's permits for a while, as did almost everyone else in eleventh grade. My mom had emphatically stated that she was too nervous to teach me, so I had been left at the mercy of my father for driving lessons. Sporadic spins around the block (interjected with sharp and biting commentary from the passenger seat) whenever my father had the time to spare, summed up my experience behind the wheel. The novelty of driving with adult supervision had worn off months ago and I was eager for the next step; the real, hard, plastic driver's license that every teenager is promised when they turn sixteen and a half.

Christian was slated to take his driving test in just a few weeks. He had been to driving school and practiced nightly with his mom so he was more than prepared to be a solo driver. I wasn't even eligible for my license until October since my birthday was a few months after his. Therefore I was totally reliant on Christian for my summer vehicular freedom. His knowledge of turn signals, passing lanes, and pedestrian rights were now of utmost importance. I swore to help him study three times a week until test day arrived on July fifteenth. I pictured him breezing through the road test as the instructor directed him into various complicated situations, passing with flying colors, then driving to pick me up in a new open-topped red convertible. Cranking Van Halen over the radio, we would make our way to the lake to swim in the fresh water until our fingers wrinkled, then cruise to the drive-in to scope out girls and catch the latest horror flick. In my mind, the summer was planned perfectly and perfectly wonderful.

The remainder of June, following our last day of school, was spent at Christian's house scheming elaborate plans on how we could earn cash to buy a car. During the school year, money had been but a fleeting thought waving a salutation as it passed through our minds, now not having enough, had become a roadblock to realizing our dreams. Reality hit when Christian's mom, Ms. Katrina Fine, took us to the local auto outlet to check out his car buying options. She brought along an instant camera so that she could take pictures to show Christian's father, whom she had been separated from for a year but still encouraged Christian to include in everything. I'm not sure if it had been Christian or me who took his parents' separation harder. I was still fond of both of them and sometimes it was hard not to take sides in their disagreements, which they always managed to put Christian in the middle of. I was hoping that his choice of car would not ignite a new argument between them.

Upon arrival at the lot, we rushed over to the new model Fords and Chevy's with a thrill. But the excitement quickly faded when we were greeted by the huge price stickers that glared unsympathetically at us like an IRS taxman at an audit. We quickly came to the realization that our meager earnings as a paper boy (me) and a dishwasher (him) did not pull in quite enough weekly profit to purchase such a fantastic vehicle. The convertible of our fantasy was now as distant as the moon. The middle-aged salesman must have noticed our disappointment and thin wallets because he promptly ushered us to the used car section.

"Check out these cars. Now *these* are some real beauties!" he exclaimed, patting the hood of the closest pre-owned.

"Yea, these are real...great," Christian said rolling his eyes. His mother poked him in the ribs with her elbow.

"These are just fine, thank you," she said. "We'll just need a moment to browse."

"You nice people take your time looking. I will be right here if you have any questions."

In truth, the cars that now lay before us resembled something of an ugly stepsister to the candy-apple-red Corvettes we had just seen. We browsed the previously owned section for what seemed like hours, finding a flaw in every car on the lot.

"Ma, I'm roasting over here. Maybe we should look somewhere else," Christian said.

For once Christian's whining had some merit, the sun was concentrating so hard on the open concrete lot that we were dragging our feet to walk. Even the salesman, who I'm sure would normally wheel and deal all day, grabbed at his collar in annoyance at our slow pace.

"How about this one? You haven't even given it a good look and I think it's very nice," Ms. Fine said.

I turned around to see a compact but well cared for automobile that we had overlooked. The seat belts were slow retracting and the salesman said it needed new brakes, but to us it was the best looker on the lot and the stereo cranked.

"Not bad. I could see myself behind the wheel," said Christian.

Ms. Fine lifted her sunglasses and read the bright orange sticker on the hatchback's passenger door aloud, "$1400– One Owner, Great Condition, Low Mileage. I would think a reasonable, good looking man like you could do better on the price than that. Couldn't you?" she asked, smiling at the salesman.

"Let's see," he said scratching the back of head and giving the car a once-over with his eyes. "I probably could do a *little* better."

"How about $900," Ms. Fine said.

"$900? No, I couldn't do $900. I wouldn't make the boss a penny off it if I did that. The absolute lowest I could go would be $1050."

"Can I tell you something Mr…I'm sorry I didn't catch your name."

"Rone."

"Mr. Rone. Can I tell you something, personal?" Ms. Fine asked, leaning in toward him.

He nodded.

"I am a single mother of a teenage boy who is desperate to have his first car. I don't make much money. I try to give him what I can, but it's not a lot. Just for once I would love to make his dream come true and the only way I can do that is if you sell me this car for $1000. Please Mr. Rone, could you do that for me?"

The salesman had been leaning in so close that some of Ms. Fine's Maybelline blush had rubbed off on his cheek.

"I would love to do that for you and if it was in my power I would, but I'll have to get my manager in on this one," he said, turning to walk back to the building.

We waited a few minutes as the two men talked. Mr. Rone motioned over at us and the dealership's portly head of sales manager glanced in our direction. He took one look at Ms. Fine, no doubt zeroing in on her tight blouse, and emerged from the sales office. He walked up to her with his hand outstretched.

"Deal," he said.

"YES!" we exclaimed in unison, exchanging our own deal closer – a high five.

We settled our hopes and dreams on a gently used 1976 blue Honda Accord. Convertible or not, any car could get you where you wanted to go, and a month before road test day wasn't the time to start getting picky.

Ms. Fine plunked down $500 as a deposit, on the desk of the smitten sales manager.

"We, or should I say – he," she said, pointing directly at Christian; "will pay the rest of the balance when he takes the car off the lot in a few weeks."

Christian and his mother had a prior understanding that she would pay half the amount of his first car and he would pay the rest. A little give and a little take was Ms. Fine's way. She could have paid the entire balance had she wanted to, but she told Christian that he would feel more pride of ownership if he helped purchase his own car. I liked her immensely, even at times, more than my own mother who preferred a sort of hands-off approach to raising children.

"I'll just put a big, fat SOLD sign on the windshield then. But, if you don't come in by the twentieth next month I'll have to put it back up for sale," said the manager, who we now came to know as Big Al. He slouched backwards into his easy chair.

"Not a problem," remarked Ms. Fine with a polite smile; "believe me, this car is top priority for these boys, I wouldn't be surprised if you had your money early. Thank you very much for your time today," she added with a nod.

"No, no, thank you," said Big Al, pushing himself to his feet. "I hope very much to make *your* acquaintance again, ma'am," he said in a breathy, labored voice.

He extended his sweaty hand once more to her as a parting gesture. Ms. Fine smiled and politely shook it, then made a beeline for the door. We followed behind, grinning from ear to ear.

"Thank you so much ma. I can't believe I have my own car! This is so mint!"

"What do you know? My kid actually remembers the good manners I taught him. You're very welcome. Just don't forget me when you are off gallivanting around town in your new car and your poor mother is home all alone," she said in a melodramatic voice as she pressed the back of her hand to her forehead.

She shot me a wink over Christian's shoulder as he gave her a quick hug. I suppressed a laugh behind the smile that I returned to her.

"I'm gonna get in the car and blast the A.C. before my pumps melt into the asphalt. You guys ready to go?"

"Just one more thing, we'll be right there," said Christian. We ran off to snap a few camera shots of our new four-wheeled blue baby for Christian's dad to see and maybe some of our friends too.

By the next day, our celebratory mood started to mix with anxiety as the looming deadline of paying off the Honda weighed heavily on our minds. We sat down with a pad and paper at Christian's kitchen table and began to brainstorm. Neither of us liked our current jobs, mostly because we had opposite schedules. I worked mornings and Christian worked nights which didn't leave much time for cruising in between shifts. Ms. Fine suggested applying for jobs at the same place.

"Wouldn't be too tough making sundaes at the ice cream place, at least you'd get to see your friends when they came in. Or how about the grocery store, stocking shelves?" she said, reaching in the cupboard for the powdered Tang.

"Ma, we don't want to waste our summer at some stupid job like that. The managers at those places always take advantage of teenagers, you tell them you only want fifteen hours and then they give you more, or you tell them you can only work weekdays and they put you on the schedule for the weekends. I am not spending my summer like that."

"Excuse me. I didn't realize," she said with a grimace.

As we continued to contemplate around a mess of crumpled paper and empty soda bottles, the aroma of fresh cut grass began to waft in through the A.C. vents.

"Don't ya just love that smell?" Ms. Fine asked.

In fact, I did love that smell. I was always eager to help my dad cut the grass on Saturday mornings, it was the only chore I didn't mind doing.

"Are you thinking what I'm thinking?" I asked Christian.

He nodded. Unbeknownst to her, Ms. Fine had just given us the idea we had been searching the whole day for.

"We can mow lawns!" Christian said.

Mowing lawns was big business in the heat of the summer months, and it could be done in the afternoon, which left mornings open for sleeping in and nights open for having fun. We just needed to figure out if it would be profitable enough. I sat down to do the math.

"Ok, so with our combined savings from birthdays and jobs, together we already have $150 saved in the bank. That only leaves $400 to be made in four weeks. If we charge $10 a lawn, we only need to mow forty lawns between now and then. The grass will grow fast, so we really only have to find ten solid people who want their grass cut once a week," I said.

Christian looked at me as if it all made perfect sense and said, "No problem."

When I got home, convincing my parents to let us use the lawn mowers was easy; I guess my father was glad to see me taking some initiative at making money.

"That's what we Davs do Sam, we work hard with our own two hands and don't make excuses for our failures. You just can't be afraid to take the first step," he told me as he wheeled the pull-start mower out of the garage.

He then proceeded to give me a half hour demonstration on how to use it properly even though I had already used the thing a hundred times before. I think it was just an excuse to give me a lecture on responsibility. My friends had always been afraid of my father and it was no wonder why; at 6'2" his height made his foreboding and he had just enough weight on his bones to back his mouth up.

I had leveled off this year at 5'7", falling right in between my father's massive stature and my mother's petite 5'2" frame. I was content because I was taller than the girls in my class but at the same time I wouldn't have minded having a few more inches on the guys. I could see my brother growing into a mini-version of my father and I sometimes wondered how different my life might have been if I had gotten his commanding genetic traits as well. Instead, I was the perfect blend of my two parents, having traits of both but resembling neither; I think my non-identity with either of them contributed to my feelings of being the outsider of the family.

"I expect this to be in the same condition when I get it back as when I gave it to you," my father said, finally concluding his tutorial.

"Dad, we aren't going to play around with it. This is a real business. We're going to take good care of everything," I assured him.

"Fair enough. But I expect that if anything does get broken, your business will be paying to get it fixed."

"Yes, dad."

With the rules firmly laid out and our equipment all set to go, we went about the task of knocking on the doors of our neighbors, asking who might want some help with their lawn. The older folks were no trouble to convince, they were glad to have some help and company come by once a week. We were also able to sign up a few single mothers who didn't want to be bothered with pushing around a heavy mower; one had just moved to the neighborhood and was still unloading boxes when we arrived. We helped her move some heavy furniture and she returned the favor with a $10 tip and a pledge to get her lawn mown regularly. When all was said and done, we had eight clients lined up as weeklies and another who signed on for a one time mowing when he would be away on business. Despite Christian's smooth talking, there wasn't anyone else in the neighborhood that he could convince to sign on with us, so we ended up just short of our weekly goal. Feeling defeated, we sulked back to Christian's house and mulled our deficit over a glass of lemonade. Ms. Fine heard our grumbles and casually chimed in.

"I know someone else that needs help with their lawn."

"You do?! Who?" Christian asked, straightening up in his chair.

"Me," she replied with a smirk. "In case you haven't noticed *Mr. Green Thumb*, there is a jungle growing right outside your own door. I can't be the only one on the block with an unruly lawn this summer." She paused. "It *is* a pretty large yard though and will probably take you twice the time, so, to be fair, I am willing to pay $20, as long as it's kept up once a week of course. I want everyone to have yard-envy of me. You think you could handle a job that big?" she asked, glancing at us over the rim of her sweating glass of ice and lemonade.

"Yeah, that would be awesome! Thanks Ms. F!" I replied before Christian had the chance to.

"That'll even out to what we wanted to have by next month. Then anything we make after that can be used for gas money and the movies and stuff," Christian said with renewed optimism.

The lemonade in my glass suddenly tasted a little sweeter as I greedily gulped the last of it and put pen to paper to write out our weekly customer list.

For the next two weeks we worked and studied driver's manuals with fervor. Each RMV regulation and blade of grass blended into the next. We settled into a compatible working routine. We muscled through the thick tufts of crabgrass and skimmed over the thinning areas. We gave easy smiles to our elderly clients who peeked out the windows; accepted sodas from the single moms who checked on us between laundry loads; oiled our mower blades at the end of the day and filled up on gasoline twice a week. Other than having to work through the perspiration caused by the noon sun, mowing lawns turned out to be just as easy a business as we conceived. In fact, it was a cash machine.

The coffee can under Christian's bed where we stashed the money was starting to spill out onto the floor. The only unavoidable speed bump along the way was my family's yearly trip to Maine. In a few days, I would be gone for a full week. I didn't feel right abandoning Christian with double lawn duty while I would be off playing volleyball on the beach in Wells.

I told this to Ms. Fine and she offered for me to stay with her for the week if it was alright with my parents. For a moment I felt confident that I might be able to get out of the trip this year. When I told my dad, he had no objection with letting me stay behind. He believed it would strengthen my work ethic, although I suspected that he wouldn't mind having one less mouth to buy lobster for either. But, my mom argued that every member of the family should be present on a *family* vacation, especially the family member who would be off to college in a couple of years. Of course, my mom and her undeviating stare never lost a battle that was fought inside the Davs house. Therefore, I was resigned to a long trip in a cramped minivan with my little brother leading a riveting game of Auto Bingo.

At the end of the week before I left, we had one more lawn to take care of. The weather had been so oppressively hot the entire week that we had put this particular job off until the last minute. Knowing that this one-time client wouldn't be home until Sunday, we had opted instead to catch a flick during the week at the air conditioned Cineplex. The Karate Kid II had just come out and we were dying to see it. Few things in life were sweeter than watching Ralph Macchio, the skinny underdog, caught in a pressing struggle between honor and revenge. Not to mention the humorous Mr. Miyagi whom we constantly mimicked in the following days with our best Asian accents, much to the chagrin of Ms. Fine who was usually an innocent bystander to our monotonous banter. The movie had been a welcome relief from the heat and the labor that had been consuming us all summer. Now we were making up for it by having to get our last job done quickly.

By the time we pushed our mowers to 372 Darcy Lane, we were already exhausted, it had been a stretch for us agreeing to do a job on this street. But at the time, we were so desperate for money that it sounded reasonable to walk the distance to the house. Now that we were actually walking the walk, we were regretting our decision. We each gave the other an oh-well look as we dragged our feet the last few steps to the house. Then the immensity of the yard came into view. We must have inconveniently overlooked the fact that this lawn was enormous when we took the job. The front and back of the house needed to be done, as well as the sides which were very narrow and where mostly weeds grew in the place of grass. I was now regretting having put it off until the last minute.

"Can you believe we agreed to ten measly bucks for this place? That guy was such a tightwad; he was even trying to talk me down to seven dollars. At this point, I don't care if it looks sloppy, let's just get it done as fast as we can," I said, tugging on my shirt to let the air circulate through.

"No kidding. When he said seven dollars I almost spit out my Coke," Christian said.

"We better get started before we lose the sun," I said, observing the sky. I bent over to start the mower.

"Wait a second," said Christian, becoming very still. "Do you hear that radio? I thought he was away."

"He is," I said. I stopped to listen and I heard it too.

A rock song played just loud enough over the speakers to be heard from inside the house. I widened my eyes as I realized the conversation I just had might have been overheard. I desperately hoped that whoever I could hear inside, hadn't heard me out here. We hurried towards the back lawn to look busy and to get as much distance between us and the front door as possible. Just as we started off, a clear voice rang from the porch.

"So, lawn boy, you think my dad's a tightwad?"

Christian breathed an exasperated sigh and stared guilty at the ground, knowing that we had been caught. Normally that would have been my reaction as well but whether it was the heat, the impending thought of being alone with my family for seven days or the accusatory tone that the girl spoke with, I went against my nature and decided I wasn't going to bite my tongue today, not for ten measly bucks.

"This lawn boy has a name; Sam. And yes, I do think he's a tightwad."

I turned around to face her with my mouth still open preparing to continue the verbal accosting but the words stopped short. My eyes squinted in the sun to take in every detail of this girl in front of me. She seemed familiar, yet I couldn't place where I had seen her before. *It's her,* my mind told me. I wrestled with my subconscious. I didn't understand how I could recognize someone I had just met.

"Well, this porch girl's name is Sara and I agree with you; he is a tightwad," she said staring directly at me with a dazzling smile spread across her face.

My cheeks grew warm as I felt the blood rush from my stomach to my head, filling my ears with the sound of a rushing tide coming to shore. *It's her,* I heard again from somewhere within me. I felt it; I needed her. I wondered how I ever got along without her before this moment. I stood there dumbstruck.

"Since we have so much in common, *Sam,* would you like to come in for a soda and find out something other than my name?" she asked.

More than you know, I thought almost out loud. More than you know.

CHAPTER 3

I followed Sara into the house, watching so intently the subtle way her hips swayed that I almost missed the step that lead down into the sunken living room. Christian was following me and he let out a snicker as I fumbled.

"Make yourself at home," she said, motioning her hand like a magician's assistant to the room in front of us. Christian and I carefully took a seat on the spotless, L-shaped sectional sofa while this mystery girl named Sara disappeared into the kitchen to get some refreshments.

"I think we've got Perrier, TAB, Dr. Pepper and New Coke, which personally, I just think is gross. What do you guys like?" she asked.

"Um, Dr. Pepper would be good," said Christian, scanning the room with his eyes.

"Me too," I said absent-mindedly.

I wasn't sure what type of beverage I had just agree to drink because I was too focused on watching Sara rummage around in the kitchen. I smiled as she lifted herself up on tiptoe to reach the glasses in the cabinet. She pushed aside beverage after beverage in the refrigerator until she found the right one, fumbled around a bit with the ice maker, and then clanked some cubes into the cups. She poured clumsily from the two liter bottle as if she didn't care if she made a mess. Her hair bounced with every move she made. I couldn't seem to take my eyes off her. Everything she did enthralled me. I felt a nudge on my arm, and realized Christian was trying to get my attention. He pointed to the entertainment center.

"Do you see that?"

I shook my head, no. I hadn't realized until now that there was anything else in the room besides her.

"Top-of-the-line stereo system *and* a VHS player. This guy's got some money. How come it's always the rich people who are the cheapest?" he whispered.

"What?" I replied, snapping my vision away from the kitchen for the first time. I had kind of been listening to him but wasn't sure if I'd heard everything.

"I said: *this guy's pretty rich isn't he?* Geez, what do you have, heat-stroke or something?"

I could hear the annoyance in his voice as if he were rolling his eyes as he spoke. I should have told him the truth right then and there, that since I'd lain eyes on her I hadn't been listening, paying attention, or caring about anything else in the world. But I didn't, and that was my first mistake.

"Yea, it's probably the heat," I lied.

I reasoned that it was better to keep quiet until I'd given myself a chance to sort out my feelings. Christian was notorious for being an awful secret keeper and I could just picture him blabbing his mouth to Sara that very instant if he knew I liked her.
She re-entered the room, balancing one glass on each hand, palm side up, like a waitress.

"One for our lawn boy, Sam, and the other for his unnamed friend," she said, raising her eyebrows curiously as if trying to get information without asking for it.

"Christian," he piped up, taking the clinking glass from her.

My mouth watered as I watched him guzzle the frosty soda. I set mine down carefully on the mirrored coaster on the coffee table in front of me. I didn't dare take a sip; my hands were sweating more than the glass. I had a reputation for being a klutz, which was not unfounded and I didn't want the cream colored carpets to become the victim of my next fumble.

"Christian it is then. So, let's see, you both already know my name, and my dad's, who we all think so highly of."

"Yeah, about that," I rushed to speak so I could clear the air on the matter.

"What about it? It's obvious he has money and likes to keep it for himself. I've been calling him a tightwad since I could pronounce the word. So, please, don't think you've offended my virgin ears, I could care less."

"Oh," I said, with a sigh of relief. "If you don't mind me asking, I was just wondering something."

"Shoot."

"How come we've never seen you around before?"

"Maybe you've never seen me because you weren't looking for me," she said sipping her drink.

I've definitely been looking for you.

I kept the thought to myself; I generally left the smooth talk to Christian. I wasn't capable of saying something like that out loud without sounding like a cornball.

"No, we would have seen you around school or someplace. And you weren't here when we met your dad," Christian pointed out.

"You didn't see me at your school because I was at another school about 500 miles away from here in Pennsylvania. I lived with my mom, now I live here. Aren't I lucky?" Her voice was rich with sarcasm when she spoke the last part.

"You're not just here for the summer are you?" I asked, probably sounding too eager.

"Unfortunately, no. I am now a permanent ward of my father's, or at least that's what the state calls it. But aside from sending some measly child support check every month, I don't see how he's been much of a parent."

She crossed her legs Indian-style on the couch with her flip-flops still on, something I wouldn't have risked doing considering the light colored fabric.

"Why do you have to live with him if you don't want to? Aren't you old enough to decide that," I asked.

I knew I was doing some serious prying but I felt compelled to get as many details as possible about her so that I could form a complete picture of her life in my mind.

"My mom passed away about two months ago, I was living with my aunt until school got out. Then they shipped me off here to be with him. Next of kin type of thing."

She looked at the floor, running her fingers through her hair as if she were contemplating something deeply. Her voice seemed tight when she spoke and I wondered if this was the first time she had talked to anyone about her situation. Perhaps because Christian and I were strangers, it was easier for her to open up. Judging by how easily she divulged information, she had probably been waiting for the chance to talk to someone about her mother for a while.

"Oh man," I said, breaking the silence; I fumbled for the right words; "I am so sorry to hear that. I can't imagine that happening to you."

"Yeah," Christian barely whispered, not contributing much in the way of a condolence.

"Thanks, I couldn't imagine it either until it actually happened. It's just weird how life keeps on going, ya know?"

She looked up and stared directly into my eyes, as if the answer to her question was hidden there. For once in my life, I didn't feel the need to look away. As we held each other's gaze, I thought I felt a connection between us but I wasn't sure if it was real or just wishful thinking.

"Thanks for the soda but we'd better get started with the lawn before we run out of time. Even if your dad is a tightwad, we still need the money. Right Sam?" Christian said, patting me on the shoulder as he stood up to leave.

Typical Christian, he'd rather be outside sweating in the heat than face an emotional conversation, now he was looking for me to back him up. I needed some more time to talk so I could see if she might be even a little interested in me. I wished he would just walk out the door and leave us alone.

"Right Sam?" he asked again.

Man he just won't let up. "Yeah, I guess so," I conceded, knowing resistance would only lead to me having to give an explanation as to why I wanted to stay. Still, I lingered on the couch defiantly a minute longer, trying to prolong the conversation. "So, if your dad's away, how come you stayed here?"

"Oh, he had a pressing business trip he couldn't cancel, even for his grieving daughter," she said, sounding a little put-off. "I wasn't about to sit in some hotel room all day anyway while he went to meetings, so I decided to stay here and unpack and get used to the place for a week."

"Cool. I mean, not cool that your dad left you here, but cool that you will be sticking around. Maybe we'll bump into you around the neighborhood?" I asked, not wanting to leave without knowing I'd see her again in the near future.

Christian continued backing up toward the door. He caught my eye for a second and pointed at the sun that was dipping lower in the sky.

Why does he have to pick now to be the responsible one? I thought.

"I really don't know anyone here at all. It would be nice to have some friends before school starts. Why don't I give you my number and maybe you guys could introduce me to some people this summer." She said the last part quickly, as if she were embarrassed to be asking.

"That would be great!" I said, with an enthusiastic smile on my face. I knew I was showing my cards here, but I didn't care. She ripped a piece of paper from a nearby notepad and scribbled down some numbers with a purple pen.

"If you don't call me I'll be reduced to sitting in my room all summer having make-believe parties with my Pillow People," she said, handing me the paper.

"I've heard that Pillow People parties can be fun, but we'll try to provide you with some company of the un-stuffed kind," I said hoping that my clever line would get a giggle out of her. I was delighted when it did.

"Awesome, I super appreciate it. It's not easy being new."

"Sam, we've really got to get started. This is gonna take a while."

I had held Christian off as long as I could, now he had become so impatient to leave he looked like a little kid about to wet his pants. I turned to Sara, smiled and shrugged my shoulders in defeat. We turned to walk away but she stopped us by the door before we could leave.

"You know, I can maneuver a mower pretty well. My dad has a ride-on in the garage. Do you want some help out there?" Her eyes revealed a child-like desperation for company which probably arose from the idle hours she was spending alone in the huge house.

"A ride-on mower? Holy crap, I *knew* your dad was loaded. Yeah, you can hop on it if you want to. It's probably the only chance we have of getting this thing done before dark," Christian said.

"Ok, let me just get changed into jeans first. I'll be right out." She disappeared down the hall.

"Wow, this is gonna go fast now. What a lucky break it was meeting her huh?" Christian said, on the way out the door.

"Yeah, pretty lucky," I answered, though I had a gut feeling that more than luck had caused us to meet today.

Christian rushed to get his mower started before the battle with daylight was lost. I was doing the exact opposite; trying to milk the time I had here with her as long as I could. With the three of us working, the job was going too fast for my liking. I stopped to take "breaks" every few steps when she was in view, pretending to wipe sweat from my forehead or tinker with my mower. Christian caught me stalling a few times but he didn't hassle me about it, probably figuring I was procrastinating because I didn't want to go home and pack the van for the family trip. By the end of a half hour, we were done. Christian started raking up his section of dead grass.

"Hey Sam! Come're!" Sara shouted across the yard after the last engine had been silenced. I practically ran to her, though I played it off like a hearty jog.

"Here's the ten dollars that my dad left for you," she said, handing me a neatly folded bill; "and here's another twenty from his sock drawer; consider it a tip." I held out my hand for the ten but withdrew it when she tried to hand me the extra.

"I can't take this. You might get in trouble if he notices it's missing and besides, you helped us with the work."

"Trust me, he'll never know. It was rolled up with his hundreds. Besides, do you really think he's going to yell at a girl who just lost her mother? And don't worry about how much work I did. I made sure to take a tip for myself too," she said with a menacing grin and a wink. I smiled back trying to mask my adoration as thankfulness.

"I guess you just bought yourself a friend," I joked. "I come pretty cheap."

We both laughed longer than was appropriate for the corny joke. I didn't mind, I preferred laughing, at the moment, it was the safe alternative to saying something stupid.

"It looks like Christian is all set to go," Sara said when the laughter subsided.

I turned my head to see Christian waiting patiently in the driveway. He was all packed up in what seemed like record time. I gave him a nod and grudgingly turned to leave.

"Oh, by the way," I said, turning back to explain my unfortunate circumstance. "I won't be calling for at least a week because I'm leaving tonight to go to Maine with my family, so, you might have to keep the Pillow People company until I get back."

"No fair, I want my twenty bucks back!" she laughed, holding out her hand for the money.

"Hey, a week's not *that* long," I said, trying to convince myself more than her. "I'll call you as soon as I get back and we can hang out."

"Sounds like a plan, Sam," she said, emphasizing the rhyming words. "You're not going to Maine too are you Christian?" she called over to him.

"Nope, not me, I don't get to lounge on a beach all day like this bum," he said, thumbing at me. "I'll be out working as usual."

"Let me know if you need help. I'll just be sittin' around watching game shows all day."

"Ok, thanks," Christian replied.

Suddenly I loathed my family vacation more than humanly possible. Sourly, I grabbed my clunky mower to start the long walk home.

"So, what do you think?" she asked, following leisurely behind me.

"About what?"

"Was it meant to be that we ran into each other today?"

"Meant to be?" I said, reiterating her question, as if the answer was obvious. "Yes, I definitely believe this was meant to be."

I hadn't thought about the clichéd sentence before I spoke it and was hoping it didn't sound silly. She smiled warmly, as if she were wrapping me in a heavy winter jacket on a cold day. When I came to the end of the driveway, she stopped, gave a final wave my way, and turned back slowly with her hands in her pockets.

"Wow," I said, barely out of earshot of the house.

"I know, I can't *believe* we finished before dark," Christian said.

"No, not that. I mean, wow, I feel bad for her. Don't you?"

"I guess so," Christian said, more clueless than unkind.

"I mean, come on, she just lost her mother and now she is living with some dad she doesn't even know. She probably had to leave a lot of friends and family behind. I think we should definitely call her and introduce her to some people."

Christian nodded his head in agreement as if he were pondering her circumstance for the first time. "Yeah, you're right. I hadn't thought about it like that. I mean, I think people will like her, she seems cool, shouldn't be tough for her to make friends here. Luckily, she'll have the whole summer to get to know people. But that is a sad thing that happened to her."

He thinks she's cool. Maybe it would be ok to tell him that I like her, I thought. "Yeah, she was really cool, wasn't she? You know I even think she's..." I started to say.

"I hate to interrupt Sammy but your dad wanted you home before dark to pack up and it's already past eight. You know how your dad is, you don't want to piss him off before vacation," Christian said, pointing to his Swatch watch.

"Oh. Yeah, is it really that time already?" I took the interruption as a sign of his disinterest and decided to let it drop, maybe my first instinct not to tell him was right and it was better to keep my feelings to myself a little while longer. "I still wanna get that glove from you. My dad always starts these family games of baseball while we're there. I'm still playing with the glove I had when I was in elementary school. I'm sick of my hand getting cramped," I said, changing the subject.

"No problem. We can stop by my house and get it on the way home. There hasn't been much time to play this summer so I think it's still in the garage."

"Sounds good. Hey, could you do me a favor and take a really long time to find it so that maybe they pack up and leave without me?"

"Uh, I think you're at the point of needing divine intervention for that van to leave without you," Christian said.

I faked a smiled knowing that he was right. I looked over my shoulder at her house on Darcy Lane until the ridgeline of the roof dipped below the horizon. I could almost hear the muffled crying that I imagined was concealed behind its walls at this very minute from a brokenhearted girl who had finally admitted out loud that her mother was indeed dead.

Twilight was spreading to every part of the sky when we reached the familiar doorstep of the Fine residence. I knew I wouldn't be receiving the welcome of a prodigal son returning home when I got to my house, which made the thought of going there all the more undesirable. So I did what I always do, I stalled. I plunked my tired body down at the kitchen table while Christian rushed to find the mitt among the accumulated junk in the garage. Truthfully, I didn't follow him because I had been hoping for a minute alone since we left Sara's so that I could peek at the piece of paper she had handed me with her number on it. I wanted total secrecy so that I could study every detail of the note. I hoped to find a delicate heart neatly placed beside the words "I like you", but I knew that was a far-fetched scenario. Carefully I unfolded the small square page which was type-headed: "From the Desk of Russell Moran." A colorful Ziggy wearing glasses and writing in a ledger was printed in the upper right corner. Words in purple ink invaded the open white space below.

Sara (porch girl/tightwad's daughter)
555-5612
Call Anytime ☺ Please!

A smile passed over my lips that I couldn't have disguised for anything. I reread it three times mouthing the words to the air. I loved the way she curled the ends of her letters. I laughed silently at how she added "Please!", as if she weren't sure I really wanted to call her. She had even described herself, probably thinking I knew other Saras and might forget which one she was. Although there was no grand confession of love, I could detect a glimmer of romantic interest. To someone else this might have seemed like an ordinary phone number scribbled on paper, but to me this little note revealed a lot. Beyond the words I saw a girl who was perhaps as insecure as I was and maybe who needed me in her life just as much as I needed her, it killed me inside knowing this was all I would have to link me to her for an entire week. I wouldn't know anything for sure about our status as a couple until after vacation. I glanced down to reread her phone number so that I could commit it to memory but before I could get another look at it, the breezeway door creaked open. Turning the note upside down, I quickly slid it under the wooden duck napkin holder on the kitchen table and pretended as if I had been staring at some spot on the floor the entire time.

"Here it is," Christian said, bounding into the room, glove in hand. "It should fit, it'll be better than a youth mitt anyway. It's probably a little stiff though, I haven't oiled it in a while," he said tossing it at me.

"Hey, beggars can't be choosers," I replied.

"Take good care of it though, my dad gave it to me and I think he spent a lot of money on it. Oh, and I also found my Walkman. You can have it for the trip. I put my Springsteen tape in there for ya. I think it goes up loud enough to overpower Mark."

"My brother isn't the one I'm worried about tuning out, I'm expecting my dad to badger me about being late the entire ride up."

"Yeah, you'd better get going, like, now. I'll see ya in a week, and then it's time for the big road test!"

"I know I can't wait!" I said, opening my eyes wide for dramatic effect.

"Now, go!"

"Ugh, ok. Say goodbye to your mom for me. Where is she anyway?"

"On a date. Don't ask, please. I'll tell you later."

I put a knowing grin on my face. "Later," I said, nodding my head at him as I strode out the door.

In a few minutes, I was back at my house, rushing to get my duffle bag into the van, getting yelled at by my parents, and giving my smirking brother a don't-say-anything-to-me-right-now, red-faced glare. I threw the baseball glove in the back and closed the hatch since everything else had already been loaded up. I leaned against the side of the van for a breather while my parents locked up the house.

One week Sam. Just one week. You can do this, I thought. But no matter how many times I repeated it, I couldn't convince myself that a week with my family was going to be fun. I put my hand into my pocket to retrieve Sara's note. At least I would have that to distract me while I was away. I fumbled around, first in my left, then my right pocket. I came up empty both times. A wave of frustration swept over me as I realized that in the rush to get here I had left it sitting on Christian's table. I felt the summer wind teasing my face as I glanced up at the moonlit sky.

Please, please let this van not start. Come on God, I need some divine intervention here, I thought.

My brother shoved past me to get the window seat, elbowing me in the ribs as he went.

"Better get in the car son, this train's leaving the station and it's not going without you," my father boomed as he hoisted himself into the driver's seat and effortlessly started the van with the turn of the key.

Thanks a lot, I thought looking up and shaking my head at the sky. Closing my eyes, I let out a hard sigh of defeat, climbed into the cramped backseat and pulled my headphones over my ears. As the van pulled out of the driveway, I let the sounds of "My Hometown" drown out the melancholy that was in my heart.

CHAPTER 4

All I could think about was getting back home to see her. The thought of it occupied my every waking moment. She seemed to be the only one that mattered anymore. I agonized, wondering what she was doing while I was gone. Was she thinking about me too, sitting by the phone, waiting for me to call? As selfish as it sounded, I kind of hoped she *was* lonely without me.

Every hour of vacation dragged by like I was in school taking some wretched mid-term exam that I had neglected to study for. My dad insisted on grilling-out hot dogs and hamburgers every night which by the third night made me want to barf when the bun hit my lips. Mark and my mom loved volleyball, so of course I was suckered into playing countless rematches until my serving arm ached so badly I could barely sleep on my right side. My face hurt from the laughter I forced in response to my dad's trite jokes. But for my family's sake, I gritted my teeth and put on a convincing front that I was a teenager happy to be living for a week "The way life should be" in Maine.

When Friday night *finally* came, I retired early to bed so that the departure on Saturday would seemingly come sooner. But my plan backfired and I lay awake for hours counting the slow laps made by the overhead ceiling fan. The anticipation of seeing her again wouldn't let my brain rest. I'm not sure how little sleep I ended up getting, but at the first sight of dawn, I was out of bed and ready to go. When my parents got up a few hours later, they knew something was awry; I had already taken a shower, gathered my belongings and stowed them neatly in the van.

"Wow, all packed and ready to go before breakfast," my father said looking at me as if some of the clams I had eaten the night before were sticking out of my ears.

"Yup, even got the boogie boards washed off like you wanted," I replied in my most chipper voice hoping to win him over with congeniality.

"Do you have a fever?" my mother asked, with one eye cocked suspiciously. "There must be some delirium behind this."

"Just thought dad would want to beat the traffic," I said, shrugging my shoulders as if I were doing them a favor.

"I do, but I'm not sure they'll be much on Saturday anyway. That's why we're leaving today instead of tomorrow," my father said.

"Don't go starting the engine *yet* you two. Mark's still asleep and I wanted to read the paper and enjoy the last few hours here before we head back to suburbia," mom said, walking off towards the bathroom.

I let out an exasperated sigh and purposefully free-fell backwards onto the stiff cottage sofa. Rolling my eyes in my mother's direction, I grudgingly accepted that we weren't going anywhere fast. I clicked on the pint-sized television in front of me, which provided the incredibly monotonous entertainment of (woohoo) nine local channels.

Slumped against the sofa, I watched the morning crawl by. I bit my tongue while every inch of the *Daily Gazette* was read by my mother; ignored my stomach growl as I watched my brother devour a hot breakfast, and cranked the volume up on the television as my father did his ritual ten minute a.m. throat clearing. I bided my time and suffered silently in my little corner of the cottage. I was being patient, *beyond patient*, with these people, who I had just spent every waking moment with for the past seven days. Then I saw my father lift the coffee pot for the *third* time to pour another round into their mugs. To take a third cup just seemed like gluttony and added insult to my growing emotional injury. Something inside me snapped.

"Don't you think you've had enough coffee? I have things to do today you know! I'm expected back to help Christian with the lawns and if I get back too late, he'll be mad he had to do everything by himself another day!"

I couldn't believe the words had left my mouth. A week's worth of my pent-up anxiety was heard, loudly I might add, by all the ears in the room.

Mom's paper lowered slowly as she peeked out from behind it; my brother stopped chewing his fluffy scrambled eggs, and my father's hand stopped pouring the hot liquid in mid-stream. My ears turned hot and red from the deafening silence, even the pine beams supporting the ceiling didn't dare make a creek. I had suffered temporary insanity and was now aware that there was a storm about to blow my way. I gripped tightly and braced myself against the couch cushions. As expected, it was my father who spoke first. He began in an eerie soft and low tone which increased gradually until it climaxed into a steady boom.

"Well...excuse *us*. I wasn't aware that you kept such a tight schedule. I think that we should all stop what we are doing right this moment and cut OUR hard-earned vacation short so that YOU can get back home AND MOW LAWNS!"

I stared at him, not saying a word. There was a long silence.

"I didn't realize it was so awful being with your family," my mother half-sobbed.

"No, I didn't mean it like that..." Against my better judgment I started to speak, but was interrupted immediately by my father.

"Oh, you never *mean it like that*, but guess what? That's exactly what it sounded like. We've had to put up with your sour attitude all week buddy but you're not going to ruin our last day here. I guess you like making your mother upset."

No, I did not like making my mother upset, and now I felt like the scum of the earth. If only I could have swallowed my words for a few more hours, then I would have been home free. But there was no taking it back now. I was in deep and I knew it. I stayed silent as my father continued. I glanced at my brother and even *he* looked scared to talk.

"Now, let me tell *you* how this day is going to play out. The three of us are going to take a walk on the beach. We might be gone for thirty minutes or we might be gone for three hours. I want this place cleaned and packed up by the time we get back and I don't want to hear another word out of you," he pointed his index finger at me daringly, "Do I make myself clear?"

I nodded my head in agreement, just in case the no-talking thing was already in effect.

"Good."

With that, the family walked out the door leaving me all alone to sort out my frustration and the morning mess.

∞

When the last bag was carefully thrown over the threshold of our ranch house, I felt it might be safe to speak my first words in over five hours but I kept it short.

"I'm sorry dad," I said, looking more at the floor than the man I was addressing.

"Don't just say sorry to me. There are two other people standing here that deserve to hear that too."

"Sorry, everyone. I know I had a bad attitude this morning and I really didn't want to ruin your vacation."

"It was your vacation too Sam. Not just ours. I hope that it wasn't as horrible for you as you made it sound," my mom said.

"No, it really wasn't. It was great. I think I was in a bad mood because I couldn't get much sleep on that bed. But it really was a great vacation. I had a lot of fun," I lied.

"You always get crabby when you haven't had eight hours sleep. I wish you would have said something; I could have put out a sleeping bag or a cot for you. Oh well, what's done is done. I was just happy to be out of this house for a week," mom said.

My father looked at me skeptically and seemed to want to say something else on the matter but mom walked over to him and rubbed his back slow and sympathetically with one hand. I could see his demeanor relax.

"You'd better get to work before you get fired," he said.

My face relaxed with relief. I was wondering if I would get a chance to make a break for Christian's today but I hadn't wanted to push my luck by asking. I guess my mother had more influence over my father than I thought.

"Thanks, I'm not sure when I'll be back but I'll call," I said quickly.

I gave my mom a hug and grabbed my work gloves. I bounded out the door letting the screen slam behind me. After a long agonizing week, I finally felt summer freedom inhabiting my body again. My mind switched to auto-pilot and my feet carried me the familiar distance to Christian's house faster than they ever had before. As I approached the steps, I heard music playing in the kitchen. Not bothering to knock, I threw open the door as quickly as I had closed the door to my own house minutes ago. I expected to see Christian and his mom sitting in the kitchen eating a snack and talking or maybe Ms. Fine would be dancing around while washing the dishes. Instead there was no one in sight.

"Christian?! I'm back!" I bellowed over the music, hoping to call someone out from hiding.

"Sam! Long time no see. You were gone so long, I thought you would have grown a beard by now," Ms. Fine joked, stepping into the kitchen. She grabbed me in for a hug with one arm and turned the radio volume down with the other.

"Yeah, the beard doesn't really grow as quick as it used to" I joked back. "Is Christian here?" I asked, looking past her into the den.

"No, he's out but he should be back soon."

"I told him he didn't have to do the work by himself today. He must have thought that I wasn't coming because it was getting late."

"Oh, actually he already got the work done this morning. But like I said, he'll be back soon."

"Really? Did he say where he was going?" I felt a little left in the dark. I couldn't imagine where else Christian would have went when he knew that I was on my way home.

"Umm, I don't think so," she said. "But you can wait for him here. I can make you something to eat if you're hungry."

"No thanks, but I'll wait if you don't mind." I sat down and scowled my eyebrows wondering where he could be.

"Make yourself at home, you know where everything is. Grab a drink or put on the T.V. if you feel like it. Like I said, he should be here soon. I'll just be reading in my room."

"Ok, thanks."

She lingered a moment longer in the kitchen looking as if she were fighting an internal struggle whether to tell me something or not. She must have decided against a confession because all I got was a half-smile before she turned and walked out of the room.

The excitement that I had felt coming here a few minutes ago was now turning to suspicion. Why was Ms. Fine acting so weird about where Christian was when she knew that he and I always told each other everything? With apprehension, I took a seat and waited. Tapping my fingers on the table, my eyes fell on the wooden duck-shaped paper napkin holder sitting just inches away from me. I shoved it aside, remembering that I had left the note folded messily underneath it. But the paper wasn't there. Maybe the table had been cleared one night for dinner and the note was pinned on the fridge. My eyes hastily devoured the room. I scanned the many announcements on the front of the avocado Kenmore for her purple handwriting but it wasn't there. Likewise, the counters and phone table were void of the note. I hoped that Ms. Fine hadn't found it, dismissed it as scrap paper and put it out with the trash. I couldn't picture her doing that, she was always respectful of Christian's belongings. Maybe he had come across it right after I left and tucked it away in his room for safe keeping until I returned. Yeah, that's what must have happened. That's what he would have done. As soon as he gets home, I can get the number from him and call her tonight.

I sat up straight, peeking over the half-curtain on the kitchen door window watching for Christian to come down the street. After twenty minutes my posture failed and I slouched down in the chair becoming mesmerized by the Kit-Kat Clock on the wall; it swung its tail teasingly back and forth and followed me with its wide white eyes. I went into a sort of transcendental stare meditation where I thought only of the slow passage that time seems to take while you are waiting for something exciting to happen.

Suddenly, I became aware of movement in my peripheral vision. I ran to the window and adjusted my eyes to the outside light so that I could see who had pulled into the driveway. There was a blue familiar looking car with two people inside. I couldn't make out who exactly they were but I remembered that it might be Ben, our friend who was getting his license this week and had promised to take us for a drive when he did. I had forgotten about that until now. That must be why Ms. Fine had been so secretive, she probably thought that I would be jealous that Ben and Christian hadn't waited for me to come home first before going for a ride. I could see how she might think that, but I honestly didn't mind. We could always go out together tomorrow for a cruise around the block.

When I heard the car engine cut off, I ran from the window and sat down at the table, leaning back casually with a Coke in my hand looking cool and nonchalant. What a surprise it would be for Christian to see me at his kitchen table relaxing with my feet up drinking one of his sodas. I pressed my lips together to try to hide my smile as I heard the door knob turn. Quickly, I thought of something clever to say.

"Hey, why don't you knock before you just barge in…"

My words dropped to the floor like an iron anchor sinking to the bottom of the ocean as the people who had been in the car walked into the room. There was Christian, just as I expected, but it wasn't Ben that he had been in the car with; it was the absolute last person that I had expected to see. In fact, it was the worst possible person on Earth that Christian could have been alone in a car with: it was Sara.

"Look who's back!" Christian said smiling, as he walked over and slapped me heartily on the shoulder.

I sat there motionless with my mouth hanging open.

"Oh, sorry, I probably shouldn't have done that," Christian said with a wince.

"Huh?" I asked, wondering if he was trying to apologize for being with her.

"I mean, you look like you got sunburnt, I probably shouldn't have slapped you that hard on your arm. It must have stung," he explained.

I didn't answer. I couldn't process anything yet. I felt the blood rushing into my head and filling up my ears. They started to pound. I wanted an explanation for the sight that was before me but I didn't know how to articulate the words. I was too befuddled to come right out and ask. So I clenched my teeth together, clammed up and slid further down the sticky plastic seat beneath me, hoping that there was a logical explanation for what, or rather *who*, I was seeing together in front of me.

"You remember Sara, of course," Christian said, motioning towards her.

She smiled looking unsure about the situation, probably aware that my attitude was a bit off.

"Before I tell you my big news, how was the vaca with the fam?" he asked, oblivious to my bodily cues of frustration.

"As good as I expected it to be," I said, hoping for no more inquiry into the matter.

"*That* good, huh?" he said, laughing.

"Just about."

He continued to press me; "Any good blowouts with the old man?"

"Nothing of interest," I said.

Christian raised one eyebrow toward me in a quizzical manner then shook his head and shrugged his shoulders.

"Well, since nothing exciting seems to have happened to *you* this week, I'll come right out with *my* good news. The RMV had a cancellation and pushed my test up to last Wednesday. So, guess what that means? I am officially a licensed driver! Can you believe it? And the road test wasn't even that hard, I mean it was everything we had gone over when we were studying and what my mom taught me while we practiced. Isn't that awesome?!"

I sat there in total silence as he looked at me for a reaction. Rightly so, I'm sure he expected a burst of ecstatic emotion from his best friend, but after the week I had, and now seeing *this*, I couldn't muster up even a single "congratulations". Confusion was leaving my mind and jealousy was taking its place. Even though I had no right to, I felt betrayed by both of them. I bit my tongue to hold back the tears that were beginning to swell. Emotionally I was tapped out and ready to give up on everyone.

"Aren't you happy for me? For *us*, I mean. I have my license and you aren't even saying anything. Man, I thought you'd be going nuts with excitement right now. Look, I know you wanted to go with me for the test and to get the car but you were gone and I just couldn't wait."

Christian seemed genuinely hurt that he was getting the reaction of a rock out of me right now. Sara leaned tightly against the door with her arms folded, probably wishing that she were on the other side of it. Christian glanced over at her and seemed to sense the uncomfortable energy in the room. For a moment, I felt badly for the way I was acting but my pride was too hurt to say so. I was bitter at them both for choosing each other over me. After all, *I* was the one who pushed Christian to study in the first place. *I* was the one who stood in the sun that hot day at the car lot to help him pick out just the right set of wheels. *I* had busted my butt all summer to afford a car that wouldn't even technically belong to me. *I* at least wanted the privilege of being in the passenger seat for the first spin around the block. Not to mention the fact that I had been the one to initiate a friendship with Sara and if it hadn't been for me, Christian wouldn't even know her. This whole situation didn't sit well with me at all.

"Hey, by the way, you didn't miss much, the test was no fun. I had to wait in line forever with blue-haired old ladies who were there to get their vision tested," Christian said, trying to lighten the mood.

"With all that on your plate, how did you manage to get the work done too?" I asked, doubting that he had done much at all. I waited to hear him worm his way out of that one with excuses too so that I could bag him for slacking and have an excuse to yell at him.

"Oh, yeah. That's where she came in," Christian said, motioning towards Sara and looking relieved that I had spoken to him; "I found her number on the table after you left and I took advantage of her offer to help while you were gone. I couldn't pass up a ride-on and an extra hand when I knew the week would be so full. She was great. We got everyone done in almost the half the time it usually takes me and you."

"So, you two got to know each other pretty *well* then?" I asked, raising my eyebrows at the end of the sentence for emphasis. I hoped the word "well" didn't imply what I thought.

"We sure did," Christian said, smiling. "I mean you can't work with someone in 85 degree heat all day and not get to know them. There is more to Sara here than meets the eye Sammy. Did you know that she is a red belt in Tae Kwon Do? After she told me that I was a little scared to boss her around. I mean she could have sent a round house kick my way anytime she wanted to. You wanna hear something hilarious that happened to us while you were gone?"

Just about the last thing that I wanted to hear right now was another hilarious moment that had happened between Christian and Sara while I was conveniently gone. However, he must have been asking a rhetorical question because he didn't wait for my response.

"On Tuesday we were at the Simmon's house and..."

My ears purposely muted the comical recollection of my friend. My eyes took over and I glanced at Sara. I was looking for some hope for me; maybe a returned glance or a rolling of her eyes to show me that she thought Christian's stories were silly and redundant. But in her face I saw only what I dreaded I would. She was fixated solely on Christian with a look that I knew well. She looked at him the way I looked at her. She laughed when he laughed, blushed ever-so-slightly when he mentioned her name in conversation and nodded her head in agreement with whatever clever utterance left his mouth. It was worse than I thought. I felt my stomach rise up into my throat. My ears tuned back into the story just as it was wrapping up.

"...and Sara tripped on the sprinkler switch just as Mrs. Simmon was walking across the lawn. Everyone was soaked! It was hysterical!" He concluded with a long laugh as if he hadn't known the ending when he began the story.

Sara laughed too, in cute shorts bursts of breath, my heart melted at the sound of it. They didn't seem to notice that I wasn't laughing with them.

"I had good company this week. Too bad it was only temp work," Sara said, after their laughter subsided.

"No way, I'm not letting my best employee go. You're too valuable to the company. My associate won't mind if we split the rest of the profits three-ways, will you Sammy?"

I shook my head no, and managed a painful smile which I offered to the new hire. She returned my smile with a thankful one.

"Good, then it's settled. It will be the three of us, equal partners, for the rest of the summer," Christian stated.

Judging by the way Sara beamed back at Christian, I doubted if there would be anything equal in our three-way partnership, more than likely I would be the third wheel.

"Let's shake on it to make it official," Christian said.

Sara and I shook first. Her palm slid smoothly into mine like a blade gliding over ice and our thumbs locked as if by bolt and switch. Our hands clasped firmly but gently; natural and easy. I let all the unpleasant thoughts of the day leave my mind as I soaked up this split second encounter with her. Too quickly Christian's hand invaded the space where mine was and I watched as Sara gripped my friend's hand a little tighter than she had mine. I saw a rush of thrill cross Christian's face as he made direct contact with her eyes. I watched them both hang on as long as they could, their hands dancing up and down in agreement with the promise that had just been made. I looked down at my own sweaty, now empty hand which was already cold from lack of touch. In that moment I knew that I had missed my chance with her. While I had been gone, she had fallen for my best friend. And there was nothing that I could do about it.

CHAPTER 5

The hanging pictures shook as I slammed the hard, oak door of my bedroom behind me. The fragile wall of emotions I had been building inside of me came crashing down, brick by crumbling brick as I threw myself on the bed. The soft, down-pillow that caught my head was soon soaked with the tears of heartache. Between sobs, the faint scent of lavender fabric softener wafted into my nostrils. My mother had been using this same perfumed brand since I was a child and it was embedded in every piece of cloth I owned. The consistency of the smell comforted me and I buried my face deeper into the pillowcase folds.

"*Sammy, what's wrong? Why don't you wanna go with us to the drive-in? Why are you acting so weird?*"

The words that my friend had spoken to me echoed loudly in my ears; an irritating playback which made me want to snap. I had deployed my old passive-aggressive standby: "I'm tired. I'll take a rain check, thanks anyway." What I really wanted to tell him was the truth; I didn't want to go because I would have to witness the hand holding and cuddling between him and Sara all night; that I didn't want to see the grand finale kiss as he dropped her off at her doorstep, wondering if he was slipping her the tongue or not. Just the thought of it was enough to push me to the brink of insanity; I didn't need to see it too. Maybe second place was just my lot in life, after all, that's where I always seemed to end up.

What I needed was some time away, not like the time away I had just had, but time away from everyone and everything so that

I could figure out what to do; away from my parents, away from my brother, away from my friend, away from...I couldn't finish the sentence with her name because I knew it wasn't true; I didn't want time *away* from her; I wanted time alone *with* her.

How was I going to handle seeing them together every day? Could I stifle my feelings enough to manage a fake smile? If I let on to having any interest in her, I would be a traitor to my best friend and I couldn't do that. The fact was that Christian hadn't gone behind my back and taken her from me, he never even knew that I liked her and if he had, I knew he never would have put the moves on her, he was too loyal. Sure, I could bring it up to him *now* that I had feelings for her but then I would be putting him in a position to choose between her and me; that was unfair.

If I just bit my tongue and let things continue the way they were, even if it wasn't in the role I hoped it would be, I would still get to spend time with her. After all, any type of relationship with her was better than none. Eventually she would get to know me just as well as she knows Christian. Then if there ever came a day that her feelings for him changed, I would be right there to scoop her up.

Wait, what was I saying? *Scoop her up?* Was I planning the demise of my best friend's relationship three moves ahead like a game of chess? It certainly sounded that way. But it wasn't. I wasn't setting out to cause their break-up, I was just taking the odds that, considering Christian's dating history, this relationship wasn't bound to last long. The pieces were being set up and I was just waiting for Sara to be plucked from his side of the board onto mine.

We will be together someday. The words came at me from somewhere deep inside my sub-conscious. And suddenly I knew it to be true. The realization hit me so quickly and in such a deep place inside my mind that for a moment I became disoriented and thought I might pass out. I clung to the bed to ground me. I felt she had a large part to play in my life, more so than even Christian, and suddenly I didn't feel devious or wrong for wanting her all for myself. If someone asked to me to explain how I knew this, I couldn't, I just did.

When the lightheadedness passed, I scrunched my pillow up tightly underneath my head, propping myself on one elbow, so that I could think this through. Could I really accept the current situation, bite my tongue, go on with life and hope that one day in the future she would fall for me? Could I make careful moves toward her and hope the rest of the pieces fell into place where I needed them to?

"Arrrr!" I screamed into my pillow out of pure frustration hitting my fist hard against my firm mattress.

How had one lousy week away from my normal life put me in this situation? The thoughts whirled around in my brain making me dizzy. With my face buried in my pillow, I did the only thing I could do in this seemingly hopeless situation - I prayed. And then I fell asleep.

∞

The next day was Sunday, a day of rest, and that's just what I intended to do. No working, no thinking, no fighting. I strolled over to Christian's with a box of Otter Pops as a peace offering and pretended that nothing out of the ordinary had occurred the previous day. Sleep had done me good, and I was feeling surprisingly at ease with my decision to accept Christian and Sara as a couple; at least for now. My conscience wouldn't let me stay angry with him.

Christian seemed genuinely happy to see me when I came strolling in the kitchen. He quickly devoured the freeze pops, never mentioning a word about our quasi-argument the day before.

"Man, these cherry ones just hit the spot don't they," he said, sucking the juice from the bottom of the tube so hard that it scrunched up into a flat piece of plastic.

I glanced in the box. The red ones were already gone. Luckily, I liked orange best; the flavor tasted more like tart syrup than the fruit it was named after but that was alright with me.

"I figured since it was so hot today, we needed something cool. I picked them up on the corner at the drug store on the way here."

"Always thinking a step ahead, that's what I like about you, Sammy," Christian said, pushing his chair back and plopping his feet satisfactorily on top of the kitchen table.

He stuck out his blood-red tongue obnoxiously. I mimicked him with an Oompa-Loompa-orange flick of mine. I relished in the joy of the light-hearted banter; it seemed like it had been forever since we had hung out together, free from responsibility.

"Let's keep the good times rolling. Whadya say about going for a ride down to the lake?" he asked.

"I'd say: is that a trick question?"

"That's what I thought. Let me just get my stuff, you can borrow one of my bathing suits."

I forgot that the car had been sitting directly in the sun all morning and hopping shot gun onto the vinyl seats of the Honda nearly gave my half-exposed legs a third degree burn.

"Wow, that's freakin' hot!" I yelled, jumping up and trying to sit lightly on the seat. "Ahh, so's that!" I said, reaching for the seat belt. The metal singed my hand when I touched it. "You better be an excellent driver because I am riding naked," I said, dropping the belt like a hot potato.

"I am, I am. Don't worry there Sammy. You're in good hands riding with me, I am an A+ driver, approved by the New Hampshire RMV," he said, pulling his laminated license from his wallet.

"Woah. I believe ya. No need to pull out the big guns."

He started up the engine gently and smiled at me as he looked over and said, "Let's roll."

After the twenty minute drive, which I will admit was smooth sailing, we arrived at the lake. Peeling our legs off the seats, we stood up and stretched. It was midday and the beach was packed with locals trying to escape the 90 degree weather; there were no spots left in the shade. I sighed, knowing that my pale skin would bake quickly. I still felt the burn on my arms from my days in the sun on vacation. We gave each other a look of exasperation that said without any words that we should have planned to come earlier.

"Let's check the other side. Maybe people were too lazy to walk that far and look for a spot," Christian said.

"I think *I'm* too lazy to walk that far," I answered, wiping stinging sweat from my forehead. The car ride over had already preheated me.

Christian squinted his eyes and used his hand as a visor to block the sun as he surveyed the surroundings. Something must have caught his eye because he looked over at me with a wide grin.

"You are never going to believe this," he said.

"What? Do you see a spot?"

"Oh, I see a spot alright," he said, nudging me on the arm. "Come on."

He took off toward an oak tree which cast yards of shade under its massive span of branches. I followed, even though I couldn't see an inch of unoccupied space beneath it.

"Here's our savior," Christian trumpeted, his hand extended towards a surprised looking girl.

"No way!" she exclaimed.

No way, I thought, in unison, unable to believe that Sara was sitting in front of us. She whipped around from where she was facing to our direction, causing her wet ponytail to plaster against her cheek. Without even bothering to wipe it away she started waving animatedly. I waved back once, quickly and silently, and gave her a smile.

"Are you guys stalking me or something? Because there are laws against that you know."

"No, I swear! We didn't even know that you were going to be here. We were just lounging around and decided to take a spin and go for a swim, for obvious reasons," Christian said, motioning towards the solar power beaming down mightily on us all.

"Where are you guys sitting?" she asked, looking left and right.

"Right here!" Christian said, insinuating us into her space.

"Um, we didn't exactly plan ahead. We just got here a few minutes ago and it looks like we're out of luck as far as premium seating goes," I replied, trying to be more tactful than he had been.

"And you saw me and automatically assumed that I was generous and kind and would invite you to sit under this gorgeous tree with me," she said, stretching her arms out and laying back like a pampered housewife.

"I'm not gonna lie. That was definitely the plan," Christian said, nodding his head in agreement.

"Don't feel like you have to let us sit here though if you don't want to," I said.

"Well, it might put you boys off to know that I am in fact not alone on my excursion to the lake today and therefore will have to consult with my gentleman companion on the matter."

She waved her hand at a man in the lake and motioned for him to come towards her. He gave a wave back, grabbed his towel off the sand and walked in our direction. *She's here with a guy*, I thought, *another guy besides Christian*. I never did ask Christian what happened last night at the drive-in. I had avoided the topic because I wanted to be spared the mushy details. He hadn't offered any either, maybe because there was nothing to tell. Maybe after getting to know each other better they decided they didn't have enough in common to go steady. Maybe they decided to just be friends. Maybe, maybe, maybe...but now who was *this* guy? A new man of the hour? If so, she was into older men.

"What honey?" the man coming toward us asked, rubbing his thick russet hair in a towel.

"Do you mind if they sit with us?"

"That depends," he said, glaring sideways in our direction. "Who are they and what do they want with my daughter?"

"DAD!" Sara gasped in embarrassment.

Phew, that explains a lot, I thought.

"This is Christian and Sam, who I told you about, like, a hundred times. Plus you hired them to mow your lawn. I was working with Christian all last week. Remember?"

"Oh, duh," her dad said, extending his hand out to both of us.

"Dad, please don't try to sound cool, it just sounds dumb," Sara said, rolling her eyes.

"I'll try," he laughed. "So, I guess we've met before then. In case you forgot, I'm Russell Moran." He shook both our hands with vigor, leaving behind a wet imprint on my palm. The coolness was a relief.

"Nice to meet you...again," Christian said; "We must have left quite an impression on you." We all let out a chuckle.

"Sara, I thought you said your last name was Sunby," I asked, wondering if I had remembered correctly.

"It is. I have my mom's last name," she answered looking down, trying to seem occupied by the pattern on the blanket.

Oh God, why did I have to ask? It had only been five minutes and I was already putting my foot in my mouth. Whenever her mother was mentioned, she looked so vulnerable; it made me want to shield her from the hurt that she was obviously facing. I was glad that her father ignored the comment; all I wanted to do was drop the subject.

"I don't see why you can't join us. It'll be nice to have some male company for a change," Mr. Moran said, as he moved the cooler aside to make room for us to sit. "Besides, I want to get to know who my little girl is hanging around with."

"Thanks, we really appreciate it," Christian said, setting his belongings down and taking the spot closest to Sara.

I slid in tentatively next to Mr. Moran, feeling awkward about the whole situation. Sara's father had probably planned an enjoyable day out with his now live-in daughter so as to get to know her better. Now we had just sufficiently butted in on any quality time alone they would have had. Christian always made himself at home around other people's families; I never understood how he could do it. He fit in wherever he went as if everyone was related to him. People warmed up very quickly to him because he always seemed at ease. For me, it took a little longer to feel comfortable around new people. There were many times I envied Christian's chameleon-like abilities, now being one of them.

"So, you ready to do what we came here for?" Christian asked me, nudging his chin at the water.

"You bet. On three?" I replied, thankful for a chance to get away from the awkward situation.

"One....two...three!" we called out in unison, making a mad dash for the shining lake. We barreled straight through the shallow area, diving head first into the dark waters. I came up faster than I went in, gasping for air. The unexpected icy cold wetness crushed my chest.

"Whoa! That's freezing!" Christian shouted.

"Yeah! I think we were supposed to get used to it first, you know, ease in!" I chattered back. "This lake is glacial run-off from the mountains."

"Oh, yea, I forgot," Christian said.

Mr. Moran had followed us down to the shore and called out, "Pleasantly surprised are we fellows?!"

"I think I'd rather be hot!" Christian called back.

I shook my head passionately in agreement. "Let's go warm up and try again later."

We swam as fast as our frozen, stiff arms would take us to shore. Mr. Moran had walked in slowly up to his waist, looking content with the temperature of his body. "Ah, so refreshing," he commented as we passed by.

"Back so soon?" Sara asked.

"I can't feel my toes," Christian said, grabbing frantically for his white tiger emblazoned towel.

"We just couldn't stand being away from you," I said.

She must have assumed I was joking, as I had made it seem, because she laughed. Only I knew there was some truth to the statement. I figured it couldn't hurt my cause to sneak in a comment of interest whenever I could.

"Ohhh, would you look at that ice cream truck over there. I swear it's taunting me. I could go for a Sno-Cone so bad right now," she said.

"Go get one. Do need money?" Christian asked.

"No, it's just that I am so hot I don't even have the energy to *think* about walking all the way over there to get one. How pathetic is that?"

"I'll go get it for you," I said. "I'll get you whatever you want." After I said it, I realized how eager to please I sounded so I pulled back and acted nonchalant; "I mean, like, if you want a Screwball or Drumstick, I could get you one of those too. I was thinking of going over there anyway."

"No, no. I wasn't trying to get you to be my servant or anything. I would feel bad. It's too hot. Look nobody's even over there because he's parked on the pavement," she argued.

"Good, that means there won't be a line. It'll be quick and easy. No big deal. Plus, I'm sure Christian wants something too. Don't you?" I asked, prodding Christian to comply so that she wouldn't feel bad for having me go for just her.

"No, not really, I'm good," he said, stretching his limbs out in the sun.

"See. I don't want to be the only one making you go over there. I can live without a Sno-Cone," she said, waving her hand to dismiss the idea.

"Yeah, but think of how cold and icy and delicious they are. Come on, I really don't mind," I said trying to entice her.

She glanced in the direction of the petite vehicle which was sitting there full of delicious treats. Finally she let out an excited, "Oh, ok! I do want one! I do. But would you really go get me one just because I'm being lazy right now?"

"Of course. It's no big deal," I replied, feeling my cheeks blush ever so slightly. I was almost bursting inside thinking that something I was about to do was going to make her happy.

"Here's the money," she said, reaching into a tie dyed bag that had a peace sign on the front and then shoving a five dollar bill in my hand. "It's on me, get whatever you want." I opened my mouth to protest but before I could say anything she said, "I insist."

As I reached into my pockets, I felt the soggy exterior of my wallet and realized that I hadn't taken it out before I dove into the water. I doubted there was a dollar bill left intact inside, so I had no choice but to take her money.

"Ok, thanks, if you insist."

"I do."

"I'll be right back then. Try to stay cool."

I bounded off in the direction of the whimsical truck labeled *Jimmy's Ice Cream and Snacks*. I must have sparked a wave of patrons because as I approached the ordering window, a line of people began forming, some of them seemingly cutting directly in front of me as they stood up from their towels. I took a spot as quickly as I could in back of a toddler and her mother. The young server behind the window looked friendly but worn-out from being stuffed inside the cramped, unventilated truck all day. Standing on my tip-toes, I tried to see over the woman's wide-brimmed hat in front of me. I wanted to double-check the menu to make sure that it included Sno-Cones. I had known of a few of these snack mobiles that stuck strictly to soft serve ice cream and left out the syrup slathered icy treat that Sara so craved.

My eyes caught a miniature picture of a half-red, half-blue round concoction on top of a white paper cone. They had them;

I breathed a sigh of relief. Planting my sandals firmly on the black tar, I waited as an indecisive young boy at the front of the line held everyone up. When he finally decided on a character-faced vanilla pop but then couldn't come up with the last five cents to pay, the woman with the large hat became exasperated and threw a nickel on the counter to get the boy on his way. I turned around to locate Sara who was looking in my direction. I gave her an "it-figures" shrug of the shoulders in reference to the line that had formed. She nodded her head in agreement.

When I looked back, it was already my turn to order. I heard the people behind me mumbling under their breath about my slowness. I shuffled up to the window and ordered two Sno-Cones. I detested the pre-packaged kind that lacked enough syrup and were wrapped in a plastic baggie, so I was happy to see the young man scoop the ice fresh from the cooler and top them with cherry flavored juice from a squeeze bottle, just the way I liked them.

"Three dollars, please," the attendant said, leaning against the counter.

Change in hand, along with two huge wet Sno-Cones, I held tightly to both, praying for good balance which had always eluded me.

"You got all that?" the attendant asked, concerned.

"Yeah, not a problem. Thanks," I said, obviously lying.

As soon as I got a few steps onto the pavement, the ice began to melt. The water made the paper cones so soggy that I could barely hold them without ripping a hole in the bottom. All I could imagine was the look of disappointment on Sara's face if I came back with two sticky dollar bills and the tattered paper remains of a once refreshing Sno-Cone. I concentrated all my effort into applying just the right amount of pressure, so as not to squeeze the ice out the top, while keeping them safely in my sweaty hand. Looking at my feet the entire time, I carefully dodged sand pails and towels as I made my way through the sea of people spread out on the grass.

After what seemed like an hour, I finally approached our spot. I confidently took my eyes off the ground and focused them forward, hoping to see Sara waiting there anxiously for my return. But instead, she was turned towards Christian, listening to something that he was whispering in her ear. She wasn't laughing, but rather listening intently to words that were very soft and obviously meant to be so. She shifted her weight to lean in closer to hear and I saw what I wished I hadn't. Christian's hand was entwined with hers.

Even though I had suspected they were an item, the proof of the fact stabbed me like a knife in the gut. My last bit of hope with her was gone. They were officially together.

"Hey, guys and gal. Are all the sharks scaring you away from the water?" Mr. Moran said, returning from a swim.

Sara and Christian quickly separated and acted as if nothing had happened between them.

"Sam! I didn't know you were standing there. How the heck did you carry these back by yourself?" Sara asked, surprised.

"Oh, I manage ok by myself," I replied, with a hint of irony in my voice. It went unnoticed.

"Here, let me take one off your hands," she said, quickly reaching for the cone in my left hand and taking her change at the same time. "They look sooo good! Hey, thanks again for going up there for me, this is awesome."

"You must've got your love of those from me. I never could pass one up," Mr. Moran said, practically licking his lips at the sight of the cherry slathered wonder.

"Actually, I got this one for you. What's left of it anyway," I said, glancing at the sticky runoff on my hands.

"Really? Thanks, you're my kind of guy." He smiled and grabbed the remaining cone.

"No, you didn't get one for him. Sam, you wanted one for yourself. Dad, give that back, he's just trying to be polite."

"No, I'm not. It's for him. Really. I don't even like them that much."

"See, he doesn't even like them. I say don't look a gift horse in the mouth. I'll take it with thanks," he said, biting front teeth first into the cold mixture.

Sara shot me a probing look but I gave her no response. Christian noticed her puzzlement and chimed in.

"You'll never get Sam to lay his cards on the table, so don't even try. I've known him for ten years and I still can't figure him out. Not that it's a bad thing; he's just not an open book."

"Funny, I've only known him a week and I think I already *do* have him figured out," she said.

She offered a smile to no one in particular and began to chew the ice, catching up with the melting in her hand. I wasn't sure how to take that statement.

"Looks like I forgot to get napkins. I'll go grab some real quick," I said, turning in the other direction before I finished the sentence, so as to avoid protest from anyone on the blanket.

Get me away from here, I thought. *I need to be alone for one minute.* I breathed deeply and pushed my way through the crowd back to the vendor. It had been much easier to come to terms with being her friend when I was alone in my room. Now that I was out here actually seeing them together in person, it was a hard pill to swallow.

"Did you have a huge spill or something?" the server asked. I hadn't realized that while I was thinking I was grabbing handful after handful of napkins.

"Huh? Oh, yeah," I quickly mumbled, dropping the last fistful on the counter and walking off.

This time I walked back slower since there was nothing waiting for me back on the blanket but heartache. I took in the expressions of the smiling people all around me and wondered what it would be like to be that happy. For now, I would have to force myself to just be content. Sometimes I wondered if it would be better to just not *be* at all.

As I got inevitably closer to my group, I noticed the flecks of her hair catching the sunlight and reflecting back all shades of brown and red. The hues danced playfully in the prism around her that my eyes were creating. I started to smile at this wonderful optical illusion until I felt the bulge of twenty paper napkins in my hand and remembered who I was to her. The friend.

The camera on my life came into focus and I began to see the scene on the blanket in front of me as if it were a movie. Set against the backdrop of the idyllic White Mountain location sat the handsome father who wouldn't let time touch him; my best friend, the dashing young man who could charm any lady; and then there was the girl, the leading lady who captivated the hearts of everyone she encountered. Vulnerable yet strong, she commanded the screen. Then here I stood, on the outskirts of the shot, a supporting character. I would never share a scene exclusively with her; never earn her affections; never be written in to further the plot of her life. She seemed unreachable, yet blissfully unaware of her position. I felt surreally removed, as if I had been written out of the story of my own life in favor of a nobler hero.

As the scene faded into darkness in my mind, I imagined I heard the voice-over speaking in my head, *"When someone has your heart without knowing it, life can become wrapped up in longing; longing for a moment, a day, a lifetime, an eternity. Your life is not your own."*

I could feel that my destiny was forever entangled with hers, and yet she might never know it. This was something I was going to have to accept. Napkins in hand, I walked back to join Mr. Moran, Christian and Sara, and took my place at the edge of the blanket.

CHAPTER 6

As the sizzling heat of July dragged on, we returned to the lake many times. Thankfully, either I became numb at seeing them together or good at ignoring them because my pride was stinging less and less. Each day seemed to get a little easier, as I gradually conceded an acceptance to their relationship. It helped that Sara fit seamlessly into our lives as if she had been there all along. We three went everywhere together. Where a duo of best friends had once been, there was now a trio, and we all felt richer for it. Though at times my heart still ached to be on the receiving end of her affection, I figured it was better to be with her as a friend than not at all.

I even found myself giving Christian relationship advice. I casually mention once that he should be more sensitive to Sara's feelings as I didn't think she appreciated hearing recounts of his dates with old flames. He seemed to take the advice to heart and never uttered another word on the subject. I silently cursed myself afterward for saying anything. I realized I wasn't doing myself any favors by making him more appealing.

As July stepped back and August moved forward, there came a sudden and welcome lift from the heavy oppression of the hot temperatures to more seasonal warmth. Everyone in town seemed to be breathing easier and enjoying the long days. On one particularly cooler day, we three amigos decided to take a forty five minute ride out to Mercury Chasm to spend the day. The Chasm, as most locals called it, was in a section of the national park where smooth rocks and jagged boulders littered the landscape. The rocks made such a peculiar formation that they seemed to have been dropped there from outer space and were thus dubbed the Mercury rocks. In the summer, teenagers flocked to The Chasm like it was Woodstock. Many of the trails were dangerous and took a lot of skill and youthful vigor to maneuver through which meant that the secluded trails were a perfect place to hang, away from the prying eyes of children and grown-ups. Christian and I had never actually been there before but the reputation of the place had reached our ears and we were eager to see its peaks for ourselves. We pulled into the wooded parking area a little after two o'clock.

"It certainly looks very...rocky," Sara commented, raising her eyebrows as she stepped out of the passenger seat and took in the scenery.

"Pretty much exactly how I pictured it," Christian said, nodding his head; "at least it's nice and shady here." He shrugged his left shoulder, indicating that the place was to his liking.

"Which trail should we start on? There's a lot of different paths to take from here." I tried to get a general consensus.

I could almost hear the testosterone pumping through his veins as Christian replied, "Whichever one looks the hardest."

"Why don't we settle for medium difficulty so that Sam and I can keep up with you," Sara said.

"Yeah, you're right. We should take it easy on Sam," Christian joked.

"Since you're all catering to me, I say we take that one there."

I pointed to a well-trodden looking path that had minimal incline and seemed to curve into the enormous mass of pine trees in front of us. They both agreed and we headed in that direction, traversing the larger rocks that we came across with ease. We shimmied sideways in between two flat slabs of granite that had been dubbed the "Orange Squeezer" and proceeded down into a short cave labeled by a wooden sign, "The Devil's Coffin". Sara shivered her way through the cold, damp rock. Christian made it through first back into the light of day as we followed closely behind.

"I'm doing *that* next!" he said.

We emerged squinting, trying to see what he was talking about. He pointed straight ahead.

"You can't be serious," Sara said craning her head backwards to look up at the massive straight-faced wall of stone fifty feet in front of us.

He nodded his head enthusiastically and ran over to the base of the rock. As I had known for a while, Christian inherited a daredevil gene from his father, now Sara was about to see his recklessness in action for the first time.

"Don't you need special equipment to climb something that steep?" she asked, following him.

"Nah. I think this is Elephant Head, I heard of some seniors last year that climbed this. If they did it without any harnesses or anything, we can too. What do you think Sam?" he asked, motioning his head towards the mini mountain.

I glanced back at Sara and could tell by the scowl on her face that she had reservations about the climb. I had some myself but I didn't want to disappoint my pal who was obviously dead-set to take on the mammoth before us. However, I also didn't want to put Sara in danger.

"How about the people that want to go up can do it and the people that don't want to can take the long way around and then we can meet up on the other side," I said, trying to be as impartial with my answer as possible, so as not to disappoint either of them.

"Does that mean that you're one of the people that want to go up or not? Because I'm going," Christian answered, with and obvious lack of patience. He wedged his foot on a jagged rock and reached above him for a grip.

I looked over at Sara to see what she was going to do before I gave my answer. She was looking exasperated by the whole situation. Probably not wanting to seem afraid, she stubbornly grabbed hold of a piece of rock behind Christian's foot and began climbing.

"I guess we're all going up," I called to Christian, who was already two or three lengths above us.

"Hey, you don't have to do this if you don't want to, I don't care," I said, tapping Sara's foot lightly.

"I know, but I don't want to feel like a chicken when he brags about this the rest of the night," she whispered back. I shook my head in concurrence. All was understood, she didn't want to lose face to a boy.

Besides my cramping hands, the climb seemed to be going fairly smoothly as we approached the quarter mark. When I looked back to see how much space was between us and the ground, a feeling of determination to finish swept over me. I figured the others felt the same because, besides an occasional grunt of heavy breath, no one said a word.

We continued in silence until a particularly crumbly piece of ledge broke off and flew by me. I looked up and could see that it had come from under Christian's fingers as he tried to overextend his reach for a higher hold. Regaining his balance quickly, he grabbed for another more solid piece but the break-off sent a flurry of rocks below him. Just as Sara's leg came up to meet her next nook, a small avalanche of dirt and dust met her there instead. I heard her struggle for a brief moment and, looking up, watched as her foot violently slid out from underneath her. She shrieked in fear as she lost her grip. Her body plunged fifteen feet downward so fast that there was nothing anyone could do.

Thud.

Her back hit the unmovable ground below. My voice was the first to call out to her.

"Oh my god, Sara! Are you hurt?! Can you move?!" I frantically screamed beginning the descent towards her.

"What the heck happened? Are you ok? Should I come down there?" Christian asked, sounding scared and dumbfounded.

"I'm...I mean...I think I'm ok...," she slowly responded, trying to make her body sit up; "no...don't come down. I'm ok...I'll be ok. Keep going up. I'll meet you on the other side. It's too slippery there for you to come down now," she said, calling back to Christian. The shakiness in her voice gave away her fake bravado.

I was already rushing as fast as I could down the face of the rock. Jumping the last three feet I knelt at her side. I looked up and saw Christian hurrying to finish the rest of the climb.

"You didn't have to come down. Like I said, I'm ok." Tears were welling up in her eyes.

"Oh, stop, of course you're not alright. Do you think you can stand?"

She winced as she tried to put weight on her wrist to hoist herself to a sitting position. I locked my arms under hers and lifted her limp form onto her feet where she freely let herself lean against me before getting her bearings to stand on her own.

"Owww," she instinctively blurted out as she tried to walk. "I think I'll just sit here for a minute until I feel better." She placed one hand on her lower back as she tried lowering herself to the ground.

"Here let me help you," I said, lowering her against a tree trunk that could support her while she sat. "Look, I know you said you're ok, but I think your wrist is as beat up as your back."

She glanced down at the sorry, swollen sight of her right wrist and ran her fingers lightly over the red marks on her arm where no doubt black and blues would appear the following morning. She looked me right in the eyes with weariness and collapsed against the tree in defeat.

"It does hurt. Like, really, really hurts. Actually everything does. And he didn't even come down to see if I was alright. I mean I know I told him not to but I didn't really think he would just keep going. I thought that he would come rushing down, like you did. I just needed someone to help me."

A few tears streaked down her face, cutting through the redness. The emotional neglect seemed to be causing her more pain than her physical wounds. I wanted to join in and lambaste Christian as well but it felt like a betrayal to utter a negative word against my best friend, whether he deserved it or not, which he most decidedly did.

"At least *I'm* here to take care of you," I said, hoping to relieve her pain.

Grabbing the bottom of my shirt, I stretched it up to her face and wiped away the mixture of dirt and tears that had stained it. She smiled gratefully and, with a sigh, let all her weight fall against me. Her head rested gently on my shoulder. I closed my eyes and drew in a long breath. I wanted to ingrain in my memory the sweet smell of her hair and the softness of her cotton t-shirt. We sat together like that for a few moments in silence until a hurried rustle of footsteps approached from behind the rock.

"Finally! I didn't think it would take so long to get over here. I don't know what I was thinking wanting to climb that thing," Christian explained in a winded voice. "How is she?" he asked me, as though I were the attending physician on duty.

"She's pretty banged up. We should get her home. Her wrist might be broken."

"Broken?! Oh god, this is all my fault. I'm so stupid sometimes," he said, smacking his hand against his forehead. "Sara what's it feel like? Do you think it's broken?" he asked, kneeling down to examine it.

"Well, I can't move it just yet. But I did break my arm goofing around with my cousins when I was little and I don't think it hurts as bad as that did. So, it's probably not broken."

"Awesome," Christian said, breathing a sigh of relief; "shouldn't we keep it elevated though or something? I think that's what you're supposed to do."

"I forgot about that," she said, as she bent up her elbow and reached as far as she comfortably could towards the sky.

"Does that feel better?" Christian asked.

"A little but can we go home now?"

"Of course. Yeah. I didn't mean for you to sit out here all day, let's get going," Christian said, nodding profusely and helping her to her feet.

He took hold of her hand and started to lead her back at a steady pace towards the car, seemingly unaware that she was limping horribly.

"She shouldn't really be walking right now. I think she hurt her back when she hit the ground," I pointed out.

"Oh…yeah, right. I guess I'll just have to carry her."

He formed his arms into a cradle and literally swept her off her feet. Sara seemed to welcome the respite and didn't object to being carried around like a baby. I followed closely behind them, carrying Sara's brown hiking sneakers, which I had suggested be taken off her feet in case her ankles swelled. Christian carried her in his arms through the entire path, dodging braches and pine cones along the way. As we reached the car, I ran ahead and cleared the back seat so that she could lay down on the ride home. I reached in the cooler for some ice but a puddle of water lay stale where it had long since melted in the trunk. The bottles of water still seemed cold enough so I grabbed two of those.

"Here you go," I said, twisting one open. "Drink this, you don't wanna dehydrate after a fall like that or you'll get dizzy."

She gulped the water down feverishly and splashed some on her face to cool down. When she was comfortably settled into the car I handed her the second bottle and said, "Put this one on your wrist. It may bring down the swelling."

"Thanks," she replied, grabbing it as Christian took off speeding down the highway.

"Oh, shoot, you *can't* take me home. I forgot, my dad's out of town for the night, he won't be back until tomorrow afternoon," Sara said in a shaky voice.

Christian and I gave each other a *can-you-believe-it* shake of the head; it must have been the third time in as many weeks that Sara's dad had been out of town and left her alone, with now being the most inconvenient time of all for him to be absent.

"What a jerk," Christian whispered.

"We can take her to your house, your mom will be able to look at her and know what to do," I said.

"Yeah, true. She did take those nursing classes after my dad and her split," he agreed.

"Sounds good to me," Sara said.

We smiled, not knowing that she had been listening to our quiet conversation.

"Hey, no one's talking to you back there. Pipe down gimp," Christian joked.

Sara smirked and continued to drink her water. The extra attention seemed to be causing her to feel better by the minute.

As we squealed into the driveway, I saw Ms. Fine peek out the bedroom window. We must have looked like a desperate troupe as we hobbled Sara to her doorstep because she promptly rushed out to help us in.

"Mom, thank God your home."

"I wasn't feeling myself today so I stayed home to rest in the air conditioning. What on Earth happened to you Sara?" she asked, escorting us into the living room.

"The boys beat me up again." Despite her obvious concern, Ms. Fine couldn't help laughing a little.

"She fell," I said, thinking that this was no time to be joking. I helped set her down on the sofa.

Ms. Fine noticed Sara's swollen wrist and deep scrapes. "Fell from where? The moon?" she demanded, in a concerned tone.

My elbow nudged Christian and I shot him a look that said, *It was your idea, you're telling her.*

"Actually, we were climbing Elephant Head at the chasm," Christian confessed.

"Christian Michael Fine! I know you put this poor girl up to climbing that elephant rock. And believe me, we *will* talk later about that. But right now she needs some ice, ibuprofen, antibiotic ointment, band aids and lots of pillows. Can you *please* go get them?" she said, addressing her son.

Christian eagerly complied and ran off faster than a roadrunner.

"It would just figure that this would happen when you are almost an hour away from home. You must be in horrible pain sweetie," she said, stroking Sara's hair.

Sara nodded in agreement but kept silent as if she didn't want to waste any more of the little energy she had on words. Having just been moved from the car to the house, she looked like she felt worse now than before. Christian returned with the necessary supplies and I sprang into action, propping up her swollen arm with three pillows and applying ice packs to her wrist and back. Meanwhile, Ms. Fine got a glass of water for her to take the ibuprofen with.

"You should feel these kick in within fifteen minutes and then the pain and swelling will go down a bit. But I need to feel your back and this wrist of yours to see if it's broken or not, ok?" Ms. Fine asked.

Sara nodded in agreement. Mrs. Fine took her time poking, prodding and moving the joint around until she was seemingly convinced that an emergency room visit wasn't needed. Then she shook her head satisfactorily in triumph.

"I've concluded my examination Miss Sunby, shall I give you the good news first or the bad news?" Ms. Fine played the role of nurse which seemed to put Sara at ease.

"Bad news first please, so that I am not kept in suspense any longer."

"The bad news is that you will need to stay in bed a few days and care for some pretty badly strained muscles in your back as well as in your carpal region, *that's your wrist*. The good news is that nothing is broken."

"That *is* good news!" Christian exclaimed.

"It certainly is good news *for her*, but it doesn't mean that you are off the hook," she said, shooting her son the evil eye.

"Don't go too hard on him, it was my choice. He didn't make me do anything that I didn't want to do," Sara said in his defense.

"I know my son, and I'm sure he wasn't as innocent as you are claiming. After all, he is of the male species." The ladies chuckled while we remained silent.

"I'd better call your father Sara and tell him what's happened. I'll make sure to send you home with everything you'll need the next couple of days."

"Actually, my dad's away until tomorrow on business. That's why we came here first," Sara said.

"Oh, my goodness. You can't go home to an empty house in your condition. And someone needs to take a look at those wounds in the morning so they don't get infected." Ms. Fine barely paused to think then said, "You'll have to stay here for the night and that's all there is to it. You can be my little patient for the next twenty four hours. I'll make up Christian's bed for you and he can sleep on the couch. That is, if you don't mind staying here."

"No, of course I don't mind. I think that sounds great. Actually, I wasn't sure what I was going to do if you didn't ask," Sara replied.

"Great! Then it's all settled. I'll get some fresh sheets," she exclaimed, setting off with a purpose.

"I've never seen my mom that happy about making the bed for *me*," Christian commented.

"She's probably excited to have a lady in the house for a change. I'm sure she's heard enough burps and farts to last her a lifetime," Sara said, rolling her eyes.

"Too bad you didn't sprain your mouth muscle," Christian joked, sitting down carefully next to her on the couch.

I understood the circumstances of the sleepover but felt strangely uncomfortable thinking about Sara sleeping in Christian's bed tonight. I figured it might be a good time to leave and mope for a while.

"I should probably get going guys. Do you need anything before I leave?" I asked.

"Yeah, I'll take a Coke," Christian answered.

"He wasn't talking to *you*! Don't go yet Sam. Sit down and relax. We've all had a rough day, let's just lounge and watch some TV."

"Hey Sammy, I'll make a deal with you. If Who's the Boss is on, then you have to stay. If it's not, then you can go."

"Sounds fair," I said, conceding to my friend's odd wager. He picked up the remote, clicked on the set and flicked through a few channels until we all heard the familiar voice of Tony Danza.

"Come on! What are the odds of that?" I exclaimed.

"I guess that settles it, you're staying," Sara concluded with a smile.

"Ha! Gotcha! Who's the Boss is on at this time every week," Christian laughed, slapping his knee for effect. Sara and I proceeded to break out into laughter as well.

"What's so funny?" Ms. Fine asked, poking her head into the living room.

"It's just Christian being Christian," Sara said, trying to catch her breath.

"That says it all," she said, turning back to her task.

The three of us sat there contentedly for a long while, letting the boob-tube pacify our minds while leaving the excitement of the day behind us. A little after nine o'clock Sara started yawning and her eyes waned behind her slipping lids. I could tell that she wanted to go to bed but probably didn't want to say so and risk being a party pooper.

"I'd better get going or my parents are gonna be wondering what happened to me," I lied, knowing that my curfew wasn't until eleven.

"I'm getting pretty sleepy myself," Sara said, yawning again.

"I didn't want to tell you what to do, but you really *should* get some sleep kiddo. I think you'll feel better in the morning," Ms. Fine said optimistically, as she slowly rubbed her hand over Sara's back to soothe her.

Christian and I helped her off the couch and into the bedroom while Ms. Fine followed closely behind. I could tell by the way she moved that she was still sore and very stiff but as she lowered onto the soft Percale sheets, the muscles in her face began to relax.

"Sleep as late as you want. We are generally lazy around here on Saturdays, especially in the morning," Ms. Fine said.

"Thanks. I never sleep late though," Sara made a point of saying.

"Why not? Did you grow up on a farm or something?" Ms. Fine asked.

"No, it's just, like, a personal choice of mine."

"I wish I was born with that kind of self-discipline. I think the only time I've seen a sunrise is when I've stayed awake all night and six a.m. happens to come before I've fallen asleep," Ms. Fine joked.

"Yeah, I used to be a night owl too. Getting up early is kinda something I do for my mom," Sara confessed.

"What kind of something?" Ms. Fine probed, having been told by Christian about Sara's circumstance and obviously trying to get her to open up about it.

"Well, it's kinda silly but, my mom loved the mornings. She said it was the only time that the world was quiet and peaceful. From my bedroom I could hear her in the mornings making coffee and turning the pages of the newspaper and I would always stuff the pillow over my head and go back to sleep. When she got sick, I started sleeping in her bed with her in case she needed anything during the night. She was vomiting a lot, you know, and I had to make sure she could get to the bathroom safely because she was so dizzy. But even through all of that, she still got up early every morning. I don't know how she did it. But it's like she had to have that time in the morning to keep her sane. So anyway, one day she crept out of bed as usual at six thirty. She was so quiet that day, I never heard a peep. I didn't even feel the bed move. I just kept sleeping. And by seven she was gone. Gone forever. She was alive for that half hour and I didn't spend it with her. She died alone without anyone holding her hand or telling her that it was going to be alright. I slept through my mother dying and I swear I'll never sleep through anything again."

Ms. Fine's eyes were brimming over with tears and she was shaking her head back and forth contradictorily in Sara's direction.

"Honey, your mother did not die alone. She died exactly when and where she wanted to. Believe me; no mother would want their child to see them die. She knew that you would be asleep and that's how she wanted it. She wanted you to remember her as she was in life, not as she was in her final moments. Do not ever blame yourself Sara. Any mother would be proud to have you as their daughter."

At that, Sara's eyes gave way to tears as well. Christian and I remained quiet as they embraced, and surprisingly I didn't feel awkward watching them cry together. Ms. Fine clicked off the light as we all walked out and retired to her bedroom, saying before she closed the door to no one in particular, "I thank God for sending that girl into my life."

As I slipped out the kitchen door and into the warm night air, I imagined Sara staring at the ceiling of the strange, but comfortable room, a wave of peace sweeping through her body as she realizes that her cozy bed was made with love by a mother. For probably the first time in three months, the burden of silence over her mother's death had been lifted. That night she felt warm, safe and cared for. And I'm sure she never wanted it to end.

CHAPTER 7

"I'm home," I called out as I passed the living room where my parents sat watching TV and made my way straight into my bedroom.

I had barely seen my parents since we got back from the trip. Whenever I spent any length of time with them, I got stressed out, so I found avoidance made my life a lot easier. I didn't understand why they felt the need to constantly pick my life apart. Christian's family was so much more laid back, especially his mom, she was never on his case about cleaning his room or doing better in school or using good posture or any of the other million things that my parents felt the need to criticize me about. I'm sure that they meant well, but their approach was definitely off-putting. Why would I want to spend time feeling crappy about myself at home when I could be around people that didn't care if I put my feet on the coffee table?

I closed the door to my room as a sign that I didn't want to be bothered by anyone tonight. I planned on getting up early to go over to the Fines' so that I could see Sara before she left. I knew my parents weren't going to happy about that since Saturdays were usually family day, but I was willing to deal with the consequences when I got home.

The next morning I left a note on the kitchen table explaining to my parents where I had gone and slipped out the door before they were awake. Hearing voices as I approached the Fines', I tapped on the door first, to be polite, then swung open the screen and re-entered the house I had just left ten hours earlier;

the smell of syrup and sizzling griddle butter greeted me. Ms. Fine was standing at the stove in her terry cloth bathrobe flipping white bread over a spatula as she giggled with Sara about the mess they were making.

"Hi, Sam. Take a seat. Christian should be up any minute. Want some?" she asked. I felt instantly welcomed.

"Sure. It smells so good, how could I resist?"

"Is that food or am I dreaming?" Christian asked emerging bleary eyed from around the corner.

"No, my son, it is not a dream. Sara and I got up early and decided to make french toast."

"I thought you only knew how to put cereal in a bowl," he said.

"Ha, ha very funny. I can cook, when I want to, which I admit isn't very often."

"No kidding. I think I can count on one hand how many times you've cooked me a hot breakfast."

"Good morning to you too sunshine," Ms. Fine replied, lightheartedly. "You're lucky we waited for you at all. We've been up since six thirty and couldn't wait any longer to eat. Sara suggested french toast which I thought was nice since usually we are always rushing in the mornings, which by the way is *why* I never cook. Actually, we should start getting up earlier; I think it would be much less stressful on both of us."

"*You* can get up earlier if you want to but I'd fall asleep in class. I don't get to take naps everyday like you," he retorted.

"We'll talk about it later when you've woken up a bit. And for your information, I don't take naps *all* the time...just lately. I think the heat's been making me tired," she said, raising her eyebrows in disapproval at her son's snippiness.

"Oh, great. See what you've started? Please don't tell her you're a vegetarian or we'll be having salads for dinner every night," Christian said to Sara.

"I wouldn't talk if I were you, last night I heard you snoring all the way in my room," Sara said straight-faced, looking down at her mixing bowl.

"You did not! I don't snore! Mom, tell her I've never snored a day in my life," Christian protested.

"Oh, yes, you certainly do. Sometimes you're so loud I think there is a cow in the next room," his mom replied with a smirk, which he didn't notice.

"Exactly! That's what it sounded like; a cow. It was more a moo than a snore. Kinda like...*MoooOOOOooo, MOOOOoooo*," Sara said, giving her best imitation of the barnyard animal.

Ms. Fine and Sara burst into laughter. Christian's cheeks flushed pink when he realized he was being played for a fool. He sat down in embarrassment to eat and I hid my smile so as not to stoke his anger anymore. He wasn't used to be ganged up on by females. Luckily, the thick and sticky sweetness of his breakfast slowed his tongue and calmed his mood.

When we were done, I volunteered to clean the mess and although Christian was supposed to help, he bailed on me after the first three dishes were dried to join the others who were setting up a board game.

"Christian, get back in there and help Sam," his mother ordered when she saw him walk away.

"No, that's ok, there isn't much left here," I lied; "I can finish by myself. You guys go ahead and start without me."

"That's not fair," said Sara. "Let me help you."

"No, really," I insisted. "Go ahead. I'm no good at Clue anyway. I'll play the next game."

"See ma, he doesn't mind. Now let's get this thing started," Christian said.

"Alright Sam, if you're sure. But Christian gets the next mess all to himself," Ms. Fine said. I nodded my head in agreement.

By the time I was done scraping dried-on egg batter off the countertop, the game was almost over. When I walked in the living room, Sara was propped on the couch with pillows behind her, Ms. Fine was leaning down to roll, and Christian was stretched out on the floor.

"Hey, Sammy. Who seems more like the murdering type to you? Professor Plum or Colonel Mustard?" Christian asked, needing some input on who he should point the finger at.

"Colonel Mustard, I guess."

"You ready Sara? Check the card to see if I'm right and no letting mom peek. I accuse..." Christian inhaled a deep breath before blurting out his accusation; "Colonel Mustard with the candlestick in the parlor".

"And you would be...correct?! No, I can't believe it," Sara said, double checking the cards. "There's no way you could have guessed right already. Did you cheat?" she asked, glancing sideways at us suspiciously.

"I've suspected for a long time now that Sam is the brains behind your operation and this has just confirmed it," Ms. Fine said.

"I didn't cheat, I swear," I said, putting my hands up to show that I wasn't holding any cards. "It's him, he's just always lucky."

"Winner cleans up the game. Isn't that right Ms. Fine? That's the rule in my house," Sara said.

"Oh, please, call me Katrina. And yes, I think that is a very good rule for our house too. I believe I will assert my parental authority and implement that rule immediately."

"I gotta get away for a while. I can't put up with these girls any longer," Christian whispered to me as he began picking up the pieces and throwing them haphazardly into the box.

"So, Sara, how are ya feeling today?" I asked, turning my attention towards her. I had been holding back this question since I walked in the door this morning so as not to appear too concerned, even though I was.

"I'm feeling better, thanks. Ms., I mean Katrina, wants me to stay off my feet for a few more hours though until she's sure that the pain won't come back. Other than that the swelling in my wrist has gone down and I'll have to live with these bruises for a while. I just hope that they go away before school starts or on top of being the new girl it'll also look like my father beats me," she said, throwing her head back with a grin.

"They're not that noticeable." I told the little white lie to comfort her.

"Ah, quit lying Sam, she looks like she was hit by a bus," Christian said bluntly but not unkindly. I shot him an exasperated glare which went unnoticed.

"Do you know what time your dad is supposed to be home?" Christian asked.

"No, I'm not sure. He didn't say, but I should probably try calling him, I guess."

"I was just thinking the same thing. I don't want him wondering where you are," Ms. Fine agreed.

Sara lifted the receiver of the push-button phone and dialed its oversized numbers. After the eighth ring, she hung up, not looking entirely disappointed.

"Nothing?" Christian probed.

"Not yet," Sara replied, shrugging her shoulders.

"So, I guess you'll have to stay a while longer then?" Christian asked.

I noticed a hint of disappointment in his voice and I'm sure Sara did too.

"Yeah, but he should be home soon so don't worry. You probably want me out of your hair by now," Sara said.

I felt an argument brewing between them.

"No, it's not that. It's nothing personally against you. It's just, remember how my friend from school asked us to go see his baseball game today against Lincoln High? Well, it starts at one and I really wanted to go but I know that you obviously can't so..." Christian left the end of his sentence unfinished as if the rest was obvious to everyone listening.

Sara picked up where he left off.

"So....you were hoping that I would go home before the game so that you could go and not have to stay here with me?"

Christian nodded sheepishly.

"Oh," she said.

The tension in the room was palpable. After a long, thoughtful silence, Ms. Fine offered a plan that would end the divisiveness.

"I know a very simple solution that will benefit everyone. We'll have a girls' day in! The boys can go enjoy their boring little baseball game, and you and I can get back in our pajamas, pig out on rocky road ice cream and watch the women-behind-bars movie marathon that's on. Who needs *men* anyway?"

"I certainly don't," Sara answered, flipping her brown hair over her shoulder, looking perkier than she had a second ago.

"Ok, that does it. Out with the boys. Boys are banned from this house until further notice," Ms. Fine said, shooing us out of the room like flies. "*Especially you,*" she muttered to Christian.

Christian began to speak a defense but as soon as he drew breath, I tugged him out of harm's way by the sleeve of his tee shirt. It was a foot in the mouth moment waiting to happen, and while I was put off by Christian's apparent selfishness, I sought to avoid any more sharp words aimed in my friend's direction. Well, besides the ones that would come from me. When we were both safely alone in the car, I sharply scolded him.

"What's the matter with you? You couldn't skip this one game and stay home with Sara today?"

"What are you talking about? You told Justin you wanted to go too," Christian said, defensively.

"Yeah, but that was before Sara got hurt and couldn't go and had to stay home all day, *at your house*."

"Hey, just because she can't go anywhere doesn't mean that I can't. It's not like we're married or anything," he huffed.

"No, that's pretty clear, but don't you feel bad for her that she hurt herself?" I asked, honestly wondering at this point.

"Of course I feel bad for her, but I'm not gonna, like, drop everything to just sit around all day."

"Don't you think you owe her at least that?"

"Why?" Christian shot back.

"Because it's your fault that she got hurt!" I blurted the statement out louder than I intended and followed it with silence.

"Oh, so you *do* think it's my fault. I didn't realize that it was me who caused the rock to crumble out from under her feet. I guess I have more power than I thought," he said in a hurt voice.

I didn't want to say any more of what I was thinking for fear that it would create a divide in our friendship that could never be bridged; I opted for more silence instead.

"So, you might as well say what you are thinking. That I am a terrible, selfish person who doesn't deserve her," Christian supposed in a rather pathetic tone.

I was pleased at the confession but not completely shocked. It was a reminder of why I had been best friends with this guy for so long. It wasn't my mind that Christian was reading, it was his own. He knew he was being self-serving; I had simply given a voice to his conscience.

"Hey, you said it not me."

"Yeah, I guess I did" he said. "I think I'm gonna call from the field and apologize to her. You're right, the whole thing stinks," Christian finished softly.

As soon as we pulled into the Lincoln High parking lot, Christian made a bee-line for the pay phone while I grabbed a spot on the bleachers. From where I was I could see him leaning against the glass as he spoke animatedly into the receiver. After what was probably the shortest apology in recorded history, he put the phone back into its cradle. He scanned the crowd for me, and I quickly turned my gaze to the field, so that it didn't look like I had been spying on him the entire time. When I heard him approaching, I squinted through the sun to see him and waved him to me.

"So, what did she say?"

"Basically, she said she doesn't like to hold grudges. I'm in the clear. It's really weird how I wasn't even looking for a great girlfriend this summer and one just kinda fell into my lap," he commented too cheery for my liking and took a seat on the bleachers next to me.

I scooted over grudgingly.

"Huh. Yeah, funny how that happened," I said, flatly.

"You know pal we were *supposed* to be looking for a girl for you this summer," he said, slapping his hand on my back.

"I'm all set," I said.

"Now, now, just because the summer's almost over doesn't mean there isn't hope left." Christian curled his hand over his eyes like the brim of a baseball hat to keep the sun out and scanned the crowd. "Now there's one. I recognize her from school. Casey Bately. Didn't you have a crush on her once?" he asked, bumping his shoulder into mine, trying to direct my attention three rows in front of us.

I glanced over in the direction of the blonde haired girl he was talking about.

"Go talk to her," he said trying to encourage me.

"No thanks," I said, shaking my head in defiance.

"No? Why not? Scared?" Christian teased.

"No, I am not scared," I retorted. "I don't have a crush on her and for your information I never did." I stared straight ahead at the player who was tapping dirt off his cleats with the bat.

"Oh, come on. *Everyone* has had a crush on her." Christian let out two compulsory laughs.

"Not me."

"Ok, then who *do* you like here? Take your pick and I'll set you up with them. You won't even have to leave your seat," Christian promised.

"No one," I replied without even looking around. "Can we just watch the game please? Isn't that what we came here for?"

"Ok, geez, Mr. Serious. I guess you're not ready to commit yet. Just take your time, think about and get back to me."

I kept looking forward as if my life depended on it, not even acknowledging what had been said, hoping that he would get the point that I was uninterested in anyone who was available. He must have realized I didn't want to talk because out of the corner of my eye I saw him shrug his shoulders as he turned toward the action on the field.

While I tried concentrating on the game in front of me, my thoughts kept drifting back to Sara. I imagined her with Ms. Fine indulging in ice cream and getting teary-eyed at the sappy drama unfolding on the television; knowing that they were probably having fun playing the role of mother and daughter. I glanced over at Christian with contempt as he raucously enjoyed every inning and out of the day. I thought about how differently the events of the past couple days would have played out if *I* were her boyfriend instead of him. I certainly wouldn't be sitting with my friend at some baseball game miles away while Sara was at home with *my* mother nursing her bumps and bruises. Of course, Sara wouldn't have even been hurt in the first place because I wouldn't have encouraged her to climb that stupid rock. I silently cursed myself for nudging Christian to mend fences with her today. I should have just stood back and watched as things rightfully fell apart.

By the time we arrived home four hours later, Sara had been returned to her father's care. Ms. Fine was very chatty the rest of the night and invited me to stay for supper; I accepted with the angle of pressing her for facts she may have learned about Sara. I didn't want to seem too obvious, so I paced my questions intermittently and seemingly casually throughout dinner. In the span of two hours I learned that Sara's favorite food was lasagna, she vacationed in Florida every year but had never been to Disney World, and that she aspired to be a writer when she grew up. I stored these facts in my brain-bank for later use.

"And why didn't you tell me that her birthday is next week?" Ms. Fine directed the question at Christian who, for the first time, looked up from his mashed potatoes and gravy.

"Because I didn't know it was next week," he said, shrugging.

"How could you not know? You're her boyfriend," she said, exasperated.

"She never told me," he answered as if that justified the fact.

"And I suppose you never asked either," she said, shaking her head in disapproval and then adding with annoyance, "*Men*!"

"Hey, don't worry. I'll get her a gift," Christian said, hurrying to redeem his self.

"You'll get her a card also. Girls love cards, it's usually better than the gift. You remember that too Sam. That's very important – *always get a card*. Make a mental note of that."

I nodded seriously, grateful for any advice that I could get on the subject and stuffed that in the brain-bank as well.

"I'd like to have a little party for her here, if you don't mind. She's such a sweet little thing and God only knows if her father will even get a cake for her. He seemed like a nice enough man but not really the parental type. I'm pretty sure he was hitting on me too," she confided as if she were talking to a girlfriend.

"Ewww, mom. I told you before I don't like hearing about that stuff. It's bad enough I have to hear about dad's dates," Christian whined.

"Your father is going out on dates? Since when?" she demanded in a tone that would have seemed more appropriate if they were still married.

"I don't know, for a couple of months I guess. I'm not even supposed to be saying anything about it."

"Well please make sure you mention to your father next weekend that I have been on my share of dates as well," she said.

"Yeah, sure," Christian muttered.

"Back to what I was saying, I think that a small party here on Thursday night with the three of us would be nice for her. Do you have any plans made yet for then?"

"No," I said, managing to slip a word into the conversation.

"Great! Then let's try to make it a surprise for her!" she exclaimed, all but clapping her hands with glee.

"Yeah, not much going on next week since school starts the week after," Christian mentioned shaking his head disapprovingly.

"Ugh. I can't even think about school right now. And homework again? No thanks," I said.

"Oh, you'll get back into the swing of things soon enough. But I do remember that feeling of wishing the summer was endless. There was always something fun going on. Now the most entertainment I get is reading a risqué romance novel. You don't know how lucky you are to be young," Ms. Fine said reminiscently, resting her chin on her right fist and taking a long glance at us sixteen year olds before she got up to clean the dishes.

We scooped up the remainder of pot roast and green beans on our plates and delivered them to her.

Some of what she said about being young stuck, and we decided to make the most of the last school-free week we had. Of course, Sara was part of that. I had to admit that the three of us fit together nicely as a group, I never felt like a third wheel and luckily they never got mushy around me. We tangled lines fishing for Kiver in the muddy pond on the edge of town, dove feet first off a sloped sandy cliff into the deep Saco River, caught a cheap flick at the second-run cinema, and frequented the ice cream stand nightly, all while managing a final cut of the lawns on our list. The only activity we purposely avoided was rock climbing.

Christian's mom made all the preparations for the party and when Thursday came we asked Sara to return to the house with us after mowing, under the guise of Ms. Fine needing help picking out a new paint color for her bedroom. As she walked through the door and her eyes caught sight of the balloons and streamers which were strewn everywhere, she lit up with a gigantic smile and you could almost see her heart pounding with excitement. We yelled, "Surprise!" in unison, and flung confetti at her wildly.

"All this for me?" she said red-faced.

"Yes it is, unless someone else you know is having a birthday today," Ms. Fine teased with affection.

"I just can't believe it. It must have been so much work to put all of this together. Thank you so, so much," Sara gushed.

She walked over and gave Christian a long, tight hug. I watched the confetti fall from her shoulders onto the floor.

"Who wants cake?" Ms. Fine asked, hurrying over to retrieve matches from the kitchen drawer.

"Me, me," answered Christian, waving his hand in the air like a child in grade school. "My mom makes the best frosting," he announced.

"*You* sit down," she said to Christian. "It was a rhetorical question. The birthday girl has to blow out her candles first. Sara, have a seat over at the chair with the balloons on it," she said, motioning to the highly decorated seat at the head of the table. She carefully lit each pastel-colored candle until the cake was radiating with heat. "Kill the lights," she said to no one in particular and Christian complied.

"Happy Birthday to you…" Ms. Fine started the song and, after a bar or two, we joined in loud enough to be heard. When our off-key rendition was finished and the cake was set before her, Sara took in a deep breath, closed her eyes and blew with all her might, trying to extinguish the candles. They went out for a brief moment and then they lit up again. She tried a second time, blowing harder than the first. Ms. Fine looked puzzled as again the candles went out, briefly followed by the return of the flame. Sara gave the cake a puzzled look and scanned the people in the room for an explanation. Christian began to chuckle and then, unable to contain his amusement, practically fell over laughing.

"Christian Fine, what did you do to her cake?" his mother demanded dumbstruck.

"Trick candles! I replaced the candles in the cabinet with trick ones yesterday. They're new. I saw them at the store. I had to get them. They're hysterical! They'll never blow out, no matter how hard you try, they just keep relighting. The look on you guys' faces was priceless!" he screeched out, in between peals of laughter.

"Oh, honestly! Things were going so smoothly. Can't you just let a nice memory be made?" Ms. Fine asked in a tone that suggested disgust.

Sara looked down at the eternal flames before her and burst out laughing as well. When I realized that she wasn't upset, my apprehension lifted and I allowed myself to laugh, which was what I had wanted to do from the beginning.

"I guess in your own distorted little way, you did just make a nice memory," Ms. Fine conceded. She reached for a long, stainless steel knife and handed it over to Sara. "Birthday girl cuts the cake," she insisted.

Sara cut four generous portions and passed them down to us. I always looked forward to Ms. Fine's delicious frosting and this time did not disappoint. The peaks were stiff, with a slight crunch to the top which gave the sweet concoction its signature style. We all greedily devoured our portions.

"Time for presents!" Ms. Fine announced.

"Gifts too? You guys spoiled me!" Sara marveled.

"You're never too old for a birthday celebration. By the way how old are you, Sara? Is this your sweet sixteen?" Ms. Fine asked, glancing over her shoulder as she gathered up the presents neatly in a pile on the table.

"Yup, but I won't be a junior. I mean, I should be, I never stayed back a grade. But I missed so much of my sophomore year when my mom got sick that I had to take incomplete grades, so, they are making me do tenth grade over again."

"But, that means we won't have any classes together," I said.

I was brokenhearted at the thought. I had hoped our schedules might put us together in a class or two that Christian didn't have, and then we might get to know each other better one-on-one. I felt like everything was working against me.

"Yeah, I know. It's a total bummer. It makes me twice as nervous. I won't know anyone in my classes."

"Oh, I wouldn't worry about it too much; you'll probably see each other in the halls and at lunch. Hey, maybe you'll have phys. ed. together. Don't they combine grades for that course? Anyway, let's not think about school on your birthday, ok? Open your gifts!" Ms. Fine said, obviously trying to ease Sara's fears a bit.

Sara looked at the three presents before her, all hiding beneath a coat of wrapping paper. She didn't seem sure which to open first, so she reached out and grabbed the smallest one.

"Good choice. That's from me," Ms. Fine pointed out.

Sara opened the attached Hallmark card first, read the poem silently and smiled in agreement at the message. She gave Ms. Fine a wink. Then she methodically peeled back the bow and shiny silver paper. A square box was revealed and she lifted the top. Her eyes lit up at the sight of a pair of dainty pearl earrings.

"Do you like them?" Ms. Fine wondered with baited breath.

"Like them? I LOVE them," Sara said, carefully picking up the small, white orbs from their cottony cushion. "These must have cost a fortune," she added, in reverence.

"Now, don't you mind about that, I feel it a privilege to have bought those for you. I am so sick of buying music cassettes, and baseball bats, and GI Joes! It's the first chance I've had to get a gift for a girl."

"All I can say is thank you. Thank you so much. They are perfect," Sara said wrapping her arms around Ms. Fine and then placing the pearls gently back in their box. If she hadn't, she might have lost them amidst the confetti.

She reached for the next package and my stomach did a flip-flop; it was mine. There had originally been a card taped to the top but I had second thoughts about giving it to her, fearing its message was too mushy, so I ripped it off right before I added it to the pile. Thankfully, there was no mark left behind telling that it had once been there. Left in its place was simple ink writing which addressed the present. The wrapping bore pink and orange polka dots and a purple ribbon secured the package closed. I wondered if she noticed the little curley-ques I had made at the end of the ribbon with my scissors. I learned in art class last year how to make them and surprisingly, they came out well.

My palms sweated as I watched her slowly rip the paper back probably wondering if the contents were as fragile as the first gift she had opened. They weren't, but nonetheless, I hoped she would still like it. Lifting the gift from the box, she held it out in front of her.

"My own journal," she said, as she ran her fingers over the embossed lettering that read *Dare to Dream*.

"It's for your poems and stories," I explained, trying to assess her reaction.

"But, how did you know that I like to write?"

I motioned my head towards Ms. Fine who smirked.

"I am going to fill up every page of this so quickly that you'll have to buy me another one for Christmas," she said, running her hand over the soft, textured fabric on the cover.

Her reaction was stronger than I expected, in a good way, and I could feel my face flush at the recognition I was getting from her. She sent me a wide grin of appreciation across the table as she stacked the blue journal under the little box with the pearls in it. She looked at her small pile of gifts with contentment.

"One more," Ms. Fine reminded.

"I wonder who this could be from," Sara teased, giving the last package a moderate shake. It was the biggest package yet and it seemed to have some weight to it.

"Just rip mine open. It's more fun that way," Christian said.

Sara tore into the shiny silver paper which was identical to the pattern Ms. Fine had used. I guessed that he had either pilfered it from her or she had actually wrapped his gift as well.

"Isn't there a card with that one?" Ms. Fine asked, searching the table for an envelope that may have fallen away from the package.

"No, I didn't see a card anywhere," Sara observed, pausing.

"Oh, don't worry about it. Maybe I'll find it later. Continue," she said, giving Christian a backwards jab with her elbow. He had neglected to follow her cardinal rule.

Sara tore into the paper until only a few stray pieces clung to the colorful box. She set it down and gave it a once over. She seemed to be mulling a reaction.

"That's very nice. Thank you, Christian," she said, patting him on the hand.

"What is it?" Ms. Fine asked, leaning over to see. It was clear now that she hadn't had a hand in the buying or wrapping of this gift.

"It's a Chia Pet," Sara said in her cheeriest voice, looking down at the gimmicky box with the pot of dirt and seed in it.

"Oh, how...nice," Ms. Fine said, studying the utterly impersonal gift in front of her.

"Yes, that's what I think. It's *very* nice and I really appreciate it," Sara said, tucking it at the bottom of her gift pile.

"I knew you'd like it. When I saw it at the drugstore I thought of you," Christian said. He beamed, obviously believing the fake sincerity being offered to him.

"And now every time I look at its grassy fur, I'll think of you," Sara said.

How she managed the sentence without laughing I don't know. Ms. Fine chuckled but quickly disguised it as a cough. I averted my eyes in embarrassment for my oblivious friend.

"Thank you guys again. This was the best party ever. I was so surprised. I just never expected this. I mean my dad didn't even get me a cake."

"See, I told you," Ms. Fine quickly pointed out to us.

"He did say that he wants us to eat together tonight though. I told him that you'd give me a ride home Christian and it's almost six, is it ok if we get going?"

He replied with a nod and a jingle of his keys.

Sara gave Ms. Fine one last warm hug and thank you. Then she turned in my direction and even though I was on the other side of the table, she stretched her arms toward me and strained her torso to lean in. I gladly reciprocated and extended my arms towards her, silently cursing the table in between us which caused a level of awkwardness in reaching for each other. She pulled me in with a tight squeeze. Her long brown hair fell lightly on my cheek. I inhaled the fruity scent of her conditioner which reminded me of fresh picked apples from the orchard. I wanted to breathe in that scent forever.

Our embrace lasted only briefly, as was appropriate for the situation. But, to my surprise, before she let go, she whispered the shortest, sweetest sentence into my ear.

"Your gift was my favorite."

The words echoed in my brain even after she walked out the door, and for the night, I was satisfied with my place in her heart.

CHAPTER 8

"You're never gonna believe what Sara got for her birthday from her dad."

The hurried sentence was blurted out over the phone line before I had barely finished saying hello. "Another birthday cake?" I guessed.

"No, actually he forgot that, but what he *did* get her totally made up for it."

"A car?"

"Sam, no, she can't even drive yet. Stop guessing and just let me tell you already."

"Ok, I give up, what did he get her?"

"Two, fifth row tickets to see Bruce Springsteen in concert tomorrow night!"

"No way! Bruce Springsteen?! Those tickets were sold out the day they went on sale!"

I had wanted to go to that concert so badly, that when tickets went on sale, I had bargained a week of chores in exchange for a ride from my dad to the venue. I waited in line for tickets all day just to be turned away when they sold out and return home empty handed.

"Can you believe she asked *ME* to go with her?!"

The words stung my ears. "That's awesome," I said with very little enthusiasm; it was the best I could conjure up.

"She would have taken you too, if there had been another ticket, but she only got two, so..."

His voice trailed off in an awkwardness that pointed out the obvious: I was low man on the totem pole in this situation. And why shouldn't I be? After all, it only made sense that she would pick her boyfriend to go with her. Despite the circumstances, I figured I should try my best to be happy for him.

"Ya got any clothes in your drawer fit to wear to a Springsteen concert? You know you have to look cool, right?" I asked, trying not to sound like a sore-sport.

"Yea, I think I have a few items that might be worthy of The Boss. I am gonna have my mom try stone-washing my jeans, and I have a leather jacket that my dad got me."

"Sharp."

"Hey, why don't you come over for pizza tomorrow night and you can help me get ready?"

"Yea, sure, why not. I don't have anything else to do."

After I said it, I debated whether I should have agreed to go over. I wasn't sure I wanted this whole experience rubbed in my face. But when the next day came, the sting had worn off and I was ready to put aside my selfish feelings to share in my friend's enthusiasm. As soon I approached the house and saw Christian's father's car in the driveway, I knew something was up. Mr. Fine was never there anymore unless it was his weekend to have Christian, which it wasn't. The door creaked as if announcing my arrival but no one looked up to greet me. I forced myself through the thick air of tension and entered the room. Christian sat fixated on the table in front of him, his face full of melancholy and anger. The anger, I had seen before on him; melancholy was a new emotion.

"I'm sorry Sam, I didn't have time to order pizza but there are some leftovers in the fridge if you are hungry," Ms. Fine said, breaking the silence.

"No, thanks. I'm not that hungry."

Christian pushed his chair away with a harsh scrape and walked out of the room. I saw a car pull into the driveway and excused myself, walking into the warm night air, thankful for a reason to escape for a moment. I waited on the stoop as Sara got out of the car. She must have busy preparing her outfit all day because she was more dressed up than I had ever seen her. On her feet were a pair of turquoise flats and black leggings hugged her calves with a denim skirt covering her thighs; a loose, bright shirt hung off one shoulder. She looked almost Madonna-esque. I could see the remnants of where her hair had been crimped, probably earlier in the day because now it hung in slack tendrils around her face.

"Thanks for the ride dad. I'm not sure what time we'll be back so don't wait up," Sara said closing the door to her father's Trans Am.

"Wait just a second," he called after her, stopping the door from closing. "Aren't you forgetting something?" He held up the tickets in his hand.

Her face flushed as she took them from him and said, "I'm glad someone remembered or I wouldn't be seeing much of anything tonight except the back side of a gate."

"That's what fathers are for, I guess. Just make sure that you don't stay out all night. Oh man, listen to me. Do you know that twenty years ago I would have been the one staying out all night and now I am dropping off my daughter at her boyfriend's house to see Bruce Springsteen. I think I am having a Twilight Zone moment here."

"Just make sure that you come back to reality before you speed off in that car. And I promise that we won't be out all night. We'll come home right after the concert. Thanks again, for the tickets, I mean."

"You're welcome. Have fun."

"Sam," she said, looking startled to see me as she approached the door.

"Hey, didn't expect me I bet. I just got here. I came over to help Christian get ready. Just giving you warning before you go in that something weird is going on. I'm not sure what's up." Just as I was finishing my sentence, Mr. Fine appeared at the door.

"Hi, you must be Sara. I've heard so much about you, I feel like I know you," he said motioning for her to come inside.

"You probably don't know who I am. I'm Stanley, Christian's father."

"Oh, yes. It's nice to finally meet you," she said extending her hand for a greeting.

"Nice to finally meet you too."

He grasped her hand in a gentle shake. We followed him into the kitchen.

"Umm, Christian is in his room right now but I'll get him for you. Wait here, ok?" he said.

She nodded her head in agreement. We heard a door slam and Christian came blowing into the room like a ferocious storm. Sara spoke first since Christian was obviously too angry for pleasantries.

"Is everything alright?" she asked carefully.

"Hmm, I'd say, no, everything is definitely not alright," Christian said choking on his words.

"What's going on? Why is your dad here?" Sara whispered, trying to contain the conversation between the three of us.

"What's going on is that I CAN'T GO TO THE CONCERT WITH YOU," Christian explained, purposely trying not to contain his end of the conversation.

"Are you kidding?! Why?" Sara gasped.

"Because we have to have some big family talk," Christian said rolling his eyes in an exaggerated manner.

"You have to have a family talk *tonight*?" I asked incredulously while still trying to bring the volume of the conversation back down. "What's so important that it has to be tonight?"

"Who knows! Who cares! My father probably got some girl pregnant and I'm gonna be a big brother. It's gotta be something about him because my mom wanted me to still go to the concert but *he* said that it was important that we talk about it right now. I wish that he would just go away and let me and mom handle our own lives. This is so unfair!"

"You are definitely, one hundred percent sure that there is no way he'll let you go, even if I am already here and have an extra ticket and no ride," Sara said, pleading her case.

"There's no way. I've asked like a million times. Sam can go with you."

She looked at me, not entirely disappointed, while my heart practically leapt out of my chest with excitement.

"But I feel bad going without you," she said.

"Don't feel bad. It's not *your* fault. Why should two awesome tickets gets wasted just because my dad is being a jerk?"

"Would you *want* to take the other ticket Sam?" she asked.

"I'd love to." Those words didn't even come close to explaining how utterly pumped I was to be going, not just to the concert but with her.

"Of course he wants to go. Who wouldn't?" Christian said sounding put off.

"I still think it's weird that you won't be there," Sara said.

"Yea, me too," I totally lied in the hopes it would ease his pain.

"If I can't be there, could you at least bring me back a program? Then maybe years from now I can pretend I was there."

"We can do that," Sara agreed nodding her head.

"By the way, you look really good tonight. And I stress the *really* part," Christian commented raising his eyebrows at her.

"Thanks."

She beamed looking down at her ensemble. I knew I should have told her that when I first saw her, Christian had beaten me to the punch and if I said it now it wouldn't seem as genuine.

"I'd better call my dad in a few minutes telling him to get right back here, otherwise we'll be late."

"Do you think I have time to go home and change real quick?" I asked looking down at my boring duds.

"Yea, it should take my dad a few minutes to get back so if you hurry it shouldn't be a problem."

I rushed home as fast as I could, explained the situation as quickly as possible to my parents who thankfully agreed to let me go without argument, and then rolled back my closet door to select an outfit. Besides the new clothes hanging there which had been purchased for me by my mother for school, nothing really stuck out. There was not an item of clothing to be found in my wardrobe that made a rock 'n roll statement.

With little time to spare, I threw on some pressed dark blue jeans and an old black t-shirt with faded lettering. At the last minute I swiped an envelope off my bureau and tucked it into my back pocket. I ran to make it there in time and arrived out of breath just as Mr. Moran pulled up and honked the horn. Christian must have anticipated my wardrobe struggle, because he bounded out of the house tossing his leather jacket at me; I caught it with a thankful wave. Sara gave Christian a consolation squeeze of the arm and approached the car. She double-checked her hair in the reflection of the window before getting in. Christian let out a deep, agitated sigh as he waved us off.

"By the look on his face, you'd think his dog had just died," Mr. Moran observed.

"Oh, it's much worse than that, his dream just died. He wanted to go to this concert so bad. I don't know why his dad is being like this," Sara empathized.

"I'm sure he has a good reason. His dad is usually really cool," I replied.

"He'd better have a good reason. I certainly hadn't planned on driving an hour each way to this concert tonight. I guess at this point it makes more sense to just stay there and wait in the parking lot than it does to come all the way home again."

"There's a lot to do in the city dad. You could go out and have a few drinks while you're waiting."

"I will not! Don't forget I'm driving. I'm responsible for more than just myself tonight you know. I think I'll just wait in the car. It's a nice night and I brought a book to pass the time."

"Do whatever you want, doesn't matter to me," Sara said shrugging her shoulders. She glanced in the rearview mirror for the third time. I was starting to think she was checking on me.

I remained quiet the entire car ride there. It was normal for me to clam up around people I felt uncomfortable around and Mr. Moran was currently at the top of that list. It wasn't that he talked unkindly to me or shunned me from the conversation. On the contrary he was very sociable and pleasant. There was just a certain way that he looked at me whenever I interacted with Sara that made me feel like my feelings for her were transparent to him. I found it best to put on a poker face, lest he decide to ask me any pressing questions about my feelings for his daughter. I had worked so hard all summer to keep them hidden from her that I couldn't bear the thought of someone else outing me in a humiliating way. I was relieved when Sara pushed a Springsteen cassette into the car stereo and blasted it.

Letting the grip of a youthful spirit grab hold of him, Mr. Moran pulled over and cranked the soft-top back. We rode the rest of the way with the summer wind whipping our hair up, down, and sideways. I looked around and couldn't help thinking that Christian was missing out on the joyride of a lifetime, riding to a concert in a red convertible, cranking tunes with the top down. It was the culmination of everything we'd hoped that summer would bring and he wasn't here to take pleasure in it. For a moment I felt a pang of guilt that I was here enjoying this time instead of him. I cursed my conscience for ruining a perfectly wonderful moment by feeling sorry for him.

"WE'RE HERE!!" Sara shouted over the music.
Mr. Moran turned the volume down as he pulled up to the parking attendant booth and handed over a ten dollar bill.

"Straight ahead that way. Follow the men waving the orange flags," the less-than-enthusiastic lot attendant droned.

"Okey dokey," he said scanning the concrete landscape ahead of him.

"If you're gonna talk like that, I'm turning the music back up," Sara kidded.

I laughed at the joke and, as I feared, I felt Mr. Moran's eyes glance backwards at me. I stopped laughing immediately and concentrated on the scene out the window. We passed one waving flag after another until we were within a football field's distance from the stadium entrance.

"Looks like you kids are walking. Hope you brought your hiking boots. Although I'm sure if you get too tired Sara, Sam will be glad to carry you," Mr. Moran said with a less than subtle grin as he opened the car door to stretch his legs.

"I don't think that will be necessary, my feet work just fine," Sara said with a flushed face.

"Of course," her dad replied smiling. "Just remember when you leave that we are parked in the Red Section, Row 3."

"Gotcha," Sara replied with a back-handed wave. She gave my sleeve a tug and we were already walking away.

"I'm so sorry about that," Sara said shaking her head in disapproval.

"Sorry about what? What your dad said? Don't worry about it. I know he was just teasing," I said, not so sure that he actually was.

In a way, I was glad that this conversation was started. I had noticed lately, in subtle ways, that she was showing less interest in Christian. At least, I thought she was. They didn't seem to be as lovey-dovey as they had at the beginning of the summer. In fact,

I hadn't seen her kiss him in over a week and she didn't laugh at his corny jokes as much anymore. Either way, this seemed like an opportune time to find out.

"I just didn't want what my dad said to make you uncomfortable."

"No, not at all. Why? Does it make you uncomfortable?" I asked, hesitating at first to ask but not being able to resist.

"Uncomfortable? No. It's just weird because it seems like he is trying to get us together. Don't you think?" she inquired.

I felt my heart skip. In one way I was excited that this conversation was leading here, but in another way I had reservations about divulging my feelings. I couldn't put out too much too soon, or risk unrequited love. After all, she had only mentioned that her *dad* was trying to get us together which really didn't make a statement one way or the other about her feelings on the matter. So, I decided to answer her question with a question, to find out what she was getting at.

"Why would you think that?" I asked.

"Oh, I don't know. It's just that he has asked me questions about you before and he looks at you funny, like he knows something."

"Knows what?"

I continued playing defense but my hands were getting clammy and I didn't know how much longer I could appear cool, calm and collected.

"Hey, I think this is it," she said pointing ahead.

I looked up at the metal archway and turn styles in front of us. We'd reached the entrance already and I wished we hadn't.

"I'd better get the tickets out."

She handed me a stub and we were ushered through a security line. In the bustle of people going left and right I almost lost her.

"I think we go this way," she said, waving her hand above her head to get my attention.

This time, I walked closely behind her. The crowd was dense and it was difficult to keep people from cutting between us.

"PRO-GRAMS! Getcha PRO-GRAMS heyah!" called an obnoxiously loud vendor with a Boston accent.

"We're supposed to pick up one of those for Christian."

"Oh yea, I'm glad one of us remembered," I said.

She tried to walk around the crowd to the vendor stand but she was being pushed around more than she was pushing through.

"I can't get over to them. Remind me to get one on the way out, ok?!" Sara yelled back at me.

I nodded in agreement making a mental note to remember. We searched the seating signs and as we finally approached the floor section, an usher greeted us with a flashlight and showed us to our row.

"Wow, someone was lucky to score these seats," the friendly usher commented.

Sara nodded her head vigorously and opened her mouth to explain but couldn't get a word in because there were so many pushy patrons shoving by. We parked ourselves in seats one and two on the aisle end of row five and commented excitedly on our clear view of the stage.

"Wow, we might even catch some of his sweat sitting here!" Sara marveled.

"I don't think I want to be *that* intimate with him, but I know what you mean. Speaking of sweat, as much as I like this jacket it's so hot out tonight that I think I'm gonna have to take it off. Don't mind my shirt, it was the only thing I could find last minute," I explained removing the leather jacket and draping it carefully on the back of the chair.

Sara glanced at my black tee and said, "I like that shirt. It's vintage. That's coming back in style you know."

I pulled the shirt out in front of my body a bit and examined it. "I guess I'm cool without even trying to be," I chuckled.

"You look good in everything," Sara said.

Sara began to fidget in her seat, looking up at the stage and eventually tucking her hands under legs. The statement seemed over-friendly to me but I didn't want to mistake kindness for flirting so, instead of directly addressing her comment, I thought it might be the right time to finish the conversation we had started in the parking lot. When I started to speak, my brain struggled to form the correct words so I opted for small talk rather than a hurried and potentially stupid statement.

"Are your hands cold?" I asked, pointing to her unique sitting position.

"Oh, no. Not at all. I guess I just always sit on them like this. I didn't even notice I was doing it."

"Really? I don't think I've ever seen you do it before."

"Actually, it's something I do when I'm nervous." She paused. "But you know my body probably just feels nervous from the anticipation of the concert."

"I know what you mean. I'm so excited I may just pee my pants."

I felt a joke was appropriate to break the underlying uneasiness of where the conversation was leading.

"Hey, when you gotta go, you gotta go," Sara said laughing.

She gently slapped her hand on top of my leg by the knee. We looked down simultaneously and I noticed the contrast of her tanned hand against my faded denim. She didn't immediately pull it away. The smiles faded from our faces and were replaced with consternation. Sara's face turned red and she slowly retracted her hand. I gulped and took another shot at trying to finish our earlier conversation.

"So, you were saying before that you think your dad is always trying to get us together. Why do you think he'd do that?"

A long silence followed. I didn't take my eyes off her as she closed her eyes lightly and took a deep breathe. When she exhaled, she opened them and spoke.

"Because, he thinks that you like me..."

I knew she wasn't finished with the sentence and I hung on the last word with baited breathe for the rest.

"...and because...he thinks that I like you."

When she was done speaking, she opened her eyes widely to watch for my reaction. What she saw was perhaps the mix of worry and relief I knew I was showing. My secret crush wasn't such a secret anymore and I wasn't sure how she felt about that. Either way, my reaction must have given her reason enough to continue speaking.

"There's something that I want to do Sam. That I feel I have to do, just so I know for sure."

"Know *what* for sure?" I asked.

Her remark took me off guard and I felt a special kind of anticipated to the answer of my question.

"What I need to know is..." Sara began as she rubbed the palms of her hands against her jeans; "friends or more?"

She wrinkled her forehead and raised one eyebrow at the end of the sentence as if the comfort of her continued existence depended on the answer to that question. I opened my mouth to speak, to let her know that I thought we were more, so much more than just friends, but before I could form the first word, her hand began inching towards mine across my lap. I could feel the heat from her palm reaching out to envelope mine. I realized what she was trying to do; it was something I had wanted to happen since we met. I felt my heart accelerate rapidly as the smooth skin of her hand easily slid into mine. She closed her fingers around my knuckles and I did the same. Her eyes locked intensely on mine and suddenly the immense crowd blurred into the background. I wondered if she was feeling the way I was at this moment – wholly and utterly complete.

"So, friends...or *more*?" I asked, subconsciously emphasizing the last word.

I gulped down the dry lump in my throat so that I could clear my ears of the surrounding noise and better hear her response. Luckily, she didn't hesitate to answer because I don't think my body could have taken one more second of the stress of not knowing.

"Definitely, more," she replied.

She breathed in deeply, as if absorbing the overwhelming change that this revelation would bring. I could feel my mouth dangling half-open in disbelief as I stared back at her, but I seemed unable to close it. There was no more hoping, guessing or praying. I had heard the words with my own ears, from the source: *definitely more*. I was so grateful that tonight she had allowed herself to feel the connection that I knew was between us.

Suddenly, before I even had a chance to fully process the magnitude of her words, the stadium lights began to dim and the stage came alive. I started to speak quickly, trying to beat the noise that was coming. I wanted to reciprocate my feelings but to my frustration, I was instantly muted by a cacophony of frenzied Springsteen fans. Bruce took the stage. The crowd leapt to their feet whistling, hooting and screaming for their idol. I didn't care.

I pressed on, determined to seize this chance to let Sara know how I really felt about her.

"YOU'RE RIGHT ABOUT ME, ABOUT US! THERE IS SOMETHING MORE!" I shouted, nodding my head up and down vigorously hoping that this kind of sign language might make her understand.

Sara pointed to her ears. She obviously couldn't hear anything I was saying. She leaned in closer to me and strained to hear.

"I SAID: THERE IS MORE! I'VE KNOWN IT SINCE WE MET!"

But again my words were drowned out as soon as they passed my lips. I wasn't even sure if they were coming out, I couldn't hear them myself. The only thing either of us could hear was the pandemonium of the crowd and the opening riff of the first song. Realizing that it was a losing battle, she shrugged her shoulders and turned her attention towards the stage. Feeling defeated I tried to focus on the band but I couldn't enjoy the scene on the stage, my unexpressed emotion wouldn't let me. Instead I turned my attention to God, the only one who could possibly hear my rants over the raucous. I looked up and shouted out my frustration at the top of my lungs, believing that only Heaven could hear me over Springsteen.

"I LOVE HER AND SHE'LL NEVER GET IT! THERE'S ALWAYS SOMETHING, ALWAYS SOMETHING IN THE WAY! WHY?"

Once the words passed my lips, my frustration gave way to a comfortable peace. I had never actually voiced my feelings for her out loud. It felt good to know that, even if she couldn't hear me right now, my confession had reached the ears of the divine.

"I GET IT SAM!" Sara replied unexpectedly.

By some miracle, she must have heard my ranting above the racket. We turned our heads and looked at each other without words, confirming by sight, that we both indeed existed together in this moment. Feeling emboldened, I brushed my fingers against hers and she softly intertwined our hands like two vines wrapping around each other. It was an unspoken gesture that meant that no more words were needed, that for right now it was enough to simply know.

CHAPTER 9

We continued holding hands and bouncing to the music as the hits blared on. I wanted to remain in this bliss forever; where time, reality, rationality and consequence didn't exist. Inside this stadium, we were just two nameless people in a sea of faces, not worrying what complications we would face later. For now, it was easy to pretend that tomorrow would never come.

Intermission came, the spotlights were cued up to illuminate the outdoor arena and we were instantly snapped out of our sublime daze. I gave her hand a tight squeeze before letting go.

"Do you wanna go get a drink?" Sara said in an even tone, as if nothing out of the ordinary were taking place between us. "I don't know about you but I'm really thirsty."

"Sounds good to me," I replied, also pretending at normalcy.

She led me by the hand past the super long line at the beer cart, to the noticeably shorter one at the lemonade stand. We slipped in behind a pair of bubbly thirty-something women who were still singing a song that had ended minutes earlier. We covertly chuckled at the fun-loving group who must have heard our giggling because they took notice of us.

"Oh my god, Anne, remember when your husband used to hold your hand like that?" the first eccentric woman said in a reminiscent tone.

"I *think* I can remember if I try really, really hard," the second female answered, scrunching up her face and tapping her finger on her head.

"How long have you two been together?" the first woman asked.

"Uh, I guess not that long actually," I said, probably turning a shade of pink as bright as their shirts.

I hadn't expected the subject to come up so quickly and, under the circumstances, I was finding it difficult to put our relationship into words. I looked to Sara for the appropriate response.

"In one way, it seems like we just met, and in another, it seems like we've been together forever," Sara said to the curious women who both sighed dreamily.

"Oh, I could tell when I saw you two that you had something special. You are just so cute together!" the first woman gushed with envy.

"Never lose the way you look at each other. Hold onto it. Believe me, it's a lonely life to live without love," the second woman advised as she turned around to order her drink.

Sara widened her eyes and raised her brows at me in delight, wowed by the compliments we had just been given by total strangers. Even though I already knew my feelings for Sara were deep, it was awesome that a third party had just confirmed that Sara's admiration for me was equal and evident. We ordered the largest sized lemonade available and happily slurped from the same straw.

"Let's find a place to sit and talk," Sara suggested.

We meandered around for a while until a patch of thick grass at the end of the vendors' row became available. Our bottoms hit grass and I gazed above, past the stadium lights, to the expansive and starry night sky, feeling as if I was seeing a work of art which had been hung for our private viewing. I contemplated whether or not to approach the delicate subject of boyfriend/girlfriend details just yet, especially considering the fact that she already had one. Thankfully, she spoke before my mind had gone into a complete tailspin of thoughts.

"Sam, what are we doing? I mean, I know *what* we're doing, but what are we *going to* do? How are we gonna go about this?" She obviously had no problem facing this situation head on.

"You mean, how are we going to tell Christian?" I presumed, knowing that this large detail couldn't be glossed over.

Sara shook her head up and down quickly as she slurped the lemonade. I paused. Before I could be comfortable formulating a conversation in my mind where I informed my best friend that Sara and I were in love, I needed to know where Sara stood. From what she was saying, she obviously wanted to break up with Christian. What I wanted to know was how deep her feelings had been for him in the past and if any still remained. I figured that she must have *some* romantic notion towards him or else she wouldn't be with him. I threw my hat into the ring of blunt speaking.

"Sara, what exactly do you think of Christian?"

She paused. "Well, it's not like I hate him or anything. I mean I'm not here doing this with you just to be mean to him," she replied sounding defensive, as if I had been insinuating treason.

I clarified for her, "No, I know that. I guess I mean…Do you still have feelings for him?"

This time there was no pause, she must have understood perfectly how she felt toward him because she had no qualms in explaining it.

"I really like Christian but only as a good friend," she said, resting her hand on my leg to assure me of the fact; "I had a crush on him that week before I got to know you, when you were away on vacation. I thought he was cute and he was the only person I had to talk to around here. Then the night before you came home, we went to get some ice cream and he kissed me. It just kind of progressed into boyfriend and girlfriend from there because we were all spending so much time together mowing lawns. I actually knew a short time into our relationship that he wasn't for me. We didn't click on a lot of stuff and he never seemed to pay attention to me the way you did. The only reason I stayed with him was because I liked hanging out with you and his mom so much. I thought of breaking up with him a lot of times but it seemed weird to say, 'Hey I wanna break up with you but can I date your best friend? Oh yeah, and can I still be friends with you and hang out with your mom?'. The funny thing is that when I first met you, that very first day, I knew I liked you a lot. But, I got to know Christian before you and that is what sent everything in the wrong direction. I just don't want to pretend anymore that

I can feel for him what I feel for you because I just can't. It doesn't work that way. Have you ever heard the saying, 'The heart wants what the heart wants?'. Well, it's true, and my heart wants you."

Until now, I had only fantasized about hearing those words. I wanted to grab hold of that last sentence and wish away all the complication that preceded it. But I couldn't. I had to face it, we both had to. I took comfort in knowing that at least we would be sorting out this difficult situation together. I was trying to form a well thought out response to what she had just said and while I did, she continued on. It seemed that she was using my silence as a time to work through her guilt. I didn't blame her, I had some guilt myself to deal with.

"I know you're trying to think about what to do but there is no nice way to tell him. I mean, it's not like we planned this, but when you really look at the situation, it's all pretty rotten isn't it? We look like really bad people don't we?" she said, her eyes getting damp.

"Don't say that. You are the sweetest person I know. It doesn't matter what it looks like to other people because, like you said, this wasn't intentional."
I took hold of her hands to stop her from tears from coming.

"So, what are we going to do?" Sara asked, letting out a tormented sigh.

I was trying to sort through the dozen or so scenarios my mind was offering, a few of which involved lying, sneaking, running away and heated confrontations. I knew Sara was looking for a quick and easy answer for a situation where perhaps there was none to be found. I offered my only balanced thought to her.

"We should just tell him the truth," I said.

My eyes were fixed on some point in the distance where the answer seemingly had come from. This was the right, albeit most undesirable, choice to make. Sara too looked off into the distance. She closed her eyes in some unknown meditation and opened them with a renewed confidence.

"You're right," she agreed.

"I am?" I half-said, half-wondered.

"Of course, you are. I think it's the only way to do it if we all still want to be friends. Maybe he will respect the truth. I mean, probably not at first, but he'll come around. He's easy-going," Sara said but waited on me for confirmation since I had known Christian a lot longer than her.

I agreed out loud that he was indeed an easy-going guy and hoped silently that his laid-back attitude also lent itself to semi-cheating, in this instance.

"What exactly are we going to say to him?" Sara asked.

The lights in the stadium started to dim as the band made their way back on stage for the second half of the show. The crowds lingering in the concession area fled back to their seats.

"Should we go back? Do you wanna wait and talk about this after the show?" I asked.

"Let's just stay and figure out what to do first, we'll only miss one song, and then we can go back in, otherwise I won't be able to enjoy myself," Sara confessed.

I too, was eager to feel a reprieve from this looming black cloud hovering over our sunny moment.

"Ok. Well, I think it's simple. Let me know if this sounds good," I said looking at Sara.

She nodded for me to continue.

"Tomorrow we both go over to his house, that way if he's at his own house, he won't feel ganged up on."

She nodded again in agreement. I continued.

"We'll start off by giving him the program from the concert as a peace offering. Then, he'll ask us how the concert was. We'll tell him how great our seats were and that we had an awesome time and all about the songs that were played and how wild the crowd was. After this, we'll say that there was something else that happened tonight that we wanna tell him about but we're not sure how he's gonna react to it. He'll question us about what it could be and, of course, it won't be anything he's thinking. I can say, 'It's something that we found out about each other last night that we didn't know before'. He'll probably be puzzled but maybe start thinking in the right direction. Then I'll say, 'I don't know if you've ever noticed before but since the first day I saw Sara, I liked her'. I'm sure he won't know what to say at this point, so we should just continue quickly here so that he won't have time to get upset yet."

"Yet?" Sara eked out.

"Yeah, yet. I'm pretty sure he's gonna be mad at first."

"Ok, I've accepted that now. Continue."

"So, then I'll say," I began and then interjected as a side note; "because I don't want you to do any of the talking if you don't want to."

Sara shook her head, no, very determinedly. I knew she'd want to avoid conflict and for some reason, opposite my character, I didn't mind taking control in this situation.

"Ok. Then I'll just say it outright that I found out that you feel the same way about me. Insert confusion, mistrust and anger here on Christian's part. Then I'll calm him down and tell him that we didn't know how else to say it to him but we really still want to be friends and that we aren't trying to be mean to him but we didn't want to hide it from him either. Then basically, we just wait to see what he says and hope that he understands."

"And if he doesn't?" Sara asked.

"I'm not sure, but I guess we deal with that when it happens."

"I think it's as good as it gets. It doesn't sound as terrible as I thought it would, and it puts it in a way where he knows that we are serious about each other and it's not just some make-out fling. I'm satisfied," she said, throwing her hands up in the air. "Now, let's try to put all of it in the back of our minds, forget about tomorrow's troubles, and make some good memories tonight."

I had no objection and with assurance took her hand and led her carefully through the dark, packed, aisles back to our seats. By the time we had scuffled past all the annoyed people in our row, Bruce was taking a breath and being handed a new guitar which had the correct tuning of his next song. As Sara had guessed, we only missed a few minutes of the performance.

"Here's an old favorite of mine by a great artist named Don McLean. Sing along if you know it," he announced with his trademark raspy vocals; *"A long, long time ago,"* began the familiar refrain which was instantly recognized and cheered loudly for.

Everyone began singing their karaoke version. I looked over at Sara as he sang. She looked so amazingly carefree and genuinely joyful. I felt a great pride and satisfaction knowing that I was now contributing to her happiness. The words of the next line rang in my ears a moment longer than the rest.

"Did you write the book of love? And do you have faith in God above?"

I looked towards the heavens again, knowing that my last words to the universe had not fallen on an unsympathetic holy ear. I offered up a grateful heart, a meek smile, and a resounding yes, in silent reply, as I realized that, for the first time in my life, I did have faith in God and everything was as He intended it to be.

CHAPTER 10

Around eleven p.m. the second set was finished and the first wave of people eager to beat the lines out of the parking lot scurried toward the door. We remained seated with the majority of the crowd, chanting for an encore. The band triumphantly emerged as if on cue and began strumming out their last song. Springsteen gave a rousing performance while sparks from finale fireworks flew through the air. When the song was finished, whistles and screams flew wildly as he took a final bow and exited stage left. We continued clapping until our hands were red and sore. Everyone had their eyes glued to the stage just in case the entertainer was going to appear for one last hurrah. When it was apparent that he had retired for the evening, the mass movement out of the stadium began.

"Let's wait until more people have cleared out. I'm in no hurry to go anywhere," Sara said, tugging me backwards by my sleeve so that I wouldn't leave.

She didn't have to pull hard as I welcomed the chance for the two of us to linger alone a little longer. We stood to accommodate the people pushing past us so that they could slide through the cramped aisle. When we were the only ones left in our row, I stepped further in the center aisle to stretch my legs and arms. We had been sitting in the same position for so long that it felt nice to relieve the tension in my muscles. Sara sat down again and re-lived the highs and lows of the concert with me. We both agreed that hearing the songs live really rocked and the band seemed tight and well-rehearsed. Sara was disappointed with how rowdy some of the fans were, especially the one who had spilled half a beer on my shoes. When it had happened, I was fairly annoyed, but as she recounted the story, I pointed out how comical the apology had been.

"'I am so sorry for wasting, like, two dollars' worth of Bud on your sneakers dude'," I said, impersonating the half-wasted offender.

Sara let out a belly-busting laugh at my surfer dude accent. While she wiped happy tears from her eyes, I noticed that barely anyone was left in the arena.

"We should probably get going Sara, your dad is waiting for us," I reluctantly managed to say.

"Aw, what's the matter? Are you afraid of my father?" she kidded.

"Just a teensy bit," I replied, creating a small space between my thumb and forefinger.

"Ok, I guess you're right," Sara said rolling her eyes in good humor.

She diligently checked the surrounding floor to make sure she wasn't leaving anything behind, which reminded me to grab the borrowed leather jacket off the back of my seat. The sight of its black shininess reminded me of Christian sitting all alone at home unaware of the news he was going to receive tomorrow, for a second I was pained, but managed to shake the feeling.

As we made our way out from under the pavilion, Sara noticed that a few refreshment stands were still open and some straggling people were lingering in groups on the pavement. Realizing that the stadium was not yet closing, she seized the opportunity to prolong the night and grabbed my arm again to stop me from walking any farther.

"I really don't want to leave yet. Do you?" she asked.

"Of course I don't. I was just worried about what your dad might think if we were the last ones out."

"Who cares? Do you know, my whole life I have been worried about what people think and it's gotten me nowhere but miserable. I am sick of it. I wanna do something that is gonna make me happy for once."

The words resounded in my head. They were an echo of my own sentiments exactly. I planted my feet and stopped moving toward the exit.

"Look at those gates," she said, pointing to the metal fencing and turn-styles three hundred feet ahead of us. "Outside of them you are just Sam and I am just Sara. That's it, that's how everyone out there sees us. But right here, right now, we are together. We are Sara and Sam and I don't want that to end yet. We are here together, *now*. Let's keep this moment as long as we can, we don't know when we'll get this chance again."

She implored me with her eyes, and I recognized the opposing passion and vulnerability that emanated from them in brilliant bursts of sparkle and color. I was drawn to her sudden display of emotion towards me. Any consequence I would have to face would be worth this uninterrupted time alone with her.

"I know. I've been waiting for something like this too and now that it's finally here, I don't want it to be over," I agreed, clasping both of her hands in mine.

"Let's sit by the fence and talk, just until these last people start to leave," she said with a playful grin.

"Sounds good to me."

Sara sat Indian-style on the ground facing me as I leaned my back against the high chain-link fence that served as a border between arena property and the outside world. In this spot, we were out of the direct line of vision of anyone else on the grounds, blocked by a tall oak tree. It was as if this private spot had been built for us when the stadium's concrete and sod were being laid.

"Let's play a little game. Go ahead and ask me a question and then I'll ask you a question," Sara said.

"And what should I ask Miss Sunby?"

"Ask me anything that you have always wanted to know about me but never had the guts to ask," she replied, outwardly excited at the pursuit of this type of knowledge.

"Anything? Even if it might be a touchy subject? I just wanna make sure because I don't know the rules," I asked with a raised eyebrow, not wanting to put her off by saying something out of line.

"The rules are simple. Ask something that you don't know about the other person and then they have to answer. So nothing is off limits. Now, come on, lay it on me," Sara said motioning towards herself with her hands.

"Ok. But you don't have to answer it if you don't want to. It's personal."

"That's kinda the idea of the game," she insisted.

"Well, I've always wanted to know a little bit more about your mom. Like, why did she die?" I asked making sure to be slow and delicate with my words.

"I did say, *anything,* didn't I?" Sara cringed but then continued. "Actually it's not as hard to talk about as it used to be, and I can see why you would wonder because she was so young. She died of breast cancer. We only knew about it for a year before she passed. When the doctors found it, she was just too far along to do much in the way of treatments but she didn't tell us that at first. She lied and said they were running some tests and it was probably nothing. We didn't know how bad it was until she started getting chemo. My aunts and I took care of her the whole time. I only wish I knew then that it was the last year I had with her. I may have acted differently, appreciated her more, you know?"

I nodded my head with true sympathy. I was relieved that she was opening up. My curiosity was only a small part of why I had asked her this question. Mostly it was because I knew that she needed someone impartial to talk about it with. I worried she wasn't getting the emotional support that she needed at home from her father.

"It sounds to me like you were a great daughter and did everything that you could. Your mom is definitely smiling down on you."

"I'd like to think so. If there is a Heaven, I know my mom is there. She was one of those people that gave anything she had to her family. I miss her."

Even though she didn't seem sad when she said this, I reached over and gave her a comforting pat on the knee.

"Ok, now that you got your answer, it's my turn to ask a question," she said.

"Shoot."

"Have you ever been in love before?" she wondered aloud, tilting her head slightly to one side and cocking her eyebrow up.

I shook my head quickly back and forth to give a *no* response.

"Not even close?" she probed.

"Not even close," I replied firmly.

"What attracted you to me?" she continued, out of turn, with the questioning.

"Besides the million obvious things, like how pretty and funny you are, I have to admit that I love the smell of your hair." I only made the superficial confession to keep the mood light after all the talk about her mother dying.

"You do?!" she squealed.

"Yeah, I'm surprised you've never caught me sneaking whiffs of it before. I actually sniffed it in front of everyone when you hugged me at your birthday party!"

"You did not! I can't believe you have been my hair stalker this whole time and I never knew!"
She rolled on her side with laughter.

"Very funny. Well, now you know, and now I know I'll never play this game again because it's totally unfair. You got to ask three questions and I only asked one," I said faking injustice and crossing my arms like a slighted child.

"That was most definitely fair because I actually gave a *real* answer with a *real* explanation to the question you asked me, and all you did was shake your head and repeat my first question back to me," she countered, sitting herself upright again.

"I guess I did do that, didn't I? Maybe I'm just not used to people being very interested in what I have to say."

"Well, get used to it because now someone is," Sara said, grabbing both of the ankles on my outstretched legs and leaning forward to emphasize her point.

"I guess I could get used to that," I said, reaching for her wrists and motioning her to sit closer to me.

She uncrossed her pretzel legs and I guided her by the waist to the space between my legs which seemed the perfect distance apart for her body to rest in. She snuggled in comfortably with her back slouched against my chest. I cautiously wrapped my forearms around her middle, being respectful not to graze any personal body areas above or below where my hands should be. I didn't want my intentions to be misrepresented.

"Have you ever seen those pictures that the gigantic telescopes take of outer space? Like the ones of dwarf stars and black holes and the milky way," Sara asked staring into the atmosphere. Her head was pointed towards the Big Dipper which could be seen distinctly on this clear, dry summer night.

"Yeah, I've seen those in National Geographic before. They are so amazing."

"Whenever I look at those pictures and then hear that they are made up of gas and matter and all that scientific stuff, it just doesn't seem to fit. How could an explosion or collection of gas make such a perfect formation? To me, it looks like a giant hand took colors from another dimension, put them on a palette and used the sky as a canvas to paint a masterpiece for all of us down here to appreciate. I mean, look at any sunrise and sunset and try to tell me that something out there doesn't want the world to be beautiful."

"I couldn't agree more."
I gave her waist a tight squeeze of approval. She took her arms and folded them over mine to hold me tightly. Sitting like this we could never be torn from each other.

"Do you think the astronauts and the teacher on The Challenger were scared before they died?" she asked.

"No. I don't think so. I think if they knew they were dying, they were ok with that because they pursued their dreams to the end. And that is one of the most satisfying ways that anyone can die, I think." The wise words sounded funny coming from my mouth.

"I couldn't agree more," Sara said parroting me with a smile.

"Since when did this game get so topic heavy? We sure are talking a lot about death," I said.

"I guess when you have seen someone die it doesn't seem so taboo anymore. It just becomes another part of life," Sara stated, adding with concern; "I hope it doesn't bother you to talk about this kind of stuff."

"Not at all, actually I like having deep conversations and until now there was no one to have them with."

"I do know one subject that you avoid though," she said.

"You do?"

"Uh huh. I still haven't gotten a real answer to the question I asked about being in love before so, I guess I have to assume that you are avoiding telling me details about a sordid past," she teased.

"If that's what I've left you thinking then I guess I'd better explain myself."

"Go on then," Sara prodded, with her head still tilted upward but her eyes fixed to the side trying to catch my expression.

"I'll say it like this. No matter what I thought I felt before, none of it was love, and I can say that with every certainty in me because since I met you, I have experienced real love and it doesn't feel like anything I ever felt before. I had always imagined it would take years of knowing someone and being in a relationship for love and trust to be built. But here I am, at the age of sixteen ready to share my life with a girl I have known until now only as a friend."

I couldn't deny that I felt a strange closeness to her that couldn't be explained, it was as if an invisible magnet were pulling us towards each other. I hadn't expected to tell her this right off the jump but since the subject had been brought up, there seemed no reason to deny it either. Still, I wasn't sure how she was going to react.

She turned her head toward my face and held it there, just staring at me as if she were still staring at the sky. I returned her gaze, unashamed to look away, sensing now that she felt the same way about me. I leaned in, almost in freeze time, for a long-awaited kiss. I could see her eyes close and her shoulders relax in expectation of the moment that was coming. Every movement toward each other was filled with anticipation. An internal tingle ran from the bottom of my feet to the crown of my head. I could feel her breath and hair wisp across my face as my lids fluttered closed and our lips prepared to embrace the way our arms had. The space between us was diminishing as I tilted my head to meet hers with ease.

"What in the hell are you doing here?! I've been looking up, down and sideways for you two." The devastatingly unwelcome and intrusive voice of Mr. Moran boomed at us.

We separated quicker than oil and water, and the kiss that never began, ended faster than the parent's eye-to-brain mechanism could compute. We sat completely still for a while, recovering from the startle, thinking how best to deal with the situation before us. But Mr. Moran's offensive strategy left no time for a defensive plan.

"I must have watched thousands of people come through that parking lot. The whole time, trying to spot you two. When the crowd started to thin and I still didn't see you, I figured you must have gone to the wrong section, so I walked around the entire parking lot – *twice*," he said, emphasizing the number by holding up two fingers. "But nope, no Sara, no Sam to be found. So, I walked up to the gate. I watched the rest of the people leave; I asked the parking attendant if he had seen you; I asked the ticket ripper guy if he had seen you; I even asked some guys smoking pot behind the dumpster if they had seen you. Nobody had seen you! Finally I convinced the manager to let me in here to look around, even though he said that everyone had left. And here you are, just sitting here without a care in the world, not even thinking that I am worried about you! For God's sake, I was one step away from calling the police! What were you doing over here?" he demanded with a mix of fear and anger.
I stood up awkwardly and brushed the dry dirt off my pants while I thought about an acceptable explanation.

"Well?" Mr. Moran pressed us, probably trying to hurry the inevitable lie along.

"We were just talking dad, and we lost track of time," Sara answered respectfully and straightforwardly.

Mr. Moran looked at me suspiciously and I nodded my head to confirm the story. He looked back and forth at his daughter and then at me before letting out a huge sigh which seemed to indicate that he had put the pieces of our love-puzzle together.

"And you never noticed this whole time that everyone else had left?" he said, calmer now, as he motioned his arm toward the rest of the empty arena.

"No, we didn't sir. When we sat down over here there were still lots of people but once we were sitting down the tree must have blocked us from seeing that everyone was leaving. I'm very sorry that you had to worry so much," I responded with more bravery than I knew I had. I didn't want Sara to take the entire rap here.

Mr. Moran searched my expression for signs of dishonesty but there were none to be found; one reason why I found it easier to always tell the truth, I could never be caught in a lie.

"Sara, let's assume I give you the benefit of the doubt and believe that what you guys are saying is true. That doesn't negate the fact that you left me waiting and worrying where you were. I don't like punishing you, but maybe there is something that *you* can think of that might make up for your carelessness tonight."

I had a hunch that it was making him feel old to assume the authoritarian role, especially when there was nothing more than innocent adolescent obliviousness to direct his anger at. Sara spoke fast to show that she was grateful for his leniency.

"What I'd like to do for you dad is to wash and vacuum your car every weekend for a month," she said.

"That is very kind of you to offer my dear. Of course, I don't want to put you out but you do know how much I like my car waxed and hand-dried too," he added facetiously.

"Of course, father. That's what I meant. Washed, waxed, hand-dried and vacuumed. Didn't I say that?"

"Come to think of it, I believe you did."

Thankfully the rousting ended there and he escorted us both back to the parking lot.

"Maybe he'll let me help you with the car, it was my fault too," I whispered when her father was a few feet ahead of us.

"As much as I'd love that, we'd better not push our luck," Sara reasoned.

Under the watchful eye of Mr. Moran, we sat in our respective seats in the car, one in the front and one in the back, as if nothing new had occurred between us. We were nearly the last car out of the parking lot as we sped off towards the highway.

"So, all the other nonsense aside, how was the concert?" Mr. Moran inquired.

"It was great. Springsteen was sooo good live, and he even played some covers too," Sara said.

"It's so much better when they play hits that you know and not just a bunch of B sides that no one can sing along too."

I wanted to nod my head in agreement but I was afraid to make a move.

"Can I see the program?" he asked.

"The program!" Sara exclaimed, smacking her hand against her forehead in disappointment.

"Oh no, the program," I said, hanging my head, equally ashamed of having forgotten the all-important souvenir.

"Uh oh, did I hit a nerve?" Mr. Moran asked.

"It's not your fault. It's just that Christian asked us to bring one back for him since he couldn't come tonight. We couldn't get to the program guy when we went in and then on the way out we just, forgot," Sara said with a dishonorable sigh.

"That's ok. Most of the time those programs are full of ads and just get thrown out anyway," her father said, trying to ease her guilt.

"I know dad. I just really wanted to have something to give to him tomorrow," Sara replied peeking at me in the rearview. I shook my head in agreement.

"Whoa, what's all this traffic?" Mr. Moran asked, suddenly pushing his foot to the brake pedal and craning his neck to see around the car in front of him.

"There's a construction sign. I think it's gonna be backed up for a ways," I said, trying to be helpful.

"Why in the heck would they be doing construction on a road near a stadium on a concert night?" Sara asked.

"Because," Mr. Moran huffed under his breath; "nobody has any freakin' common sense, that's why. Welcome to the real world kids."

CHAPTER 11

We made a plan to meet at Christian's house early the next afternoon. Without the promised program in tow, we had nothing to offer him but bad news and neither of us was much looking forward to the planned confrontation. I knew that a wonderful reprieve would follow once the liberating words were spoken; I used that knowledge as motivation to press on. The next day came too fast and before I knew it, we were standing on his door stoop.

"Are you ready to do this?" Sara asked with wide eyes and trepidation.

I thought back to the previous night's conversation about what we had planned to say. Now I hoped I had the courage to actually say it. I was doing this for Sara - to be with her. I didn't have any other choice.

"Well, I don't think I'll ever really be ready," I said; "but the only alternative is to lie and sneak around. I think we owe it to Christian to be honest."

"I know, I know. Ok then, here we go," she said with a sigh. She took two steps toward the door and stalled. "You knock. I can't. My brain won't tell my hand to do it," she said.

I understood. Boldly walking up to the familiar door, I knocked. It was probably the first time in my whole life that I hadn't just barged in; if that didn't seem suspicious, nothing would. We stood for a minute staring at the white door with intent but it wasn't opening.

"Knock louder. I don't think anyone heard you," Sara nervously insisted.

I knocked harder this time and directed my blows to the small panes of glass so that I could be heard easier. After another long minute without any reaction from inside the house, I peeked through the window to see if there was someone home. I saw Christian lounging on the couch in the living room, no doubt with the television volume turned up so high he couldn't hear an elephant on the stairs if there was one. I gave up on the idea of knocking and let myself in as I was accustomed to.

"Are you sure it's alright to just walk in?"

"I've been doing it all my life," I assured as I crossed the threshold and called out to Christian in my friendliest tone; "Hey, couch potato, you've got company."

Christian's legs were propped up on the arm of the sofa; he twisted his torso to address us.

"You're not company, you're Sam," he remarked flippantly.

"And Sara," she added with perkiness.

"Oh, I didn't see you back there. You *are* company," he consented but still did not get up off the couch to greet us.

Sara looked at me with hesitation regarding the welcome we had been given. I wasn't about to back down now, so I planted my butt on the sofa, right next to Christian, and tried to loosen him up with small talk.

"Whatcha watching?"

"The Warriors."

"I love that movie. There are some rad fight scenes in that. The baseball gang is cool."

"Yeah," Christian agreed, but not with enthusiasm.
I knew he wouldn't be able to resist talking about baseball, so I figured I had the perfect segue into a subject that might put some life into him.

"Speaking of baseball, the game's on. Have you checked the score yet? Who's winning?"

"Eh, I don't know. I gotta pee, I'll be right back."

The response was as flat and uninterested as if I had been talking about interest rates. He let one leg fall off the couch then used it as a crutch to pry the rest of his body up and into the bathroom. As soon as the door closed behind him, Sara dashed over and grabbed onto my elbow.

"He knows. I don't know how, but he definitely knows what is going on with us," she whispered in a panicked rush.

"He *is* acting really depressed and weird. But how could he possibly know what happened last night? We were the only ones there."

"*My dad!* My dad was there too. Maybe my dad called and told him!" Sara quietly huffed.

"I can't picture that happening. I think Christian just suspects something is going on because we showed up together today. He's probably noticed for a while the way we act around each other and…"

"Shhhh!"

Sara let go of my arm and stood up as the bathroom door swung open and Christian stepped back within earshot.

"Feel better?" I asked.

"Much."

"Maybe he just had to go pee badly," Sara said talking out of the side of her mouth at me in a barely-there voice.

"How was the concert?" Christian asked seemingly out of obligation.

"Oh, it was great…but you didn't miss much that you can't hear on his tapes," Sara said.

I was glad that she was downplaying the fact that he had missed the once-in-a-lifetime show and thankfully, she didn't mention the program we had neglected to get for him. With any luck, it had slipped his mind.

"Yeah, it was fun. We walked a mile to our car and some guy spilled beer on me," I said, trying to point out the downsides of the night before I laid the biggest bummer of all on him. "Something else crazy happened last night that we wanted to tell you about too," I began but was interrupted by the sound of a small dog yipping through the house.

"A puppy?! Oh my goodness! It's so tiny and cute," Sara gushed, bending down to pet the curly furred pet.

"Oh, hi kids," Ms. Fine said trailing behind the petite poodle. "Christian, she needs to go out. Can you take her? I don't want her getting bad habits and going on the carpet. I'm going to lie down. Just keep her out here with you guys for a while. Ok, sweetie?"

"Sure mom, no problem," Christian replied solemnly as his mother covered a yawn and retreated to her bedroom.

"This is *your* dog? I didn't peg you for the poodle type," I chuckled, reaching down to pat the puppy's palm-sized head.

"I didn't pick it out. My dad got her," he said.

"I thought your dad said you were too irresponsible to own a dog."

"She's not for *me*. She's for my mom," he explained.

"That's why he wanted you to stay home from the concert last night? Did he get a dog for your mom because they are getting back together?" I hoped out loud.

"No," Christian said without any indication that he was going to continue the sentence.

"No? Then why *did* he make you stay home?" I pressed.
Sara looked up from the puppy to show her interest in hearing his answer.

"My dad got the stupid puppy for my mom because she just found out that she's sick...she has cancer," Christian declared.

Sara let out a short gasp and covered her mouth with her hands. If I were a girl I would have done the same. My brow furrowed in disbelief and after the initial shock passed, I tried to comfort my friend with a hug. Christian returned it at first but soon pulled away in frustration.

"You know, those doctors are totally to blame for this. My mom started getting these headaches and feeling tired like six months ago and she kept going to the doctor and they kept telling her it was her hormones and just take some aspirin and you'll be fine. You're over-reacting; all women your age go through this. Blah, blah, blah. Now finally, someone listened to her and ordered some tests and they found advanced cancer and they say they don't even know if she's going to live or not. I don't care what they say, I know she's not gonna die. They're all idiots anyway, why should we listen to them?"
He picked up a pillow and chucked it across the room at the wall.

"Christian, calm down. She's gonna be fine. Your mom is strong." I tried my best to offer encouraging words but it was difficult considering the news I just got.

"I know that. I know. I know," he repeated, pacing back and forth as the dog whined at him. "Ok, ok, I'll take you out. I'll be right back guys."

Christian scooped up the puppy and walked out the kitchen door. We looked at each other in stupor at what had just occurred. My fear at a confrontation with Christian had just turned to guilt at the thought of revealing our secret now and I'm sure Sara was feeling the same thing. Reluctantly I shook my head very slowly back and forth, giving the signal to Sara that we would not be divulging any unnecessary information today; my empathy wouldn't allow it. She nodded her head with melancholy in her movement and a tear on her cheek. Somehow it seemed easier and less real to say it without words. I grabbed her hand and stroked it tenderly, wondering how long it would be before I got the chance to hold it again.

"I guess everyone feels better after they pee; she stopped whining," Christian said, sounding more like himself as he reentered the house.

I separated from Sara as quickly as I had last night when I heard her father approach us. There was no way he could have seen us together for that brief moment. We were in the clear.

"Bring the little sweetie over to me," Sara said to Christian as she wiped away the tear that had fallen to her chin. "What a doll she is."

Sara was succeeding at masking her gloom. She took the puppy into her arms and began playing with its paws.

"Hey, I'm sorry I flipped out and threw the pillow like that. I've just been so upset ever since they told me last night. I don't want to talk about it with my mom because I know it upsets her to hear those things and my dad has just sort of gone into hero mode and taken over. It's kind of annoying."

"Everyone deals with it differently. It's totally normal to yell like that. I was really mad at first too, but I was mad at my mom, not the doctors. Try living with *that* guilt," Sara explained giving her attention to the puppy as she spoke. "By the way, does this little girl have a name?" she asked.

"My mom named her Delilah. Like it's not bad enough that I have to take a poodle out for a walk, now I have to call out, 'Go pee Delilah'," he said imitating a southern bell's genteel voice.

We all laughed more than the joke warranted but at least some of the sadness broke. Sara continued playing with the puppy, moving Delilah's feet forward and backwards to make the dog appear to be performing a minuet. The mood in the room was lightening considerably thanks to the convenient distraction of having a new pet in the house.

"Chris, are we being too loud for your mom? Isn't she resting?" Sara asked with concern. "When *my* mom was sick it was really difficult for her to get rest so my aunt made sure the house was totally silent. I had to be so quiet all the time the neighbors probably thought that monks lived there."

"No, she'd tell us if we were being loud. She said yesterday that she didn't want anyone acting weird around her or for our routine to change. She said if we acted like everything was normal then maybe it would be." Christian shrugged as a comment to the end of his sentence.

"Well, I've known your mom for as long as I've known you and there has never been anybody or anything that's gotten the best of her. She's gonna beat this," I said.

I reassured my emotionally unstable friend with a couple of gentle pats on the back. As much as I knew I needed to be strong for Christian right now, my insides wanted to sob. I turned away to hide my weak eyes from present company and preoccupied myself by fiddling with a loose string on the couch. The thought of possibly losing the woman who had treated me like her second son for eleven years was heartbreaking.

The sound of the bickering birds outside the window began invading the acoustics of the living room as the conversation inside dropped. Interestingly though, the quiet seemed more appropriate than awkward.

"What's going on out here?" Ms. Fine emerged from her bedroom still looking tired.

"We weren't being too loud were we?" Christian said with worry.

"Oh, *much* too loud. How am I supposed to sleep with all this noise?" Ms. Fine said sarcastically plugging her ears with her fingers. "Are you kidding me, Chris? I thought you'd murdered the dog and was burying her in the back yard, it's so quiet in here."

"I'd never let him do that. She's too cute to kill," Sara said, protectively clutching Delilah close to her chest.

Christian's shoulders relaxed noticeably as he realized that we hadn't disturbed his mother. I looked up from fidgeting with the string and grinned happily knowing that a devastating medical diagnosis had not suppressed Ms. Fine's sense of humor.

"She *is* cute isn't she?" Ms. Fine concurred, reaching down and scooping the puppy from Sara's arms into her own. Delilah lavished rapid fire kisses on the cheek of her new owner.

"I guess she's taken to you already," Sara said.

"Yes, she has, she loves her mommy," Ms. Fine acknowledged, in between licks.
The squirmy puppy wriggled in her arms and she set her down on the carpet to run free for a while.

"The television isn't blaring, the radio isn't cranking tunes. I hope this house isn't in a premature state of mourning," she said almost scolding us. "Could you guys please turn up the volume out here so that I can get some rest? All I can hear is my air conditioner buzzing and it's driving me crazy."

"I think we can do that," said Christian and I shook my head in agreement.

"Thanks sweetie. Love ya," Ms. Fine bent over and kissed her son on the top of the head, something that normally would have embarrassed Christian but didn't seem to faze him now.

She walked carefully into the kitchen, watching the placement of each foot in front of the other. Then after filling a glass with tap water, she followed the same path back to her bedroom.

"Have fun," she insisted over her shoulder, disappearing behind the solid oak door of the dimly lit master bedroom.

"She seems to be feeling good," I pointed out to Christian, hoping to encourage him.

"Are you blind? Did you see the way she was walking? She can't even keep her balance anymore," he snapped back at me.

"I, I, just meant that she seemed like she was in a good mood," I stammered, the lump in my throat constricting my voice.

"She's obviously just pretending. Anyone can see that," Christian scolded.

"I'm sorry I didn't mean anything by it. I was just trying to point out..." I started.

"The obvious? Ya, thanks for that. Now can we talk about something else?" Christian finished the sentence with his own interpretation of my thoughts and turned towards the television.

I stood silently blinking back tears, my throat so tight now that I would have been unable to speak had I wanted to, which at the moment I did not. Sara fidgeted with unease, sliding her eyes back and forth between myself and Christian as if torn on what to say to whom. I'm sure she was able to identify with Christian's internal strife while also empathizing with my wounded feelings over the words that had just been exchanged.

"Why don't we make some lunch? Is anyone else hungry?" Sara asked.

"Yeah, lunch sounds good to me. I can cook up some grilled cheese sandwiches," Christian offered, as if he hadn't just bitten my head off.

They looked over at me to see if I was in agreement with the meal choice.

"Actually, I think I'll just go home for lunch," I said trying deliberately to sound casual about my choice to leave.

"Ah, come one. Stay. I know you love grilled cheese," Christian said, trying to convince me to change my mind.

"No, not today. I've barely been home all summer and my mom has been bugging me to spend more time with the family. Maybe some other time though," I said refusing the offer as politely as I could.

"Yeah, ok, next time," he said with regret in his voice.

I was glad he stopped there because I had the feeling that if we exchanged any more words right now it was not going to be good for either of us. I'd always had trouble being around Christian's blunt brand of anger, especially when he started directing that anger towards me, and today was no exception - even if his mother was sick. I knew my continued presence would lead to a fight. I patted my friend on the back to let him know I was still there for him, while I made my exit. From the driveway I heard Sara inside.

"I'll be right back Christian. I forgot to give Sam the five dollars I owe him from last night."

"Sam! Wait a sec!" she yelled, jogging a few feet on the uneven gravel to catch up to me.

I turned around immediately but waited for her to speak.

"Are you ok? You *do* know he didn't intentionally hurt your feelings back there, right?"

I shrugged my shoulders with an air of indifference. My pride was still injured.

"Well, he didn't," she continued. "It's just the way that he's grieving right now. He's in the denial and anger stage. It's in all the books. It's exactly how I acted when my mom told me she was sick. I blew up at her and my aunts all the time at first. It's almost like you can't control your emotions and it's usually the people you love who take the brunt of it. So, don't take anything he says personally right now, ok? It's gonna take a while for him to start feeling like himself again."

"Sara, I understand. It's just that I was being made to feel like the bad guy in there and it wasn't fair. I am trying to process this all right now too, she is like a second mom to me. It's just, I don't want this to be about me right now and my feelings, that's why I need to leave. He obviously needs someone to talk to and who better than you? You can relate because you've been through this before."

"I know, but I want to make sure that *you're* alright with everything that's happened today. I know she is like your mom. You've gotta be hurting; never mind the way Christian snapped at you, and then we had to put all of our own plans aside. We haven't even talked about what we are going to do about that yet."

"I think we agree that there's nothing we can do. Christian needs you right now. He's got no one else. We know how we feel about each other and that's what's important. Everything else will fall into place," I said.

Each word stung as it came out of my mouth.

"But this isn't the way I wanted it to go. I know he needs me but I just want to be with you. I have this awful knot in my stomach right now," Sara said.

I pulled her in for an embrace and she let her sadness spill out on my shoulder in the form of sobs. I knew Christian couldn't hear our conversation and I figured if he saw me holding her like this, he would just shrug it off as me comforting her over the news of his mother.

"Please don't cry, Sara. We're not saying, *never*, we're just saying, *not right now.*"
I tried to assure myself as well as I cupped her tear soaked face in my hands.

"But I don't know if I can do this again, Sam. Can I watch another person die?"

"You won't have to. She's not going to die. She's going to be fine, it's in her name, it's part of her; she will be just fine."

"Ok but as soon as this all blows over and she's in the clear and Christian is back on solid ground, can we end this charade?" Sara asked.

"Just give me the word. It can't come fast enough," I said, trying hard to repress the intense feeling of helplessness that was pushing to overwhelm me.

Sara held onto me tightly, grasping her hands together like a lock on the back of my neck and burying her face in my shirt. I could feel her inhaling the musky scent of my deodorant the way I had done with her hair. Slowly, she loosened her grip and let her arms fall away from me.

"So, I'll see you tomorrow right? As friends, I mean?" Sara inquired, wiping the remaining wetness from her cheeks as if she were hiding evidence.

"I'll be here just like I always am," I confirmed adding; "but not just as a friend, as a best friend."

Sara managed a smile and nodded at the arrangement. She maintained eye contact as she slowly started to back up in the direction of the house. She hung onto my hand until the distance between us was greater than the length of our arms. As the tips of her fingers fell from mine, she turned and walked with haste to face the obstacles that lay ahead of her.

I stood rooted to that spot, watching the wind catch her hair and whip it back at me into knots. I thought of how only minutes ago she had come bounding out of the yellow ranch house seeking me and now she was reentering it, going back for Christian. I looked down onto the pavement at the miniscule wet marks left by her tears; dark gray spots so insignificant that no one else would know of their existence. Only me, who had felt the heartbreak that caused them to fall, could see them clearly. But she had left something other than these little messengers of heartbreak behind; her gentle spirit still clung to the warm afternoon air. Even though I felt a bit silly doing so, I spoke to it.

"Don't forget I'm waiting."

Not wanting any more pain to be drawn out of this moment, I turned with uncertainty and walked, alone, back to my house.

CHAPTER 12

Strangely, when I arrived home, no one greeted me. They all seemed dispersed around the house, busy with other things. I counted my blessings that I wasn't being immediately roped into family time, and customarily headed straight to my room. I was excited at the idea of listening to some music on my headphones and tuning out the world for a while. A soulful melody was what the doctor always ordered for an aching heart.

Barely an hour had passed before my mother was knocking on my bedroom door. I slid my headphones down around my neck and turned the knob. She poked her head through the opening.

"Come downstairs Sam, your father and I need to talk to you and your brother."

Those words, 'need to talk', we never good, especially when it involved both me and my brother. I had been slacking on my chores and since it was summer, Matt was probably doing the same; I'm sure my dad was ready to lay into us both. I put my Walkman on the bed and followed her to the parlor. My brother was sitting straight up against the back of the couch and my father was standing tall with one arm propped on top of the fireplace mantel. I prepared myself for the lengthy lecture about familial responsibility that I knew was coming. But to my surprise, when I entered the room, my father sat down in his easy chair and my mother went to stand beside him. He never sat when he was about to lecture us, usually preferring to tower over us instead. I could tell this wasn't going to be his usual sermon tonight. The mood seemed very serious and, for a split second, I wondered if he was about to tell me that *my* mother had cancer. God forgive me for even thinking it, but I did.

"I called this meeting to tell you kids about something very exciting that is happening to this family. There have been a lot of changes going on in the company that I work for. Many of these changes, I don't like one bit and frankly they are taking hard-earned money out of my pocket. I haven't told you two, but I have been interviewing at other places for different positions. One of the places where I interviewed made me an offer and I accepted it. It is more money, shorter hours, and has wonderful benefits. This new job will affect the entire family for the better. I am proud to inform you that I will now be working at Northeastern College. This means, of course, we are moving."

I felt like he had just thrown a bag of rocks at my stomach and for a moment I couldn't speak. I went into denial mode, just as Sara said happens when a person is handed news that is unfathomable. I didn't believe I had heard him correctly. I couldn't believe this was true and not some cruel joke. I looked at my brother. He was dumbfounded, confirmation that he had heard the same thing as me. My denial turned to rage. My brother and I had to unite and fight to stay. Being the oldest, I spoke first.

"Moving?! When and where exactly?!"

"First off, I don't like your tone. But I can understand that you are taken back by this so I'll let it slide. To answer your question - soon. I gave my notice at work and your mother and I already put a down payment on a house in a nice suburb right outside of Boston. It's newer than this one and you and your brother will each have your own room. We'll put this one on the market immediately but we don't have to wait for it to sell until we leave. They need me at the college right away and I can't pass this up. You may not like it at first, but like it or not, we're moving."

We're moving. Moving. Moving? MOVING! The words pounded in my head like a migraine. If he said it one more time, I was going to be sick. We weren't just packing up and heading across town to a bigger ranch house. We were completely and certainly leaving the state where I was born and raised. Life, as I currently knew it, was about to drastically change. We were moving far enough away that I would have to leave everything and, more importantly, *everyone* behind. I was being taken away from Sara. Any chance I had with her was gone.

Once that realization hit me, I totally lost my mind. I spewed the most hurtful versions of, I'm-not-going-you-can't-make-me, that I could think of. My brother dissented as well but even his calmer and more innocent arguments were bounced right back at him. My father was not changing his mind. I looked to my mother for some compassion, but she just nodded along like a puppet, agreeing with every selfish word my father said.

After an hour of banging my head against the brick wall that is my father, I began to realize that nothing I said mattered; nothing I said would change his mind. I felt about as insignificant to him as a stray ant that he had stepped on simply because it was in his way; by the end of the conversation all that was left of me was the residual mush on the bottom of his shoe.

I sat there, numb and dumb, absorbing the details he was divulging about the place and time that my life was going to change. When I was excused from the conversation, I walked like a zombie up to my room, slammed the door so hard behind me that the wall shook, plopped myself face down onto my bed and didn't come out until it was time to say goodbye.

∞

Dear Sam,

I don't even know what to say. It seems like we were just getting started and now you've been ripped away from me — literally. I'll never forgive your father for moving you all the way to Boston. It's like he didn't even stop to think about how it would affect you. And me. But of course, no one else knows about that. I know we decided that me remaining Christian's girlfriend for a little while is the right thing to do but it's been really hard. Honestly, I think about you constantly and knowing that you're not close by makes me want to just crawl under my covers and hide from the world. Christian's trying all the time to make me laugh but it just doesn't feel right being with him and having fun knowing that you are all alone and so far away. Even though he hasn't said anything to me about it, I think he can tell I've been distant from him, I don't think he's connected it to you being gone though, so that's good. I'm over his house every day because of his mom. She's really weak from the chemo so I try to make sure that all the laundry and cooking is done so that she doesn't have to do any housework when she finally gets a little bit of energy. I didn't think I'd have to go through this again so soon. The worst part is, not knowing how it's going to end (if you know what I mean).

So I know you just left a week ago but do you have any idea when you'll be able to come back for a weekend? Chris and his mom want you back almost as badly as I do. It doesn't feel the same around here without you. My dad says I've been moping around ever since you left. I didn't think it was that obvious but apparently it is. It's weird that just a year ago I was living my life, not even knowing that you existed and now that I know you're out there, I can't live my life right without you in it. Please come back soon.
You're too far away for comfort.

 Love, Sara

THIS SPACE BETWEEN US

To My Sara Sun,

You don't know how awesome it was to get your letter! When I went to the mailbox and saw your name in the return address, I torn the envelope open and read it before I was even in the house. Then when I got in the house I reread it about 5 more times. In a strange way seeing your handwriting made me feel close to you again. Believe me I will never forgive my father either for taking me away from you. I've probably only spoken 2 or 3 words to him since we've been here. I think he's gotten the hint that I'm furious. As happy as I was to see the letter from you, it did make me sad to hear that you've been sad. Even if I'm not there I still want you to be happy and have fun. It's not right for us both to be miserable over something that we can't control. I'll give you a break and continue to be miserable enough for both of us, ok? Just kidding. Tell Chris and Ms. Fine that I miss them too and that I hope that she feels better soon. Actually, on second thought don't. It's probably better if people don't know that we are writing secret love letters to each other. As of right now, I am not sure when I'll be home again. I say "home" because my real home is wherever you are. I've been begging my mom to go back within the next couple of weekends but she hasn't committed to a date yet. I'll let you know as soon as she does. Until I get a car and a Massachusetts license she's the only transportation I have. I know Chris would drive and come my way but I don't think his car can handle the trip and I wouldn't want you stranded on the side of the road somewhere with a blown gasket.

This whole thing is torture. Every day I'm away from you I want to see you more. I don't even have a picture of you to look at. But that doesn't really matter because the picture that I have of you in my mind is clearer than any camera could take. None of these girls in Boston come close to comparing to you. Stay strong for Chris and his family, they need you now. I need you too but I guess we can't always get what we want. See you very, very, very soon (mom permitting).

Love you too,

Sam

P.S. Do you like my new nickname for you? "Sara Sun" because you are like the sun, wherever you are there is warmth and light.

Hi Sam,

Hey how's it going? Nothing much here. Oh man I can't believe I have to write to you to ask you that! This sucks, like majorly sucks. I want to kill your dad. Boston for God's sake! That seems so far away and I definitely can't picture you going to some big city school. I hope you don't like get beat up or anything. I heard that there's gangs and stuff in Boston. Not that I wanna make you think you are going to get beat up or anything, I'm sure you'll be ok. Forget I said that. I hope that you like your new school and new house. I think I heard your mom say it was going to be bigger and that you and Mark wouldn't have to share a room anymore. That's cool, I guess. So there's not much new with my mom yet, I know it's only been a few weeks since you left but I thought I'd let you know because I know you've probably been wondering about her. I'll let you know as soon as anything changes. My dad's been hovering over us a lot and I think that's aggravating her. But I've gotten used to the dog a little bit and I don't mind so much taking her for walks anymore. School is ok, well it's school, you know. Everyone was wicked bummed when they found out you wouldn't be finishing senior year here. Wow, that's even weird to say that. Justin said to say hi, so "hi". They want your new phone number when I get it. By the way, when will the phone be hooked up? Seems like it's taking forever. Hey! Maybe you can come back for prom? That would be fun. Not that I want to go really but I'm sure Sara will. Well actually, maybe not. I mean I'm sure she'll want to go but maybe not with me. I don't know. It's weird. Suddenly she seems like she isn't really interested in me or something. She's really nice to my mom and she takes care of her a lot but sometimes I think the only reason she comes over is to be with my mom. She's acting kind of like she likes someone else but I have no clue who. She barely talks to anyone at school besides a couple of girls that she made friends with. I know one thing, if she does dump me for someone at school I won't be able to stand seeing them together every day. It would be too hard to stay friends with her, I know some people can but I couldn't. It would hurt too much. I don't know maybe I am just being paranoid or maybe everything just seems different because you aren't around anymore to make fun of. Ha Ha Just kidding. Actually, Sara has been really helping me get through some of this stuff with my mom. We talk a lot about how to handle it and me being prepared, just in case something happens. Ugh, I don't even want to think about that. It's scary to think that you're gone, there's a chance that my mom might die and now I might lose Sara too. I really don't want to lose her. I don't know what I'd do without her right now, she keeps me from falling off the edge. She is the only one I have to talk to. You can probably tell I like her way more than any of the other girls I've dated. But it's more than that. Can I tell you something? I think I'm starting to lean towards more than just liking her, I might end up in L--- with her. Fill in the blanks! But you know how easy it would be to L--- Sara, she's so different from any other girls. She likes all the same stuff as we do and we have so much fun together. My mom would be happy if we stayed together I know that. <u>SHE'S IN LOVE WITH HER!</u> Ha Ha. I think it will work out alright though, I just have to be extra nice and pay more attention to her and I'm sure she'll come around. By the way, have I said how much I hate this stupid year, it is the worst year of my life! Yours too I'm sure. Remember when we cared so much about getting my driver's license, that seems like forever ago but it's only been four months. I just can't wait until the summer when you can come back all the time and visit. My mom bought an air mattress for when you sleep over. I think she's secretly hoping that she can adopt you and you'll stay. WOW! This letter is way too long so I'd better stop. I hope you don't fall asleep reading it. I've never written this much to anyone before! That should make you feel special. Call me as soon as the phone's hooked up or write back – whatever comes first.

Christian

P.S. Even though I'm three hours away, I've still got your back and I know you've got mine!

∞

The letter *was* long, but I read and re-read it over and over, focusing on the part where he confessed that he might be in love with Sara. He was being vulnerable and opening up to me about his feelings, which was unprecedented for him. I knew he couldn't possibly love her as much as I did, but still, it made me pause to hear my best friend reveal these intimate feelings to me. I didn't know how I could ever tell him that I loved her too, and even more devastating, that she loved me. That last post script, in particular, echoed in my mind and haunted my conscience. *I've still got your back.* How could I betray Christian's loyalty at the most delicate time in his life?

I threw the letter on the floor and stomped on it, wishing I had never even opened the stupid thing. But now that I *had* read it, I couldn't ignore it. As much as I hated it; this letter changed everything. The fact was, I was a state away, with nothing to offer in the way of a real relationship and Christian was right there with her. His mom loved her. They were good people and could give her what she needed - physical and emotional support. All I had to offer her were letters and hopes to visit on the occasional weekend. I realized that she might have a real chance at happiness if she stayed with Christian and I didn't want to be the one to get in the way of that. I thought and thought and thought and finally sat down to pen a letter, telling her the truth.

~~Dear Sara,~~

~~I just got a letter from Christian and he is suspicious that you like someone else. It is killing him. He said that he could never be friends with you or the guy that you like if you dumped him. You are the only person that he has right now. If he ever found out that you and I have something together he would lose his mind. You have to stay with him and forget about me. I am so far away and as it is he is right there with you. Please forget about me and try to be happy with Christian.~~

~~I'll always love you,~~

~~Sam~~

I realized she would never go for it. As much as I wanted to tell her the truth, I knew she wouldn't accept it as a reason to stay with Christian. She would simply write back and tell me that Chris would be ok in time and that we needed to do things for ourselves in order to be happy. I knew she would be right, because that was what my inner voice told me as well. But the voice of my logic was louder and insisted that my distance from her did not serve either of us well. She was better off being forced into being happy where she was than to choose being miserable, waiting for me to come back. Still, my hand was cramping at the thought of writing a lie. Instead, I wrote back to Christian. Hoping it would remind me of why I was about to do what I was about to do.

Hey Chris,
Yeah that really was a long letter, you weren't kidding. But it was good reading. The phone line is being put in on Monday so I will call you with my new number then. Our house was just built so they basically had to wire the entire thing to the pole. School sucks just like I thought it would. The building is huge and it is so hard to find my classes. Plus I have no one to sit with at lunch so I just go outside and sit on the stairs. At least I will only be here for like 7 months before I graduate. Get this, my dad's already talking about enrolling me in college here! I told him I wanted to go back to NH for college but because he works at Northeastern now he can get me free tuition, he said it's one of the reasons he took the job and that there is no discussion about it, that's where I am going! He'll probably make me live at home too because I'm sure

that room and board isn't included in his free deal. I can't wait until I am an adult and I can finally make my own decisions. I feel for you with having your dad around all the time now, I think that we are both sick of them. I guess no news with your mom is better than bad news. She'll hang in there, she's strong. Just let me know if anything changes.

I can't wait for the summer. Tell your mom she'll be sorry that she ever bought that air mattress because I'll wear it out! Also, don't worry about Sara, she'll come around. I'm sure that there is no one else that she likes. She is probably just being weird around you because of what happened with her mom. I'm sure this is hard on her too. Stick it out and keep being the best boyfriend that you can be. Spend lots of time with her and buy her flowers and tell her thank you for helping out with your mom and stuff like that. She needs to feel special and get some attention too right now. But like I said, don't worry, everything will work out for the best.

Your friend,

Sam

P.S. Believe me, I've got your back more than you know!

∞

Writing to Christian made me feel like I had a purpose and it was to preserve his happiness. If I could do that, then at least I had done one thing right. It made what I had to write to Sara seem like a means to an end. I reminded myself that it was seemingly improbable that Sara and I would be permanently reunited in the near future anyway, due to the fact that a giant granite state had wedged itself between us. Still, it took all of my life long good sense to overpower my self-serving will and come to the final decision that I was not going to pursue Sara at the expense of my best friend's sanity. Even though I was convinced that what I was doing was right, my hand shook as I wrote.

> Hi Sara,
>
> Please read this alone. I didn't want to call because I don't have any privacy on the phone around here.
>
> We never got much of a chance to talk before I left about how this would work with me and you. I don't know how long it will be before I'm able to come back for good since my dad has already enrolled me in Northeastern College for the fall. I guess we never really know how our lives are going to turn out, especially when we are teenagers and have no control over anything.
>
> I'm not sure how you feel about it. Us staying together, I mean. But I think it would be better if we didn't feel obligated or attached to each other. You're in New Hampshire with Chris and I'm in Massachusetts now with all the new people I've been meeting. I think it would just be way too hard to keep our relationship long distance. When I am back in NH for good then maybe we can reconnect in that kind of way.

> Please don't be upset or think that you did anything wrong, that's the last thing I want. I'll see you when I come back for visits and I still hope that we can be best friends like we promised. It just seems to make more sense this way for everyone. Let me know what you think.
>
> Sorry, Sam

As I re-read it aloud, the words in this disingenuous note burned my insides like swallowed poison. I felt ugly and sick, as if my self-loathing would never relent. I needed to get the letter far away from me before I ripped it up or threw it away in regret. I sealed my gloomy fate, as I licked the postage stamp that sent the letter traveling from Massachusetts to Sara's mailbox in New Hampshire. How I had convinced myself that this was the best solution for all involved was beyond me. There was nothing left to do but wait in dread for the reply. When her return letter arrived a week later, I still wasn't ready to read its contents but my curiosity made me open the envelope.

> Sam,
> No hard feelings.
> You're right, I totally understand.
> Of course, we're still best friends.
> See you when you visit.
> Sara

I studied the curly handwritten note. I knew Sara well enough to interpret the unwritten message on the page. The notepaper was void of her signature purple ink, a sure sign that she was in a serious and somber mood while writing it. The content seemed too sparse to be spontaneous so I guessed that the few sentences she had written were well thought out. No greeting such as the customary "hi" or the more formal "hello or even the obligatory "to" was found on the page. I hadn't expected that she would close the letter with "love" or "yours truly", but I was hurt that she hadn't even bothered with "bye" or "sincerely". She signed very simply "Sara" which I felt purposely left no hint of affection for me. And why should she? I'm sure her heart had been broken, along with mine, in my attempt to preserve Christian's.

Looking at this, I was now almost positive that I had done the wrong thing. I should have gone with my gut and sent her the first letter I wrote and at least been honest so that she could have made up her own mind about the situation. Now I had made myself look like a selfish, horny teenager who couldn't be bothered with waiting for the occasional weekend to make-out with his girlfriend. I crumpled up the letter she had written to get it out of my sight, and with one hand, tossed it into the wicker waste basket which sat next to my queen-sized bed.

A half hour passed while I stared at the floor contemplating my decision. I stopped pacing, pulled the note from the trash, smoothed it out and re-read it. I wasn't upset with her over the short words she had written because I knew I had warranted them. I thought about the events that had led up to this letter; events that seemed totally and wholly out of my control, except one - the last letter I had written. I imagined how the tears must have stung her face when she read it. I wanted so badly to right my wrong. I began to write to her again, stopping a dozen times, crossing out and crumpling up the candid words that I knew she would never accept now that I had already done the damage with a lie.

The only hope I secretly harbored was that the natural course of time would cause Sara and Christian to grow apart, thus allowing her and I another chance to be together, free from the guilt of our current circumstances. Until that time came, I had to assume the role I knew best, being her trusted friend. I hoped that she would at least want to remain *that*, even if it did take some time to get over what I had done. I would wait as long as I needed for it to be right between us.

I gave up on writing a confession and placed her letter next to Christian's in my dresser as a reminder of whom I had done this for. Maybe as the days went on, I would find some solace in knowing that I had helped out someone in this world.

Looking around, I realized that I didn't even have my brother in shouting distance anymore to take out my frustrations on. He was busy playing video games down the hall in his own room and I was beginning to realize that sharing a room all those years with him wasn't as bad as I had made it out to be. I guess I was just going to have to get used to being alone.

Plopping myself down on my soft bed which had become my new best friend, I covered my head with the goose-down pillow and let out a weighty sigh releasing enough hot air and heartache to fill every corner of my new, oversized, empty bedroom.

CHAPTER 13

About a month later, my old house sold and my father returned for the weekend to tie up some loose ends. I hitched a ride back to New Hampshire with him; it was the first time I had been back since I moved. The minute we pulled into the familiar driveway, I unbuckled my seat belt, grabbed my backpack, and bolted for the Fine house. Christian and his mom were waiting for me in the kitchen when I bounded through the door. I saw lunch sitting on the counter: tuna salad stuffed in split-top hot dog buns, one of my favorites.

"Sam! Get over here young man, you're mine now and I'm never letting you leave," Ms. Fine gushed, opening her arms wide. I walked to greet her, setting my backpack down at the door, but before I could reach her, Christian practically tackled me to the floor with an enthusiastic bear hug.

"My man! Long time no see," he said as I pushed my way to standing.

"If I had known everyone was gonna be this nice to me, I would have moved a long time ago," I said.
They chuckled.

"It's just so good to have you back. We missed you around here. I feel like I've lost my son," Ms. Fine said.

"Gee ma, thanks. What am I, chopped liver?" Christian asked.

"Oh, stop. You know what I mean. Anyway Sam, we are all set for your stay with us," she said motioning to the living room.

As promised, the newly-purchased air mattress was blown-up and waiting for me upon my arrival. She had even put sheets and blanket on top with some throw pillows to make it look like a real bed.

"Aw, thanks. You didn't have to go through all that trouble though."

"Enough. You are no trouble at all. You are *family*," she said.

"Do you think I can steal the golden boy away for a little while? A few people from school want to see him and I promised them we'd stop by," Christian said to his mother and turned to me; "Sara was supposed to come too but she's sick."

Sick or trying to avoid me like the plague? I thought. *Probably the latter.*

"I suppose you can go, but only after you've eaten lunch. I made Sam's favorite."

"Yea, of course, I'm starved," Christian said.

"You're always starved," his mother replied.

"That's because I'm a growing boy. You should know that," he said, stuffing the first mouthful of food in.

I sat back and watched the easy conversation between Christian and his mother, wondering why my family couldn't be this laid back. It felt more like home to be here in this house with friends than it did to be in my tidy over-sized new house with my own mother and father. I longed to have this life back.

The day turned out to be a blast and would have been perfect if Sara were there. Christian called her at least a dozen a times to join us but she kept insisting she wasn't feeling up to it. At one point, Christian called her bluff but she wouldn't relent, finally telling him that it was a girl problem. That shut him up pretty quickly. So, we went on without her, visiting friends, fishing in the trout pond and staying up past midnight laughing at cheesy cop movies until we spewed soda all over the carpet.

The last time Christian called her, I could hear her voice over the phone and I desperately wanted to grab the receiver, tell her to come see me and plead with her to forgive me. But I couldn't. I never got to talk to her, never got to see her, never got to find out what she was thinking or how much she probably hated me.

When Sunday afternoon came, I wanted to hide in the Fine's garage until my father was in another state, but instead I reluctantly got into his van to return to Massachusetts. I left with a sense of unease that things were still unresolved between Sara and me. The weekend had gone by too quickly and the worst part was, I wasn't sure when I was going to get the chance to come back.

Turns out I never did go back until I got my license two months later, my parents always had some excuse as to why they couldn't go which translated to me as they just didn't care about my happiness. Once I had my freedom on wheels, I took the almost three hour drive to the Fine house every weekend. Sara didn't fake sick the second time I went back and when I first saw her, my heart leapt out of my chest. It had been so long since I laid eyes on her, I felt like I was seeing her for the first time. Thankfully, the initial awkwardness didn't last long and as soon as the first laugh rolled into our conversation, I felt the invisible ice break. Our time apart seemed to have healed the wounds between us.

As I hoped, each time I returned we grew to be closer and closer friends. But we were only as close as the huge distance between us would allow. I still missed out on a lot of day to day happenings. Sometimes when I was around her and Christian, I couldn't help feeling like I was sixteen again returning from vacation, a third wheel who couldn't keep up with all their private jokes. I saw them enjoying each other's company; walking the dog together, racing each other to the car or squirting playfully with the water hose. But they also bickered, sometimes incessantly, over the smallest tasks. Whenever I took the long drive up, I hoped it would be the day that Sara would tell me she had dumped Christian. I waited with baited breath for the big fight between them that would end it all, but it didn't come; after more time passed, I gave up hope that it ever would.

In accordance with what my father told me, I was enrolled at Northeastern College and stuck in Boston for the next four years with nothing to do but study in my dorm room (I promised to pay for room and board myself) and try to stay out of trouble. Luckily, Sara kept an interest in the happenings of my life, and being the lover of the penned word, she faithfully wrote weekly letters to "keep me company in between classes." Every Friday I checked my student post box with anticipation of another correspondence from her. My stomach fluttered whenever I saw the familiar *S. Sunby* in the left hand corner of an envelope. I relished in the fact that she shared every detail of her life with me in those letters; her poetry, her annoyances with community college, her low paying job. She even wrote about her aversion to organized religion in a three page rant one night when she couldn't sleep. Getting a glimpse at all her private thoughts sometimes made it hard for me to remember that she wasn't my girlfriend. I wondered how much of this stuff she shared with Christian too. But then, she probably didn't share much since he was more of the talker in the relationship and *I* was more of the listener; something that was for once, playing to my advantage.

    I wrote back to her, gladly and faithfully, answering all her questions and adding some of my own, but always keeping the tone friendly. Even though I felt like I could tell her anything in those letters, I never brought up my feelings for her again, for fear that some aspect of our friendship would change and I would lose her forever. In a way it made me miserable that emotionally she with me, but physically she wasn't. She was a sun out of my orbit where her rays of light and warmth couldn't penetrate the thick cumulus formations which hovered above me daily.

    After what seemed like a lifetime, the day came when I finally walked the stage to receive my bachelor's degree. Ms. Fine, Christian and Sara were there to cheer me on and I could hear their whoops and hollers above those of my own family. My graduation was a marked release from academics, college life, and my father's grasp. I no longer had to wander amongst the crowds and smog of Boston. I was free to make my own decisions. My first one was to return permanently to my old neighborhood in the White Mountains of New Hampshire. Even before I graduated, I had been scouted for a lucrative, high salary position with a Boston advertising firm. I knew that most other grads would have killed for the chance to put their degree to use right out of school but I had turned it down without a thought. If I had told my father about the offer, he might have strapped me to a chair and made me stay, so I didn't. I planned my move back to my hometown quietly and quickly. As far as I could tell, the rural area held no job prospects for me but I didn't care. I was moving back to be near Sara and nothing else. I figured the rest would fall into place when I got there.

I hadn't so much as dated one person my entire college career; not because I hadn't had the opportunity but because I could never bring myself to be with any other girl but Sara. There hadn't been one pretty face I'd seen that equaled her's; not one laugh that sounded as genuine; not one conversation that held the deep meaning ours did. Everything had gone contrary to my belief that if time didn't bring us back together, at least our separation might make me not want her so badly. But instead of dissipating, my love for her had only intensified with the passing days, months and years. I knew now that it wouldn't be enough to just be friends with her, I needed more. And I needed to tell her.

I had shared so many private moments with her through our letters that I was confident our connection was stronger now than it ever was. Plus, Ms. Fine was in remission from her cancer and Christian was wrapped up in his job as a river guide. He led many overnight trips with his groups, and he and Sara seemed to be spending less time together because she was taking college classes and working too. I felt that the time was finally right to come clean about my feelings and see if she would grant me another chance. I planned on revealing everything honestly and completely as soon as I got settled into my new apartment.

I had rented a rather small one bedroom, which was attached to a single family house. The people I was renting from seemed amiable and the price was right for my currently unemployed budget. I planned on living off my savings until I could secure a job. Being native to the area (I was only three blocks from where I used to live) would work in my job hunting favor here since most of the businesses preferred to hire locals. If after three months I couldn't find a job that would pay enough to live on, I was willing to expand my search to some nearby cities.

My brother took the drive up with me on moving day to help load and unload my furniture into my new pad. He was still at Northeastern *and* holding down a minimum wage job like I had, because our parents refused to pay for extras. He had to get back for work that night and couldn't stay to help me unload everything. I had hoped for Christian's help, but he too couldn't get the day off of work, so I was stuck carrying boxes in and out of the moving van by myself a hundred times. I didn't realize I had accumulated so much stuff in my short life.

Plopping the last box onto the floor, I plunked myself down at the kitchen table which had been left by the previous occupant of the apartment; the chair's vinyl padding was almost nonexistent and the Formica table top had seen better days, I was considering whether I even wanted to eat off of it. If I got some extra cash soon, this would be one of the first items to be replaced. I looked at the bland vanilla colored walls and outdated carpeting; the place reminded me a lot of my dorm room. I made a mental note to ask the landlord if she'd mind if I painted. Just as I was thinking about which color scheme I should explore, Christian came bounding through the entry door which I had left half-open in my haste to get the last box in.

"Well, *you* have perfect timing don't you?" I said.

"Don't tell me you're done already?"

"Literally, just brought in the last box," I said motioning to the heavy heap of cardboard on the floor which housed my college texts.

"Bummer. I didn't know what time I'd be done today. I just got out and I figured you'd still be unpacking. Not my fault you're an overachiever." He gave me a kidding smile as he strut the few steps from the entry past the living room and into the kitchen; "Nice digs."

"Thanks. It's something," I said shrugging my shoulders. "For now."

"I hope you're not too mad about me not haulin' boxes today because I have a favor to ask."

"That depends on what the favor is," I said leaning back in my chair, gesturing my chin upwards for him to continue.

"Ah, it's nothing really. Just wondering if you'll be my best man?"

The sentence shot from his mouth and hit me like an atomic shock wave. He casually took a seat from me across the table.

"You're *WHAT?*" I asked, tilting my ear in his direction to make sure that I had heard correctly.

"My BEST MAN! Dude, I asked Sara to marry me last night and she said yes, of course," he added as if he didn't need to mention that little detail; "Whaddya think? Are you up for the job?"

Christian sounded ecstatic. He searched my face for excitement where there was none.

"You're kidding right?" I said blankly.

"Why? Do you think marriage is a joke?" Christian chuckled as if I were playing a game with him.

"Only when *you* talk about it," I replied without humor. Christian looked taken aback.

"Well, it's not a joke and I'm not kidding. We've been together for almost six years. You must have known I would ask her sooner or later."

"Maybe, but you never actually mentioned it to me. Have you and Sara even talked about it before now?"

I was positive Sara had never brought that up in any of her letters and I definitely would have remembered if Christian had ever talked about it. I felt completely blindsided.

"Nah, not really. We've both been kinda busy so it never came up. I just figured it was the right time," Christian explained.

The right time, I thought. That sounded familiar. Evidently it felt like the right time for everyone. Why was I always preempted by this knucklehead standing in front of me? Why did *he* have to open his mouth just as I was about to spill six years of pent up feelings?

"Why now?" I demanded, I was sick of mincing words. "Why not next week or next month or next year?" I was livid but trying to control the anger in my voice as best I could.

"Because, if I didn't ask her now, she wouldn't have enough time to get a dress," Christian replied grabbing a piece of pizza out of the takeout box on the counter and nibbling it.

I was obviously doing *too good* of a job at masking my emotions because he wasn't picking up on them.

"What are you talking about? When are you getting married?"

"A week from Saturday."

He leaned back in his chair as if there was nothing more to say on the subject. I wasn't about to let it go so easily.

"Hold on, hold on. You're telling me that you and Sara are going to be married, as in husband and wife, in two weeks?"

I held up two fingers like a peace sign in Christian's face so that he would know I required a thorough answer.

"Yup. The town of Jackson is having a communal marriage ceremony under the wooden covered bridge a week from Saturday. Anyone who wants to come can get married all together at the same time. Then after the ceremony they are having a band in the gazebo and food and dancing..." He started to trail off as if he was going to end it there but instead perked up with an animated voice; "oh, and get this, my mom and dad are gonna go and renew their vows! They've been acting all love-y dove-y ever since they got back together. It's so weird. My mom's gonna get all dressed up and do her hair, she hasn't cut it since it grew back from the chemo, so it's really long now."

"How many other people will be there?" I asked wanting as many answers to as many questions as possible.

I purposely glossed over the last comment he made about his parents, wanting only to focus on Sara and Christian. At this point, anything else was a distraction.

"Probably a lot. I'm not sure. But it sounds like a really cool time," Christian explained as he munched on a mouthful of pizza.

"And *this*, communal wedding thing, is something that you *both* want to do?" I asked not believing that it was.

"I mean she seemed alright. We haven't talked too much about it yet. But it'll be a great story to tell our kids someday," he commented as he swallowed the last bit of crust. "You can ask her yourself. She'll be here in a few minutes. She said she wanted to see your new place."

"She's coming here. Now?"

My pent up anger was starting to spill out. Now that this wrench had been thrown into my plans I wondered what, if anything, I should say to her about us. I wasn't even sure I was capable of carrying on a pleasant conversation right now.

"Yeah. Sorry I invited her over without asking, I just figured you'd want to congratulate her and all that stuff."

I stared off into the distance, nodding my head numbly in agreement; trying to process the news I had just been given. It seemed as if suddenly I had been removed from the altar of the future I had been imagining all these years and replaced by Christian. The only possible explanation of why she had accepted a proposal from him, someone who could never love her as much as I did, is because that after all this time, she didn't know that I still loved her.

As Christian reached into the pizza box for his second slice, he turned on the beat-up looking radio in the corner which had also been left by the previous tenant. Suddenly, the contemplative silence of the room was broken by a loud-mouthed sports commentator. I couldn't contain the fire that was building in me any longer. I shot him a glare that, had it been a weapon, easily would have killed him. Reaching backwards I snapped the dial off with force.

"Whyd'ya do that?" Christian said, puzzled, as he paused from his pizza binge.

"Because I'm so sick of hearing the blah, blah, blah," I spat out.

"What's up your butt today?" Christian finished chewing and wiped his mouth with the back of his hand.

"Nothing." I waved my hand dismissively at the question.

"Yeah…Ok." Christian rolled his eyes at my obvious lie.

"Why does there always have to be something wrong just because, for once, I don't want to do what you want to do."

"Whoa, whoa, whoa. Hold on a second here. So, now you *always* do what I want to do. I thought we were just talking about the radio."

"You would."

"What the hell is that supposed to mean?" Christian folded his arms and sat back in his chair waiting for an explanation.

"Whatever you think it means," I said under my breath as I turned to walk away.

"No way," Christian said. He got up from his chair, grabbed my arm and pulled me to sit down with him at the table. "You are not going to avoid this like you avoid every other confrontation. Obviously you have something to say. Now say it."

"Don't touch me!" I pulled my arm back from Christian's grasp and gave him a shove on the shoulder.
He stood up at the challenge and I met him where he was, staring him down with intensity.

"Back off, I don't want to get into this right now," I said.

"There we go again with the avoidance. Come on, get it out. Speak now or forever hold your peace."

Christian sat down again, obviously feeling that the moment for a physical altercation had passed, or trying to avoid one. I doubt he realized the irony in his statement. I pictured the altar and the priest speaking these final words before pronouncing Christian and Sara husband and wife. He was right; now was the time to speak my peace.

"Alright, you wanna hear it. Here it comes...you're not good enough for her."

"Are you serious right now man?" he asked, scratching at the back of his head.

I nodded and continued challenging him with my eyes. He furrowed his brow.

"Where the hell do you get off, huh? What do you even know?" he said, rising to his feet. "You've been off at college for four years sitting in some classroom, with no girlfriend I might add, while we've been here living life, day in and day out, together. We've been getting along really good."

I could tell that he was going to continue talking, but I didn't want to hear it. I threw up my hands in disgust.

"I'm not just talking about getting along. I'm talking about everything. Really knowing each other. I mean, did you even stop and think about this wedding that you are having. Well, yeah, you probably did think about how convenient it would be for *you* but did you think about Sara at all? I would put money on the fact that she doesn't want to be standing next to fifty other women in gowns on *her* wedding day. But see, it's that kinda stuff. You don't even think about what she wants."

Christian went silent for a moment and plopped back down into the chair. He slumped forward in a posture of defeat.

"Holy shit, you're right," he said staring at the wall. "I'm a selfish asshole."

As much as I wanted to continue laying into him, I couldn't now that he wasn't being a selfish jerk. This new Mr. Remorseful was really hard to yell at. Maybe this was the right time to lay out all my cards, here and now, while he was being reasonable and we could sort things out man to man.

"Look, I'm not trying to make you feel bad. It's just, I know Sara better than you think and I wanted to tell you," I began to say.

"Ding dong," a sweet female voice chimed in, interrupting me mid-sentence.

Sara slid off her cheap plastic flip flops, leaving them at the entryway, as she waved excitedly at me. Her lightweight top flowed behind her as she ran barefoot across the room and wrapped her arms around me.

"It's so nice to have you back!" she exclaimed.

Her messy ponytail hung low, practically falling out of its loose, purple elastic band as she squeezed me. I pulled her in and grabbed tightly. The fruity smell of her hair was still the same.

"Welcome to Casa de Sam," I said motioning my arm around the room.

"Nice place you've got here. When can I move in?" she joked.

"There's always an extra bed," I replied, wanting to throw a sheet on the mattress right now and sign her name to the lease.

"Don't mind the way I look." She gestured at her torn jeans; "I was just working in the garden."

"You look great, don't worry about it."

I didn't have to fib, even with no makeup and dirty clothes her eyes sparkled. Christian silently scooted himself up onto the kitchen counter as I showed Sara around. When I got to the master bedroom she plopped backwards onto the king sized bed.

"Big bed! I'm impressed with all this. You did pretty good for yourself. But then again, I knew you would," she said sitting up.

I couldn't help blushing at the compliment. I looked down quickly so that she wouldn't notice.

"Yeah, I got so used to the queen I had in my room that I missed a big bed when I was in the dorm so I spent some graduation money and bought this," I said patting the mattress.

"When you graduated *with honors* you mean," she corrected.

"What else did I have to do but study?"

"Sure smarty pants. I just hope this means that you're sticking around for a while. We don't wanna lose you again."

I nodded instead of speaking my plans. After what I heard from Christian, I didn't want to comment on my now-uncertain future.

"So, what's Chris been chewing your ear off with?" she asked.

"Um." I gulped down the lump in my throat so that I could say the words without my voice cracking; "He told me that congratulations are in order. That you guys are, engaged."

There was no mistaking the sadness that darkened my voice as I spoke.

"He *did* tell you then."

"Yeah, he did. Two weeks, huh? That doesn't leave much time. How do you feel about that?"

"I don't know." She paused slightly and locked eyes with me before continuing. Then she spoke softly, almost in a whisper, "How do you feel about it?"

I sat down next to her on the big mattress, inhaling deeply as I prepared to give her a candid answer.

"What's so great in the bedroom? Are you guys hiding a TV in here?" Christian peered around the doorway and flipped the light switch up but the room remained dark. "I guess the last guy took the light bulbs too," Christian commented pointing up to the ceiling fixture.

We separated slightly and shifted our body weight away from each other. I was sure my face betrayed me with guilt but it seemed to go unnoticed by Christian. I was starting to think that some unseen force was working against me, preventing me from speaking the words that had been on the tip of my tongue twice today.

"So Sammy did you agree with her that she is making the best decision of her life?"

"Wouldn't the best decision of her life involve some sort of a ring?" I retorted quicker than my brain-to-mouth filter could connect.

I had noticed Sara's bare left ring finger when she came through the door and I was pouncing on that now as a superficial excuse as to why she shouldn't have said yes. Christian looked hurt by the comment which made me regret it slightly.

"Maybe we should go and let you finish unpacking. We did just kind of barge in on you. I'll call you tomorrow when you're settled," Christian said, already walking toward the door.

"Yeah, that's probably a good idea. I'll talk to you tomorrow," I said resigning myself to the fact that a meaningful conversation between him and I wasn't going to happen today.

"My dad wanted to us to stop by today anyway for a celebration dinner, and also so that Christian can meet his new girlfriend. That should be interesting," Sara said.

"Oh yeah? How is the old man anyway?" I asked.

"As good as ever. We're getting along better than we used to but I can't wait to move out. It's ok when he's by himself but he keeps bringing these woman home and it's like he thinks they are gonna be my new mom or something. It's weird."

"Yeah, that is weird."

Christian was halfway out the door but he called back, "By the way, nice place. I hope there's gonna be lots of fun times here."

Thankfully, he was still being nice to me, which meant I hadn't wounded his pride too badly. Sara lagged a few feet behind Christian, pausing to slide her sandals back on. Once he was out into the hallway she grabbed me, as she had done when she first walked in the door, and hugged me tightly again. This time she held on a little longer than I expected.

"Bye Sam," she breathed into my ear, releasing her hold on me.

I said nothing, only closed the door lightly behind her as she walked out. I leaned my back against the wall, hating the feeling of a room after she left; it was as if all the joy had been caught up and taken out with her. I walked back to the bedroom and sat in the imprint of where she had been. I hadn't made the bed yet and just looking around at all the unopened boxes was making me tired. I decided to crash on the couch instead.

After hooking up my small seventeen inch dorm TV, I tuned into the only station that the antennae could pick up. The channel was airing a romantic comedy which I had seen before. The dim-witted and hapless main character hadn't garnered my sympathy the first time I watched the movie, but now I found myself rooting for him. Cheesy montage aside, I noticed some themes that mirrored my own life. Even though I knew the ending, I stayed up until the last scene when the lovers finally got to share their first kiss. I stared at the screen trying to imagine that I was the lucky, persistent guy and Sara was the gorgeous, adoring girl. But it only ended up exasperating me further to be confronted with the image of what my life could have been, had things gone differently.

I wanted to continue to blame my father for moving me away from her; I wanted to blame Christian for his magnetism that attracted her in the first place; for God's sake I even wanted to blame Ms. Fine for getting cancer at the most inopportune time. But when I honestly faced the mental review of the years that had passed, I came to a conclusion. There was only one person to blame for Sara and Christian's impending marriage…me. And I was also the only person who could stop it.

CHAPTER 14

In the days since Sara and Christian's engagement announcement, I had purposefully avoided spending much time with either of them while I tried to figure out exactly the right way to go about telling her my feelings. So of course she was understandingly suspicious now as to why I was standing here, on the threshold of her door, the night before her wedding, saying that I had something to tell her.

"What is it? Come on Sam, you are killing me here!" Sara said.

"Are you really, really sure you want to know?" I asked. I was trying to stall, not having totally convinced myself that I should be here doing this.

"I'm *really, really* one-hundred-percent-triple-sure that I want to know. Sam Davs if you stand there a minute longer staring at me with those brown unassuming eyes and not saying anything, I will be forced to tickle it out of you," she said, moving her fingers menacingly in my direction.

I fake laughed, still not sure if I should utter the words that might turn her world upside down.

As I tried to get up the courage to speak, my mind floated in and out of memories; memories of me and her together, me and Christian together, and even Christian and her together. I felt as if every encounter between us since we met was converging at once, side by side, in this present moment. I realized in hindsight, that each painful event of the past had come about as a result of definitive choices that I had made; choices that now made me sick to recall.

What if I had never opened Christian's letter? *What if* I hadn't let it affect me so much? *What if* I had never acted on the pity I felt for my vulnerable friend? All the, what-ifs in the world weren't going to change the position I was in now but I couldn't help but wonder. The ghosts of the decisions that I *didn't* make were haunting me.

I looked at her. She seemed so oblivious to what I was about to say and for a moment I wanted to give her a simple "good luck tomorrow", and turn and walk away from the hardship this moment was causing me. But I couldn't. It wasn't time to clam up and walk away like I always did; it was time to make a new choice for myself, one that would lead her back to me. This was my last chance to tell her how I felt because after tonight, she would be a married woman. And not just *any* married woman, she would be the woman married to my best friend. There were no tomorrows left for us.

"Umm..." I started to speak with hesitation.
I had tried, so strenuously, since we met to repress my feelings for her that it was now proving exceedingly difficult to articulate what I wanted to say.

"Did Christian put you up to something?" she prodded.

My face grew grave as I contemplated my next sentence. The words that I was trying to manifest gnawed at me, as if they were the final statement granted to a prisoner on death row.

"Is he backing out on me? Does he not want to go through with the wedding?"

She must be picking up on my uneasiness or she wouldn't have asked that. But, then again, she didn't pose the question disconcertingly, which was odd considering she thought her groom might be dumping her the night before the ceremony. Perhaps she was hoping somewhere deep inside that Christian *was* backing out. That thought gave me the confidence to continue.

"No, I couldn't be so lucky as to have that happen," I replied in almost a whisper.

"What do you mean?" Sara crinkled her eyebrows together like a reporter asking for an elaboration on an intriguing lead.

"What I mean is...it would make what I have to say a lot easier if he did back out," I explained cautiously.

Sara relaxed her eyebrows and bit her lower lip, waiting to hear more from me before she spoke. I took her cue and continued. The flood gate had been opened now and I could barely hold back the words that rushed forward.

"I've been wrong Sara, so wrong for a long time. I've stood back and let all of this happen for the good of everyone else. All the while, I've been miserable and I feel like if I don't say this now, I will stay miserable for the rest of my life." I paused slightly only to catch my breath. "I don't know what's been implied over the years about our relationship but I feel like I need to clear up once and for all how I feel about you."

I looked over to gauge her reaction to my speech thus far. She had gone from standing to sitting down on the last step of the porch. Her knees were curled up to her chest and her elbows rested on them. Her hands were on the top of her head, grabbing her hair softly with her fingers. I couldn't see her face because she had tucked it down. I knew I was giving her a lot of information to digest all at once but I couldn't stop now, there was so much more to explain. I continued.

"I feel the same way about you as I did that night at the concert when we confessed to each other that we were more than just friends." I glanced at her again; she remained unchanged. "No, I take that back, multiply the way I felt about you back then by a hundred and that's how I feel about you now. I've gotten to know you on so many more levels since then and each new thing I've learned has only made me crazier about you. There is nothing about you that I don't love and there is nothing that you could do that would make me stop loving you. It's like, you were made for me."

I stopped there as I noticed that Sara was shaking her head slowly back and forth. I waited for her to speak what was obviously on her mind.

"But, the letter. You wrote me that letter after you moved and broke up with me. You said you didn't want to feel tied down," Sara said incredulously lifting her gaze to directly meet my eyes with the hint of a challenge.

"I only wrote that and said those things because Christian had written *me* a letter telling me that he loved you and would go insane if he didn't have you in his life. I did it to protect him and give you guys a chance without me in the picture stealing you away. It was the hardest thing I've ever done, if I had to do it over again, believe me, I wouldn't. There are so many things I would do different."

I spoke passionately, wanting to grab her hand and make her understand. But out of respect for the emotions she must be facing now, I kept a firm boundary between us. When I was done speaking, I noticed her eyes sharpen as if the meaning behind this long-standing mystery had finally revealed itself to her. She released her hair and let her hands fall to the ground, bending her head back she looked up at the night sky. I thought she was about to cry. I had to say something to comfort her.

"I'm sorry that I'm saying all of this now. I know this isn't fair to do the night before your wedding."

My apology was sincere but I despised my timing.

"No, no it's not that," Sara half-chuckled to the air, letting a pained smile cross her face; "I based every decision I made with Christian on that one letter I got from you. At first, I thought you had found someone else and then when I never heard you mention anyone, I just figured you hadn't wanted me. All these years, I tried so hard to stay away from you; to make sure I didn't sit next to you or talk with you on the phone for too long or look overly excited when you were around and all along…" she trailed off deep in thought.

"And all along we both wanted to do this."

I finished her sentence and, as if on cue, I tenderly took her shaking hands into mine. Her despondence melted into relief as we held a cathartic gaze for several quiet minutes.

"I have to show you something. I wrote it last night. It's about you. Wait right here," Sara said jumping up suddenly, as if she were a patient waking up from a coma.

Before I had processed what she said, she had bounded into the house and was gone. I smiled blissfully after her, feeling as though the weight of a thousand worlds had been taken off my shoulders. The sense of everything being as it was intended returned for the first time since the night of the concert. I knew I'd never allow us to be apart from each other again.

While I waited for her to return, I took a stroll down the driveway inhaling the details of my surroundings, wanting to cherish every part of this night. All the things I saw that made up the familiar landscape: the large white porch, the untended rose bush and the asphalt driveway, seemed to have significance now. This was the very porch where I had met Sara for the first time; she had laughed when the thorns from those roses had pricked me as I clumsily mowed into them, and that driveway was where we had lingered talking and exchanging phone numbers at the age of sixteen before I left for vacation. I marveled that any time had passed at all since that day, everything seemed so unchanged.

The hot night air was filled with thick humidity that was almost drinkable and I appreciated the way it created a smell like fresh rain. I listened closely to the symphony created by the sounds of this mountain neighborhood in the middle of summer. I was so much happier listening to the chirps and ribbitts of the crickets and frogs communicating in the darkness than I was hearing the incessant beeping traffic and cursing of the Boston cabbies. The only interruption to nature's cacophony out here was one random passing car. The crackling speakers of the old beater that cruised the block were blaring the chorus to some unfamiliar song.

The screen door creaked open and Sara came springing out with a white lined piece of paper held crookedly in her hand, she had obviously grabbed it in haste in order to rejoin me quickly. I watched with amusement while she let the screen door slam loudly behind her as she clumsily fumbled down the stairs towards me.

"I found it!" she called, hurrying so fast down the driveway that she almost tripped over her own feet.

Suddenly, a strong gust of wind came down off the mountains, stealing the weightless paper right from her grasp. It was carried up and over her head. The hair that whipped across her face made it impossible for her to see where it was going as she reached her hands out in vain to grasp it.

"I'll get it! It's coming my way!" I called out to her.

I stepped forward and sideways, mini-jumping and grabbing at the air, as the paper continued to elude me. I craned my neck back to look above my head and I noticed the wind begin to subside. The paper was floating down within my reach. I took a step backwards off the curb as I reached and twisted to grasp Sara's treasured paper securely in my right palm. Suddenly, I heard Sara cry out my name in terror.

"SAAMMM!!"

I looked up in confusion and caught her wild eyes for a split second before I felt the impact. In one swift motion, my feet were uprooted from the ground and my head was thrown violently against the cement. The vicious screech of four halting tires shrieked in my ears. A surge of heat like a fever spiked up my body into my head. Sharp, knife-like pains shot through my limbs. My eyes wanted to close instantly but I fought against them, blinking rapidly to help maintain consciousness; each movement of my eyes caused warm blood to drip onto my lids. Still, I continued blinking until the bright clustered stars in the sky blurred into focus.

"SAM! OH MY GOD! SAM!!" Sara screamed.
I could hear her footsteps crunching through glass as she ran to me. I felt her kneel by my side.

"Sara..."
The weakness of my voice startled me. Instinctively, I tried to get up to reach for her, but my legs felt too heavy to move, as if they were anchored in place.

"No, no, don't get up! Stay there! Don't move." She instructed with extreme concern in her voice. "We don't know what's broken yet."

Everything.

"I don't know what happened! It was an accident. It was an accident. I just didn't see him! He wasn't there when I came around the corner. I don't know! I don't know what happened," a despondent teenager whose voice I didn't recognize began babbling hysterically.

I realized the unfamiliar song I had heard blaring from a car a few minutes ago was playing, softer now, a few feet from where I lay. *This must be who hit me*, I realized.

"Oh God! Look at all the blood!" he wailed.

ALL the blood? I only felt a little on my face.

"SHUT UP AND GO IN THE HOUSE AND CALL 911! NOW!!" Sara screamed, scolding the young man severely.

He must have sprinted in the direction he was directed to because the chatter quickly ceased. I felt Sara softly rest her head on my chest. With her against me I could feel the faint *thump, thump* of my weak heart struggling to pump more blood than it was losing. I felt the color draining from my face and I wondered how pale I must look. Still, the physical contact from her felt so welcoming that my nerves relaxed against her tender touch even as my body gasped for air.

"You're heart sounds so weak," she muttered in shock, then shouted, "WHERE IS THE AMBULANCE?!"

"On its way," the shaky voice of the driver assured.

"You're gonna be ok, Sam. The paramedics will be here soon. Just hang in there," Sara pleaded. "I can hear your heart. It's still beating. As long as it's beating, they can save you."

But I thought otherwise. With each breath that I took, I could feel the life draining from my body. It was only a matter of time before there wasn't enough blood left to propel my heart; physiology was the only thing keeping my heart beating right now and I knew it. I had to finish my mission; I had to say what I came here to say. I ignored the excruciating pain in my arm as I lifted my hand and placed it on my chest. I sucked some air into my failing lungs and managed to get out some words.

"Sara, my heart was never in here." She affectionately clasped her hand over mine and I guided both our hands to her heart. "*This*...is where my heart's always been...with yours."

She grabbed my hand tightly in recognition and held it greedily, refusing to let go. "No Sam. This can't be it. Not now. This is our beginning, not the end. Don't leave me. I can't live one more day without you."

Her words mixed with the puttering of the car's idling engine and the words "without you" hung heavily over us for what seemed like an eternal moment. My chest heaved as I tried to take in enough oxygen to speak.

"Read it to me."

"What?" she asked leaning closer to my mouth to hear.

"Read," I whispered.

She looked puzzled for a moment until she saw the paper grasped tightly in my hand.

"You want me to read this? Now?" she asked.

"Yes," I mouthed but no words came out.

"I can't. It's too much." She began to cry.

"Please." I spoke faintly but clearly.

She nodded her head reluctantly, smeared the tears away with the back of her hand and read from the paper.

"There is no black and white, Only gray rests here.
It fills the space between, Forcing us farther apart
Than we ever intended to be.
God may have other colors To fill the space, my love,
But where they hide I cannot see.
When will He bring you back from there,
To close enough to me?"

Her voice cracked on the last line and gave way to a gut-wrenching sob. The tears began to leak from my eyes too, stinging my skin like acid. I didn't want to accept this fate. Mustering up some might, I took several deep breaths and then spoke.

"Sara, I don't know where I'm going after this…"

"Sam, please don't say that," she pleaded chocking back anguish.

I didn't have the breath or the time to object so I continued.

"…I can promise you one thing…that no matter how much space is between us…I will always find you."

A soft, steady wind began fluttering through the giant oak trees that semi-circled me; the breeze was a comfort to my feverish skin. My ears drank in the sound of the green leaves rustling harmonically against each other. Nature was creating a sort of whispering lullaby that only the still could hear. The trees sang, *"Hushhhh, Hushhhh, Hush. Sssleep, Sssleep, Sssleep. Hushhhh, Hush."*

My vision started to grow hazy and my eyes locked onto some far away point in the sky. Everything in my line of sight was fading to black. I wrestled with weak ocular muscles, trying to coax them to stay open but gravity took control of my lids and they dropped slowly over my eyes. Before they closed I rushed to catalog every detail of Sara's face in my mind, trying desperately to sear this last image of her onto my sight, trusting that it would cross over with me to whatever was beyond this world. Soon my eyes were completely shut and her image stared at me like the shadow of a ghost that I couldn't be sure I had really seen. I hoped it was enough to remember her by.

"Sam? Sam? Can you hear me?"

I could feel Sara shaking me urgently, but there was nothing I could do to comfort her. When she didn't get a reply she pressed her ear to my heart and listened.

Thum,Thump…Thump…Thump…..Thump……..Thump…………

She waited for the next *Thump*, the hope of life that she so desperately needed. But it never came. I heard her scream out in defiance as the sirens vainly blared towards us. She clutched my shirt with both her fists and pressed her face against my now cold skin.

"Find me," she whispered. It was desperate plea.

They were the last words I heard before my consciousness drifted a million light years away, removing me from the chaotic scene where my lifeless body lay heavy on the pavement.

CHAPTER 15

I seamlessly joined the sky, as if on the crest of a wave riding a gentle tide, going out at day's end, slowly lapping the shore, caressing each grain of sand, hanging onto this beautiful beach I was visiting, not wanting to leave quite yet, but also not being able to resist the unending sea which called me back at once, to rejoin the vast unknown. A warm velvety blackness embraced me. I sensed an absence of gravity which caused complete weightlessness as if I were floating down a stream. I felt as though I had drifted into the most comfortable sleep I had ever known and was being ferried by an all-consuming presence into a dream. The intense pain in my body quickly faded into a memory that was so distant I wasn't sure it ever existed. There was a perception of unlimited space around me that seemed dense rather than vacant, filled with molecules of stillness that vibrated at high frequencies. I doubted there would be an echo if I called out. I wasn't sure how long I rested in this timeless place before I produced my first cohesive thought.

"Where am I?" I wordlessly asked the void, somehow knowing that I would be answered.

"Where do you *think* you are?" a gentle voice asked.
The voice spoke in a tone which transcended the highs and lows of gender and I couldn't tell if it was a male or female.

"Hell?"

"And what do you suppose that hell is like?"

"I guess dark and black. Lonely and full of despair."

"And how do you feel right now?"

"Loved. And peaceful."

"Do you imagine that love and peace can exist in hell?"

"No, and I think I see your point," I said realizing the contradiction.

"If you aren't in hell, then where are you?" the still-gentle voice asked.

"Purgatory?"

As soon as I said this I heard a chorus of celestial giggles.

"That's where you think you are? Purgatory. May I ask why?"

The voice was not at all condescending, although I felt it had the right to be. I sensed that it had all the answers and was patiently waiting for me to catch onto them.

"I guess I think I am in purgatory because I am just waiting here for the next thing," I replied, not able to come up with any spectacular reasoning.

"And what do you expect that next thing to be?"

"I don't know," was my nonverbal reply.

"And that's why right now it is nothing. The next thing is whatever you want it to be," the voice revealed.

"Whatever I want it to be? You mean I create my own heaven?"

"Yes. Or your own hell."

"Why would I create a hell?" I asked.

"The more pertinent question is: why would *I*? Every soul is a divine spark that originated from me, the Creator and Eternal Fire. Therefore, every person on Earth is a perfect part of me. How can I punish myself?"

"Then, you *are* God," I said.

"Yes. But I'm more of a Creator than a Governor as you think God is."

"But not the Creator of hell?"

"No. In your forgetful state of physicality, you imposed rules, sins and penalties on *yourselves*. I stay out of that."

"If you're God and you didn't create hell, then how could you even let us make our own hell to go to?"

"Do you remember when you were a child and you pretended that Godzilla was attacking you? One minute you were being chased by the monsters you invented and the next minute you were conquering them. I always know that your reality will change the second you think of a new one. There is no real danger in your imagination. Every parent on your planet knows that."

"Then why do some people create a hell for themselves, wouldn't everyone want to go to heaven?" I asked.

I was genuinely confused at the idea that anyone would want to enter into the place with weeping and gnashing of teeth that I had read about in my Sunday school bible classes. The subject of hell had always caused me uneasiness toward God. When I was six and received my first communion I had asked my pastor why God had created a hell if He was good and loving. Not even he could give me a satisfactory answer. He just said, "There are some things we will never know on this Earth." I guess he was right; one of the perks of dying was that you got to find these things out.

The voice continued to speak, "Everyone wants to go to heaven, yes. But here is the revelation - it is not about what you *want*; it is about what you *think*. If someone crosses over to this realm and *thinks* that in their last life they committed unforgivable deeds which dictate punishment, they may create a perception of suffering for a time. But as soon as they *think* they've been punished enough, the suffering will end and their new reality will take over. Every being is in a constant process of self-creation."

"So, am I imagining you right now?"

"No. I am one of the few Absolute Truths. Everyone eventually comes back to Me."

"Then why can I only hear you in my thoughts? Why can't I see you?"

"Because child, you still expect to see with your eyes. Realize first that sight does not exist, only *thought*, and then you will see me."

Suddenly, the space around me illuminated. In an instant I forgot about the darkness that had just enveloped me. A shape began to take form in the center of the light which looked like a man in purple robes with straight, golden hair and sad piercing blue eyes.

"God?" I asked the apparition.

"In a way," the Being explained. "This is the form which you have chosen to see Me. People often see Me first as they pictured Me in life. In your case, I am the image of the risen Jesus Christ."

"Yes, from my catechism books."

I marveled at the likeness.

"You know, in His human incarnation, Jesus actually looked more like this."

The body of the finely clothed, porcelain skinned Jesus fell away and a dark featured man with tattered garments and rough hands took his place.

"He also looked like this," God said, changing form again. This time the pauper Jesus transformed into an Asian male with a loose yellow robe and hands clasped in prayer.

"Buddha?"

"Yes. And how about this one?" God asked.

The serene face of Siddhartha Gautama faded and was replaced by a man with a black beard, pale skin and of large stature. He smiled and lowered his gaze. I did not recognize the image of the man standing before me.

"I am also Muhammad," God replied to my confused thoughts. "These are just a few of the many incarnations of the spirit you know as Jesus. He has been a teacher for many generations."

"So that answers my question about reincarnation, but what about Jesus? Is He really You or just your Son? He must be special to have been so many important people."

"Everyone is special. The whole of Me could never be in one man, but as I said, the parts of Me are in every man. Jesus is no more special to Me than you. He was however, the first, and therefore stronger in spirit."

"The first what?" I wondered in thought.

"The first spark that burst from my Fire. In every age, on every planet and in every realm He never forgets, He remembers All."

"Wow," I marveled. "That means religion has gotten it all wrong."

"Eternity is more than any human mind can conceive and it is not limited by rights and wrongs, only Truth is held here."

Suddenly the Mohammed figure melted away into a female draped in white flowing thin linen with a careworn face whose arms extended out to me with a motherly invitation for an embrace.

"How can I hug you, I don't have a body," I contemplated.

"But you do now," the compassionate, now feminine, God-voice said. "You just thought about it. Look."

I looked down and saw feet, hands, arms and legs. All the parts of my body as I had known it at age sixteen were there as if I were in the flesh again. I felt my face for the blemishes I remembered hating so much during my teen years.

"They aren't there. You have recreated your body as the perfect representation of yourself at your most happy time in life," She explained.

I went slowly to Her, feeling the sensation of legs even though I was gliding more than walking. When I reached Her, I leaned willingly into Her embrace, letting Her arms engulf my being. A simultaneous thrill and absolute calm rushed in, around, and through everything that sustained me.

"That's You, isn't it? The real You," I said, barely able to contain my thankfulness at this Love that She was giving me.

"You are correct. I am not this body or any other. I am the thought, the feeling, and the achievement of absolute Love."

"What else *is* there?" I asked, feeling enraptured by the presence of the Divine.

"Precisely. This is the only Truth. All else is illusion."

"I understand," I said.

"Now what will you do with that understanding? What will you create next for yourself from the place of absolute Love?"

My consciousness was so clear now that thoughts came quickly and lucidly. I reflected on simple pleasures from Earth that had pleasant memories attached to them and suddenly they manifested before me. First a warm summer breeze blew by filling my nostrils with the sweet scent of roses and tiger lilies. Then, I was surrounded by bleachers and a ball field holding a plump, juicy hot dog in my hand, squeezing the soft bun between my fingers and taking an eager bite. When I turned around, the sky was dusk and I was sitting in the plush grass of a campground field, listening to the crickets create a tuneful orchestra of sound. As the scenery changed, the serene Being looked on with delight.

"Why does everything keep changing so quickly?" I asked.

"Your world now changes at the speed of thought. If you prefer to stay in one place longer, just continue concentrating on the feeling that place gives you and your thoughts will not stray. You can stay for as long as you like anywhere you want," She explained and then reached out towards me. "Here, hold My hand, I will ground you."

I willingly reached for Her hand. For a minute I thought I wouldn't be able to grasp it, as it seemed to be composed of particles of light and no substance. But when I touched my hand to Hers, my flesh melted into the light and our arms became one.

"Concentrate strongly on the feeling you just experienced when I embraced you in my arms. Let your thoughts remain there and they will manifest the deepest desire of your heart," She instructed.

I closed my eyes, which I knew wasn't necessary since they were only a projection of thought, but going through this act seemed to make concentrating easier. I let myself be consumed by the feeling of serenity that buzzed around me.

"Open them," She gently instructed with a smile.

I slowly pushed up my lids to reveal the object of my most cherished thoughts. Standing in front of me was the flawless image of Sara at sixteen, she was wearing a striking blue sundress, and her brown hair was wavy and wild. Soaring pine trees and distant mountains scattered the landscape. A translucent stream meandered through the meadow to our right. We stood together, barefoot, in the lush green grass.

"Sara?" I asked in disbelief.

She stared back at me with a gleaming smile.

"Sara?" I asked again but received no reaction from the doll-like girl in front of me.

"Why won't she answer?" I questioned the Divine Woman.

"Because, you haven't thought of what you want her to say yet," She replied matter-of-factly.

"Are you saying that this is just my imagination? This isn't really Sara?"
I was confused.

"I'm sorry dear heart, but Sara's soul is still on Earth."

I could feel the whole of my being sink into sadness. The Divine Woman saw my unhappiness and responded immediately.

"Do not despair my budding flower. You *will* be reunited just as you wish to be when she takes the journey Home. Until then, you can be kept company by the piece of her spirit that you hold in your memory."

She waved her hand and the scenery around me transformed into a gorgeous garden alive with pink apple blossoms and violet wisteria.

"But it's not the same. I can recreate her hair and mannerisms and body parts but I can't recreate the true things that make her who she is. She's always just beyond my reach. If this is Heaven then why am I feeling this way? Aren't I supposed to be happy all the time?"

"This place where you are now is not the end-all to the universe. Neither is it absolute Truth. This is just another realm where you can create experiences without the restrictions of geography, time, body, and consequence. The Heaven you imagine is actually what is called - *The All*. The All is my home, where I reside, a place of sublime bliss where individual souls rejoin The One and ego consciousness ceases to exist."

"Who can go there?" I asked.

"No one is excluded. Everyone can travel to and from there as they please. The All is the epicenter from which all of life flows."

"Then I want to go there now. I'll come back here when Sara crosses over. I just can't bear to miss her any longer."

"You cannot merge with The All right now. You still don't remember *anything* do you?" the Divine Woman commented with a crinkled brow.

"Why *can't* I go there now? What is there to remember?"

I was feeling confused and frustrated. What I wanted in Heaven was to be with Sara and it seemed like that wasn't going to happen.

"Here let me show you."

She reached out Her opaque finger and touched it lightly to my forehead. I saw a mirror image in my mind of the current moment, and then a sudden rewinding started. A swirl of pictures invaded my sight, changing so rapidly in my mental vision that I almost didn't recognize they were flashes of my life. I was traveling back through my memories, pausing at the most crucial points. I saw myself being struck by the car; the night at the concert; meeting Sara for the first time; growing up with Christian. Then foreign images invaded my mind and it was as if I were watching a time-travel flick that I had never seen, except I was the star.

First, I was admiring a beautiful girl across the room at a formal ball. Then, my young wife was helping my carry wood through the snow back to our cabin. Finally, an elderly woman read to me in a rocking chair next to a grand fireplace. Slowly I became aware that this set of memories was just as real as the first ones. The sights, sounds, and feelings associated with these time periods were becoming clearer. I wasn't watching a movie; I was reliving my forgotten lifetimes. I snapped my eyes open wide in amazement.

"That was me and Sara. We've always been together. I remember all of that. It's like I still know that I'm me, but I also understand that I was all of those people too," I marveled.

"Yes, you understand now that your physical bodies have changed many times but your spirits have not. Now come to comprehend *this* and you will be wise - you are in fact all people at all times and still uniquely you."

I nodded my head in recognition but not full comprehension.

"How come we never remember any of this until we die?" I asked.

"When you are children you remember much, but can only communicate a little. By the time you are old enough to communicate everything, you have forgotten it all. The finite, physical body has been encouraged and nurtured to develop but the infinite spiritual part of you has been stifled. However, sometimes humans draw things to them in their current lives that apply to their previous ones. Their spirit does this subconsciously as a way to help them recognize and remember their soul. It becomes a way to reconnect their conscious to Me."

"You mean, like, when someone is drawn to a particular era in history," I said.

"Yes. Or, as in your case, when they are drawn to a specific person or persons."

"Persons?"

"Sara *and* Christian."

"You mean I've known Christian before too? That must be why I could empathize so easily with his feelings."

The ethereal Divine Woman nodded her head and spoke, "Your relationship with Christian has not always been the same as it was in your recent life. Once, quite contrary actually. Christian served under you, as your roadie, on a music tour."

"You mean I was famous once?" My eyes lit up with excitement at the thought.

"Yes, on one occasion you desired to experience that particular kind of admiration and willed personal fame into existence. Most everyone has chosen that life at some point. But, if you notice, that wasn't a lifetime that you called to mind just now in your review. The moments that you brought to consciousness so easily were of love and simple contentment."

I slowly nodded my head in acknowledgment and She continued; "But please, close your eyes, there is more."

She placed a single slender finger back on my forehead. This time the depth of the memory that she brought to the forefront jolted my body back forcefully. My vision was flooded by a never-ending clean, black sky, which somehow was unlit by the massive ball of white fire burning in the center of the darkness. There was a scattering of sparks that looked like shooting stars bursting from the light which streaked across the blackness and left a trail of sparkling dust behind them. As the sparks journeyed into the vast expanse, red, blue, and green planets exploded into existence and they directed their course towards them.

I felt the Divine Woman direct my sight to a bright spot of concentrated energy near the core of the blazing fire. I saw a slightly bigger, slightly brighter spark catapult hastily from the center. My heart leapt at the familiarity of the scene. I watched as the eager Divine offspring flew off on its own, shaking and vibrating rapidly as it struggled with the downward descent. Just as the atmosphere of the green planet it was heading for came into reach, the intense heat that the spark possessed caused an internal explosion. A flash of light briefly illuminated the darkness and when it faded, there were two sparks in the place where there had just been one. The explosion had divided the energy in half and created two. I felt a pang of sadness as I watched the two parts of the split spark land on opposite sides of the green planet. At this image the Divine Woman withdrew Her supernatural hand from my forehead and spoke.

"Now do you fully remember? Now do you understand why you can't go to The All yet?"

I didn't respond. I remained still. My thoughts were overwhelmed with a million different memories flooding my consciousness.

She explained, "You cannot enter The All if you are not whole. Sam and Sara, Sara and Sam, have always been, since before time was recorded. They are a Yin and a Yang, two parts that fit together to complete a puzzle. Without one the other would not exist. They are not soul-mates or twin-souls as some are. They are the *same* soul. They are the *same* spark. You are in love with the part of you that you have lost. Just as every soul comes back to their Creator, you two will always come back to each other."

Upon speaking Her last word, an invigorating wind swept by and carried Her away, molecule by molecule. The lovely Divine Woman was replaced now by a kindly faced, silvery long-haired woman with petite pruned hands.

"It's still You, isn't it?" I asked.

She nodded her head in agreement.

"Why are you appearing to me now like this?"

"You are projecting onto Me the image of what you want for yourself. You want to grow old with Sara in the physical body. Even though you are not fully aware, right now a part of you is trying to imagine what that life would look like."

"I didn't even realize I was thinking about that."

"Much like I am able to be in many places at the same time, you are capable of thinking many complex thoughts simultaneously. Especially in this realm. Sam, I am sensing a question in your thoughts right now and I need to explain the answer to you. Please bear in mind that honesty is the only response I can give, no matter how painful it may be to hear."

"Yes, go on."

"You need to be prepared for the fact that Sara may not come directly here to be with you when she dies."

"What? I don't understand. You said that we always come back to each other. If I am here, won't she want to be here too?"

"Where you go immediately after you die is wherever your thoughts take you. Sara still has a long mortal life ahead of her and if her thoughts move away from you during those years she may not remember when she passes that ultimately her final place is with you. She may choose reincarnation or a Heaven of her own. There may be a long period of time before her thoughts come back to you."

"But how could she not remember me if we have been together for so many lifetimes?"

The idea that she might continue to live her life without thinking of me was hurtful.

"It is not something to be taken personally Sam," the Creator replied to my thoughts; "when you first got here, there was little that *you* remembered either. That does not mean that your love for Sara is any less. Each transition is a new process."

"I think I understand," I replied with a heavy heart.

The matronly old woman took my hands in Hers.

"It does not satisfy me to see you down-hearted but it is better for you to be prepared for what lies ahead."

I had so many more questions to ask but before I could speak again another voice broke into the silence from, what seemed like, beyond the frame of the space I occupied.

"Sam," it spoke.

"Yes," I answered off-guard.

I turned around to find its origin, and there was a bright concentration of light where none had existed before. My eyes squinted as if unable to process this new light. The voice was coming from within it. I attuned my ears beyond myself and began to hear whispering. As I focused and listened longer, I began to distinguish some words and phrases. By the pitch of the voices, I determined that two women were talking, but I couldn't quite piece together the conversation.

Are they speaking a foreign language? I wondered.

"In a way, they are," God answered. "They are speaking English, your previous native tongue, but you have been in this realm so long now that you have forgotten what it sounds like."

"But aren't I speaking English right now?" I asked, puzzled.

"Not only are you not speaking English right now, you're not speaking at all. We are just *understanding* each other."

I nodded in agreement, sensing what was meant by this.

"What are these women saying that concerns me?" I asked.

"They are calling for you Sam, listen."

As soon as God revealed this, the voices came into focus. I heard, *Sam. Sam Fine. Sam.* My name was being repeated almost chant-like. I looked to God for an answer.

"Someone on Earth is calling for you. Calling for you to go back."

"Me? Why are they calling for me?" I asked dumbfounded.

"That is for *you* to find out, but only if you wish. Those on Earth frequently call on their loved ones to make appearances from this realm. Some choose to go back, others don't. Some appear once or twice on Earth to provide closure for loved ones; others prefer to stay in the serenity of this realm far away from the grief that making an appearance can bring."

"But what should I do? Who's calling me?" I implored.

"I cannot make that decision for you or reveal that answer to you. The only guidance I give is this: follow the desire of your spirit."

"My desire is to go back," I said, knowing that I wouldn't be able to move on if I didn't find out who wanted me back on Earth. I was hoping desperately that Sara was on the other end of that voice.

"If that is your desire, then why aren't you there now?" the Creator asked.

I wondered the same thing. In this realm just the desire of being somewhere, caused it to manifest. I looked around and realized that the bigger part of me did not want to leave the bliss and beauty that I was surrounded by here. This place held contentment which I hadn't felt since my childhood, before the dangers of the world had corrupted my sense of security.

"Sam. Are you there Sam?"

I could hear the voice clearer now. It was her. My head snapped back, looking in the direction the voice came from.

"Sara."

As soon as I uttered her name, I was back on Earth.

CHAPTER 16

My transition from one realm to another was surprisingly easy. Other than my eyes having to adjust to the brightness of the room, my senses acclimated quickly to the new climate. Before I was able to make out their faces, they spoke again.

"Is he here?"

Her voice was clear and coherent now that I was here with her; it was Sara.

"If he is, he's not telling me," the other woman said.

Their features slowly came into focus and I saw that a middle-aged woman sat across from Sara conversing with her. I looked around to see where I was; the walls were light purple with white stenciling boarder and I heard soft, new-age music playing in the next room. I didn't recognize any of it. I had never been here before.

"But, if he is here you'll be able to see him?" Sara asked.

I could tell that she wasn't the same age as when I had last seen her. She seemed to be in her early thirties now which surprised me since it felt like I had been on the other side for only a few minutes. Her assumed age meant that I had been there for nearly ten years. She had never been one to wear very much makeup, but now her cheeks were flush with pink blush, and her tinted lips suggested that she had applied lipstick. Her hair was different too, slightly shorter and straightened, though these cosmetic changes weren't the largest difference I noticed. Her demeanor seemed defeated and worn-out, very unlike the bubbly, vivacious girl I had always known. Her frown lines were thick, and tired, dark circles lay heavy under her eyes.

"Sorry if that's a stupid question, I just don't know how this whole psychic medium thing works," she said to the woman.

Psychic medium? Is that who is calling me here?

"That's ok sweetie, don't be shy. I'm happy to answer any questions that you have. Sometimes I do see spirits, and other times I get a feeling. Usually the departed will give me images of events or places that mean something to you and I can pass that on. Then again, sometimes they don't want to speak to me at all. Sometimes they would rather communicate directly with their loved ones."

Damn right, I thought. *Why would I want to waste my time talking to you when Sara is sitting right here in front of me?*

"But, how would he communicate with me? I don't have any special ability," Sara said.

"He might move things; make a knocking sound; touch you. It's really individual."

"Oh ok, I think I understand. Do you think it would help to use a picture of us and ask again?" Sara said as she pulled a 4x6 photo from her back pocket.

"Yes, that would be great," the medium said.

Uncrossing her legs, the woman smoothed the front of her loose-knit pants as she leaned forward to grab the picture. A pleasantly scented candle flickered on the table in front of her and she placed the picture next to it. Closing her eyes, she continued her ritual.

"Sam...Sara would like to speak to you. Please come forward and give us a sign or speak to me so that we know you are here with us. Sam, are you here? Please come forward," the medium asked again.

They don't know I'm here. I've got to do something.
As soon as the thought left my mind I became aware of an electric-pulsing force running from my core to the tips of my fingers. It was the pure life energy I had felt on the other side.

I'll give it a shot, I thought.
I slowly ran my hand down the lace curtains next to me.

"That just moved!" Sara exclaimed pointing to the billowing curtain.

The medium turned around quickly and nodded her head to confirm that she had seen the fabric move as well. I could barely contain the elation I felt. When I had touched the curtain I had the smallest hope that it would move but I hadn't imagined that it would sway as strongly as if a breeze had blown through it. Now that I knew I could manipulate physical objects, I felt the energy rising in my fingertips and surging powerfully. I was ready for more.

"He's here. I know he is. I can feel him," Sara declared with certainty, rubbing the goose bumps on her arms.

"I can too. Let's keep going," the medium suggested.
Sara nodded her head firmly in agreement. Her palms looked sweaty as she rubbed them on her jeans. I saw her eyes scan the room, searching for signs of movement.

"Sam," the psychic was addressing me with certainty in her voice; "Sara is going to ask you some yes-or-no questions and if you can, we would like you to respond with knocks. One knock means, yes, two knocks means, no. Go ahead please Sara," she said, turning the conversation over to her.

"Um," Sara said fidgeting nervously in her seat on the couch. "Sam? Just knock if you are here with us."

I walked slowly over to the coffee table. I now stood only three feet away from Sara. Being this close to her again I felt the familiar magnetic pull in her direction. I used all my strength to concentrate on the task at hand. I looked down at the dense wooden surface of the table in front of me and wondered if my spirit body could create enough force against it to produce sound; it seemed almost impossible. I was beginning to doubt whether I had physically moved the curtain at all or if it had been the wind produced by my energy that had made it sway. If that were the case, I wouldn't be able to have any effect on this solid structure.

As these thoughts began to take over, I felt the electricity recede from my fingers. In haste, I took a swift punch at the table; my hand sliced through it like hot butter without making any contact at all.

It's impossible. I'll never be able to do it. I stood there for a moment dumbstruck.

"Sam?" Sara's voice came again.

Suddenly it occurred to me that I wasn't really in a body, even though it felt like I was; therefore I wasn't operating on the physical principles of Earth. It was only my own belief and limitations that were controlling the circumstances. As long as I believed that I couldn't affect my surroundings, I never would. I looked at the table again, now in a different way; the table wasn't made of a material that was greater or even inferior to me, the substance of the table was my equal, made by the One Creator from the same energy that I was. This time I didn't bother putting any force behind my knuckles; I just brought them to the table and tapped lightly on the surface.

Knock. Knock.

I heard the audible noise that my efforts produced, and judging by the look on Sara's face, she heard it too. Appropriately, she went pale as if she had seen (or heard) a ghost.

The medium was obviously pleased with the contact she made and she spoke to me again, "Thank you Sam for letting us know that you're here. Sara wants to talk to you, so please stay with us for a while." She turned her attention to Sara and said, "Keep going. I think he wants to communicate directly with you."

The look on Sara's face turned to surprise and elation. She complied eagerly with the direction she was being given and started talking.

"Oh my gosh, ok. Thank you Sam for letting us know you're here. There are some things I need you to know and then something I need to know from you. First and foremost, I loved you Sam with all my heart and I still do. I'm not sure why I latched onto Christian, he's so similar to my dad and I think I may have used his attention as a substitute. But what I need you to know is that I always wanted it to be me and you. In my mind I always thought we'd end up happily married, but we never got that chance, did we? The night you died you were at my house because you were trying to tell me that *we* were the ones meant to be together, not me and Christian. I feel guilty, sooo guilty, for your death, and I need to know if you forgive me?"

My mind raced to take it all in. Everything that she said was what I had always known in my heart but had wanted to hear directly from her. I was pained to think that she felt at all responsible for my death. I knew I needed to answer her, to let her know that I could never blame her for anything, especially my death. If blame was to be put on anyone, it would be on me. I had been careless with every decision I made in my life and that was the reason I was there that night.

I wanted to knock my answer on the table and put her mind at ease but after everything I had heard, I couldn't remember if one or two knocks meant yes. If I answered incorrectly, it would be devastating; she might drown emotionally in her guilt for the rest of her life and, no doubt leave here with a diminished sense of my love for her. I had to think fast.

Knock, knock, knock, knock, knock, knock.
I tapped on the table repeatedly to let her know that I was still here and I wanted to answer her question. The medium and Sara both looked around quizzically.

"What does that mean?" Sara asked.

"I don't know. But it's an answer. Ask again, this time with specific instructions on how to respond. He may not know what you want him to do."

Yes! Exactly! She is here for a reason.

"Sorry if I confused you Sam. Please knock once for, yes, or twice for, no.

Knock, came my singular and swift reply.

"Oh thank God," Sara said through a cracking voice.
Tears streaked down her face. The medium reached over sympathetically and pulled her in for a hug.

"It's ok to cry dear," she said patting and rubbing Sara's back.
After a few moments Sara sat up and wiped the last large tears from her face. She sighed heavily as she composed herself to speak again.

"Sam, are you happy?"

Knock.

Her face lit up.

"Can I ask another question?"

"Go for it dear," the medium said.

"Sam, will we be together again someday?"

I walked slowly to where she sat, taking note of every stray hair and worry line on her face that distracted from her beauty. I sat down next to her and placed my hands on top of hers.

"As long as you don't forget me," I said.

Sara jumped back in her seat startled; "I thought I heard something."

"What did you hear?" the medium asked, sitting on the edge of her seat leaning in towards Sara.

"I don't know, I'm not sure. It wasn't words exactly. More like a high pitched babble. But I couldn't make it out. And I've got goose bumps," Sara said rubbing her arms vigorously.

"He's trying to tell you something. It's not surprising you couldn't make it out. It's very hard for us to understand what the other side is saying, our ears aren't tuned to their frequency," the medium explained. "That's why I have this." She tapped her hand on a digital recorder that was on sitting in front of her on the table. "I record all my sessions for clients to take home with them in case a message comes through that they may need to review and think about later. But it's also a great tool for catching spirit voices. When we play this back, you might be able to hear a clearer response to your questions."

I was ecstatic to hear that I had some verbal means by which to communicate with. I sprung up, walked directly over to the recorder, and began speaking into it. I hoped that the digital device would translate something back to Sara in words that she could understand.

"Sara, if you can hear me on this thing, please know that I love you beyond love and it's not my choice to be separated from you. If there were any way for us to be together on this Earth again, I would do it."

I spoke the last part through gritted teeth, still not wanting to think that my time here with her was temporary.

"Would you mind if we play it back quickly now? I'm sorry but I just can't wait until I get home, and I'd rather have you here to listen with me in case I have any questions," Sara said to the medium.

"Sure, sweetheart I understand. Let me just rewind that last part and let's see if we can hear anything, ok?"

The medium gave her an understanding smile as she fiddled with the buttons on the recorder. I thought about how, in life, I had dismissed these people who call themselves psychics and mediums as quacks. Now here I was, in spirit body, communicating with a medium that obviously had the ability to break over to the other side and call me here. In fact, she seemed genuinely caring towards Sara, who was obviously in a fragile mental state. I regretted now that I had passed judgment on others like her simply because I had not wanted to consider the fact that such abilities might exist. My perspective on this side made me realize that, although I was tolerant of others in my last life, I had been narrow-minded as well.

"What do you think he was trying to say?" Sara asked as the medium continued to fiddle with the electronic device.

"There's only one way to find out, isn't there?" she said as she pushed the play-button.

Quiet static popped over the small speaker and Sara leaned in closer to hear.

"This should be right before you asked your...oh yes, here it is," the medium said as she was interrupted by Sara's voice on the recorder.

Turning up the volume knob almost to full blast, they both went silent. At first loud static crackled through the room then a sound like a mumble broke in.

"What was that?" Sara asked.

"I don't...I don't know. There was something different there wasn't there? Indistinct though. Let me go back," the medium said furrowing her brow in concentration as she rewound back to the static.

"...*please*..."

The word I had spoken came out short and quick followed by more static.

"*Please?* Is that what it said?" Sara asked.

"Yes, yes. I think so. We definitely got something dear and I agree, I think it said, *please*."

"Huh...," Sara breathed out almost in the form of a question.

"Like I said sweetie, it is very hard to communicate with the other side. We only get snippets of words when they may actually be trying to have a whole conversation with us."

"No, you're hearing it wrong. There's more!" I screamed wildly in frustration. But my voice echoed only in my own ears.

"It's so amazing, unbelievable really. He was trying to say something to me," Sara said open-mouthed.

"You may not get the answers to your questions exactly the way you want them, but at least we got something. He reached out to you and that takes a lot of strength and power for a spirit to do. Honestly, I am truly amazed. I have been blessed with abilities as a psychic medium for nearly fifteen years and I have never felt anything like this love. There is some deeper spiritual bond between the two of you than I ever thought was universally possible," the medium said. She gestured her hands in the air and turned her palms upward toward heaven, "And now he is communicating with visual and audible signs *on command* in *this* room for us to see. Let me tell you, what's happening here is extraordinary."

She motioned her pointer finger back and forth between Sara and the air which held my invisible spirit.

"I've always felt that," Sara stated.

"We might not get anything else and that's ok. He came through for you," the medium said patting Sara's knee.

"But there's more! I need you to hear what I said! I never got a chance to tell you these things when I was on Earth. Please listen to me now!" I yelled in complete frustration.

Bringing my arm back, I swung at a yellow vase on an inset shelf; it smashed forcefully to the ground shattering into colorful ribbons of pieces. I heard the women scream and saw them jump back. Then my vision became strangely out of focus. I narrowed and strained my eyes in concentration, but to no avail. I couldn't distinguish the features on her face anymore; everything appeared blurry, as though I needed glasses to help me see.

"SAM?!" Sara blurted out in surprise.

"Holy Krishna! I didn't see that coming!" The medium clutched her chest as though she were about to have a heart attack.

"Sam? Sam?" Sara asked trying to elicit a response from me, the unseen force, who had caused the uproar.

For the moment, I couldn't speak. Nothing but silence answered her. Frantically, I reached out to touch her, but I was stopped short by an almost invisible mist which now surrounded me. In frustration, I pushed and shoved my body against the force field, but it wouldn't bend. Instead, it moved as I moved, following my every step, encasing me like prison bars. It was a barrier. There was now a line between her world and mine that I could not cross. I pounded my fists against the hazy walls in anger.

"Sam. Do not do this," the gentle voice of the Creator spoke.

"You're here? You can see me?" I asked ceasing the fit I was throwing. I was relieved to know that I was not completely alone.

"I am always here Sam," the Creator replied.

"Can you get me out of this thing?" I asked pushing more thoughtfully now against the barrier, trying to find a weak place where I could slip out.

The material of the invisible bubble was cold to the touch and chilled me to my core. I began to shiver.

I shouted at God, "She needs to know I'm still here! She has to know I still love her! Why did everything suddenly change?! How come I'm right here and they can't hear me?!"

I was becoming increasingly frustrated again at my confinement.

"First be calm, and then you can understand."

"Why don't you just show yourself and explain this to me?" I said.

"You cannot see me now and soon you won't be able to hear me either; you are getting further away from me. You have been here too long. You are forgetting that you are spirit body and not human. You cannot communicate with Sara like you did in the flesh. Your thoughts are becoming confused because you expect a certain outcome and are receiving another. You are isolating yourself from both worlds. You are becoming a wayward spirit."

I thought I sensed concern when the last part was spoken.

"What does that mean?" I asked.

"You are becoming a ghost."

"A ghost?"

"Sam, you are a loving being. I urge you to come back with Me before The Anger consumes you."

The Anger? The way the Creator said those words made me believe that the emotion of anger was a living entity and it was bent on separating me from God. As I was contemplating this, Sara spoke.

"I don't feel him anymore. Do you think he's still here?" she asked.

I strained to watch her through my foggy lens. The medium remained still, allowing a long moment to pass before she shook her head back and forth solemnly.

"I'm sorry sweetheart. I don't think so."

Sara's hand fell heavily on her knee; she sighed and got up to leave.

"You don't have to go sweetie. Stay and have a cup of tea. I have some chamomile I could whip up real quick," the medium offered.

"Thank you so much but, I think I'd better get going. There's a lot to take in and I think I want to get home and process it all, you know?"

"Don't say another word about it," the medium said putting her hand up as a gesture of understanding. "It has been a privilege my dear to talk with you and your one-true-love today. You just let me know if there is anything else I can do for you sweetie." She got up and grabbed Sara's hand in hers, looking her straight in the eyes. "And I genuinely hope that you can find happiness in this life. You deserve it."

"Do you think we'll ever be together again?" Sara asked tearfully.

"Sweetheart, I don't know much about much. But after today, I know one thing. You and Sam will most definitely be together again."

Hearing those words spoken out loud was a sweet confirmation of what I already knew to be true. Sara wiped the forming tears from her eyes and walked to the door uttering, *thank you*, as she exited. I couldn't bear to see her walk away from me again.

"Don't leave Sara, I'm still here!"

I craned my neck to try and see her out the window as she left but the blurriness of my vision overwhelmed me. My feet felt like lead as I tried blindly to follow her.

"She doesn't know that you are here anymore. Your confusion is separating you from her, from Me and ultimately from any sense of self that you had. You are becoming nothing more than a bang in the night, a creak on the stairs, a shadow out of the corner of her eye," the Creator explained.

"Then reincarnate me. I need to be with her now here on Earth," I stated with resolve.

"I ask you to think harder on that. Choosing reincarnation would not fulfill your purpose. Your paths would not cross in the way you hope. You would be placed in a new, previously uninhabited physical body. You would be starting over as an infant. Sara would continue to age. There is a very high possibility that you won't even be born in the same country."

"Alright, then I'll stay here, like this. I'll figure it out," I said with defiance.

After I spoke, a mirror appeared in front of me. I came face to face with my own hollow, sunken, desperate eyes. I refused to care that the sallow skin which hung loosely from my cheekbones was my own.

"It doesn't matter what I become. I need to protect and take care of her down here. I can't leave her alone. This planet has so many dangers. Not the least of which being loneliness," I said turning to shun the image.

"I have shown you the lowest form of yourself, an image which haunts even the most ambivalent souls, and you are saying that you would settle for that? You would forgo your own soul's contentment so that Sara would not be alone on this planet?" the Creator asked.

I nodded my head with resolve in agreement.

"Love over Self is the greatest sacrifice of all," the Creator said.

Suddenly the Creator came into my view. I saw her as a light-haired woman with a care-worn face. There was a long pause before She spoke again.

"Sam, I want to give you a gift. Come near to me."

I walked humbly to where She stood, putting aside my misplaced hostility, I surrendered myself completely to Her. She took my face in Her hands and as She did, I closed my eyes, letting the warm Divine Light soak into my being again. She bent down and whispered softly in my ear: "Now, wake up Sam, and cherish this day."

CHAPTER 17

The room around me buzzed with light, sound, taste and touch. My senses were in overdrive, hearing, seeing and feeling everything around me. My heart beat heavy with the anxiety of over-stimulation.

"Time to wake up Sam," a female voice called out.

My name rung loudly in my ears and the sound pierced my eardrums. *Wait...my ears?* I felt the sides of my head and, to my surprise, there they sat, flat against my skull, in the flesh. I stirred my body and felt the softness of a fluffy pillow pressed against my cheek. An airy down-comforter lay strewn across my legs. As I shifted onto my side to prop myself up, I felt the heaviness of my bones pushing against my muscles. I tried to glance at my surroundings but my eyes fluttered instinctively against the sunlight which was filtering into the room where I lay. I strained them opened and closed several times; it took some adjustment to use a retina and cornea to see again but I finally got the hang of it. The powder blue color on the walls came into focus and the digital clock on the nightstand lit up the numbers 7:30. I was in someone's bedroom.

I wanted to sit up and find out more, so I pushed myself to the edge of the bed. Because of my skewed sense of reality, I misjudged the distance to the floor and my feet hit the hardwood with a clumsy thud. Having just been in ethereal form, I was really feeling the burden that the physical body imposed on me. I stretched the stiffness out of my limbs and prepared to greet the voice calling my name.

"Sam, come on. Rise and shine."

As the woman continued calling out, I heard her footsteps approaching my room. I pushed myself to my feet and grabbed for the robe hanging on the chair beside me. I wasn't sure who I might encounter and I didn't want to be caught red-faced in boxers, which was all I was wearing at the moment. Just as I thought she was going to burst in, she walked right past the door, knocking instead on the one across the hall.

"Samantha Christina Fine, I said get out here right now before you're late for school again," the woman said.

I peered around the door jamb and watched as a small girl about five or six years old with a long, brown ponytail, turned the knob and came bouncing out of the room.

"Ok Mommy. I'm ready. I couldn't decide which color to wear today," she pointed down past her denim overalls at a pair of mismatched socks; "so I wore both."

"Good choice," her mother replied. "Now go eat your cereal."

The girl skipped merrily off to gobble her breakfast. Just then, the woman turned around, and for the first time, I saw her face. I was amazed I hadn't recognized her voice: it was Sara and she was coming my way.

I was so taken aback by the sight of her that I had to force myself to sit back down on the bed. Besides a change of clothes, she looked exactly the same as I had just seen her, the time lapse must have been only a matter of days. I was grateful for that, last time it had been difficult seeing her changed so much.

"Oh. Good morning," she said with surprise. "Sorry if I woke you up yelling for her. I wasn't trying to. You can go back to sleep. It's only seven thirty, you don't have to work until eleven today, right?"

She grabbed some dirty laundry off the floor while she waited for me to respond. I shook my head, perplexed, still unsure of where, when, or what I was doing here. The last thing I remembered was talking to the Creator and now I was here in a seemingly parallel universe, playing house with Sara.

"Christian, did you hear me? Eleven, right? Or did they change your hours?" she asked me.

My head snapped up in confusion.

"Did you say Christian?"

"Oh come on. It's too early for jokes. I just want to know if you're going back to bed or not," she said exasperated.

I walked slowly over to the full-length standing mirror in the corner of the room. I was afraid of whose reflection might be staring back at me. I stood for a moment in front of it with my eyes closed. When I got the courage up to open them, I gasped. Every feature staring back at me was familiar but not in the way I thought it would be. Reaching my broad hands up to my head I combed my fingers through the thick black hair. I moved my square chin from side to side and flexed my muscular forearms back and forth. Sara stopped gathering clothes to watch me.

"It's all the same at it was yesterday," she said.

"No, it's not. Not at all," I whispered to myself.

I took one last long look at the handsome, well-built man in the mirror before turning around and declaring my identity out loud: "I'm Christian."

"And I'm Sara, nice to meet you. Are you ok?" she asked chuckling.

I thought for a moment before I answered; not sure if any of this phenomenon I was experiencing was actually ok. Then an echo of a voice rang in my mind, *"My gift to you. Cherish this day."* I understood. This was the gift that the Creator had given me. I had another chance with Sara, in the role I had always wanted, as her husband.

"I'm ok," I said. "Actually, I am more than ok. I'm wonderful! This is going to be the best day of my entire existence!"

I ran to her and joyfully scooped her high up in my arms. She smiled despite the laundry that fell back to the floor in heaps.

"Wow, Chris what's gotten into you?!" she marveled.

"Sam," I joked.

"Sam? Did she tell you to play a trick on me this morning?" she asked.

"No, no, never mind," I laughed and dropped the subject.

"Are you gonna put me down now? Not that I don't like it, but I do have to get her to school and try to get to work on time."

"School? Work? I don't think so. Today we are all taking the day off. We'll call it a mental health day," I declared.

"You *are* crazy," she said, wiggling out of my arms.

"Yup, crazy for *you*!" I clarified.

She eyed me suspiciously as she gathered the laundry in her arms again and made her way towards the door. Suddenly the patter of small feet came barreling around her and the child jumped into my arms.

"Daddy says no school today! I heard," the little girl boasted.

"Well, actually that's up to mom," I explained, realizing now that this was Samantha.

She looked over at her mother with a cute little pout that I knew Sara wouldn't be able to deny.

"Oh, alright! Mental health day for everyone," Sara conceded.

"YAY!" Samantha and I shouted simultaneously.

"So, what should we do on this lovely day?" I asked, hiking Samantha up onto my back.

"Zoo, zoo, zoo!!" she begged.

"Hmmm. The zoo would be nice. It's a beautiful day and there won't be a crowd on a weekday. What do you think Christian?" Sara asked me.

At the moment, I was thinking that I didn't want to be called Christian; it reminded me that this situation was most likely temporary.

"I think that the zoo is an excellent idea honey. Hey, I like that...honey. Nicknames are nice sometimes; why don't you just call me honey today," I said.

"I thought you didn't like being called that."

"Oh yea, I don't usually. But today I do. Today seems special somehow, don't you think?" I searched her face as I said this, hopeful that she might recognize something other than her husband; something familiar that might tell her it was me, but she didn't return my eye contact.

"Yes, it is definitely *different*. I'll give you that," she said.

"Let's not waste a minute of it. I'll finish getting dressed and then we'll head out," I said, shooing them out of the room.

"Wait." Sara stuck her hand up in a stop motion. "What excuse are you gonna give work?"

I didn't have to think twice, I would tell the truth; "I'm just gonna tell them that I'm not feeling like myself today."

"Ok," Sara said shrugging her shoulders; "probably wouldn't be a lie."

"See you in a few minutes," I said closing the door behind them.

I quickly threw off my clothes, adding them to the pile in the hamper. I hurried to dress as fast as I could, feeling resentful that this mundane task of dressing was causing me to squander valuable time that could be spent with Sara. I searched for underwear first and as I bent down to open the bottom drawer of the large oak dresser, I caught the foreign reflection of myself again in the mirror. The sight of it continued to startle me. I had never seen this body naked before and I felt a deep embarrassment for looking at it now. After all, I was still Sam, no matter what lies the mirror told. Putting my hand firmly on the wooden moveable frame of the mirror I flipped it around until it reflected only the wall.

I returned to rummaging through unorganized drawers until I found clothes that matched. I hastily threw on white striped black athletic shorts and a white fitted tee to make an outfit. The shirt felt stifling and I tugged at the chest to loosen it. I had never been one to wear clothes that hugged my body, probably because my body had never looked this good in tight clothes. But I decided against changing and embraced my new fit look.

A pair of sneakers peeked out at me from under the bed; I grabbed them and set about tying the laces as fast as my fingers could fly. I heard phone calls and preparations being made as Sara and Samantha excitedly bustled around. I walked out to meet them, ready to start this miracle of a day that had been given as a gift to me.

"Daddy! We are ready, ready, ready to go to the zoo, zoo, zoo!" Samantha half-sang, extending her arms out at the end as if she were part of a chorus line.

I smiled at the adorable child in front of me. She looked like a mini-version of her mother, especially when she flashed her dimples.

"Yup, we'd better a get a move on before all the animals go out to lunch," I joked.

Sara grabbed her purse and I started for the door.

"Wait," Samantha said, running in the opposite direction. When she came back a minute later she had a plastic bottle in her hand. "We need to bring some medicine because Mommy told her boss at work that she is sick."

I looked at Sara who covered her face with her hands to hide her laugh.

"Yea, I guess we'd better," I replied, taking the bottle from her and humoring the serious child. I bent down on one knee so as to be face-to-face with her and said, "Mommy is very old, and old people needs lots of medicine."

I pretended to whisper but I spoke loud enough so that Sara could hear me. She slapped me on the back with a faux-appalled look on her face and grabbed the aspirin from my hand. I laughed slightly and continued to address Samantha; "You have to look out for Mommy and make sure that she doesn't get too tired today, ok?"

She nodded her head as if she agreed with every word I said.

"How old *is* Mommy?" she asked.

"Half past a hundred," Sara said jokingly before I could respond. "Now can we please get going? I'm getting older by the second waiting for you two slow-pokes."

"Yay!" Samantha exclaimed, jumping up and running for the door.

"Everybody ready now?" I asked.

Sara grabbed her over-sized purse which was now full of aspirin and probably every other necessity known to females. She flung it over her arm with one hand and, as if we were teenage best friends again she plopped her other arm buddy-style over my shoulder.

"We're off," she said. "Your little family is ready for their adventure."

My heart swelled.

CHAPTER 18

The zoo was quiet and besides the occasional mother pushing a stroller, we felt as if the entire place had been reserved just for us. Samantha raced from exhibit to exhibit, scoping out each animal in its re-created habitat. We saw kangaroos, elephants and zebras all within the first fifteen minutes of arriving. Sara and I followed at a close pace behind trying heartily to keep up with the energetic kindergartener.

"DADDY! Look! This monkey is making funny faces at me!" Samantha yelled through her giggles.

"I think he likes you sweetheart," Sara replied, walking over to check out the primates.

"If you think that's a funny face, look at this one," I said.

Samantha spun around to see and, for her amusement, I contorted my face into a gnarly expression which rivaled the chimps. My musing worked as I hoped, and she began laughing hysterically, firing back at me with her own silly tongue-twisted version of a monkey face.

"Don't hold it too long or you'll get stuck like that," I teased, having remembered hearing that from my own father when I was young.

"No it won't!" Samantha cried in horror, obviously not realizing that I was joking.

"Daddy's just kidding," Sara said, patting her daughter on the head.

"Just jokes kiddo," I reassured, feeling sorry that I had frightened her. "Now how about we go check out the lions' den?"

"Roar! Race you there!" Samantha said as she took off down the pavement path, giving herself a head start.

I followed with just enough speed to make her think I was trying to pass her, but not enough to actually do so.

"I win!" she shouted, slapping her hand on a fence to signal that she had reached the destination point first.

Pretending to huff and puff, I jogged up behind her and admitted defeat; "You're just too fast for me, kid."

She flashed a victory smile and then turned her attention to the exhibit. The lions were supposed to be pacing back and forth behind the glass wall in front of us but nothing besides patches of well-trodden grass could be seen. She searched the landscape with her eyes, craning her head back as far as she could and stood on tip-toe to try and catch a glimpse of moving fur.

"Where are they Daddy?" she asked, seeming frustrated with the lack of entertainment at this particular stop.

"Hmm, maybe they're sleeping in the shade," I said, wandering around the perimeter to scope out the area.

"Nothing over here either," Sara said, standing at the other end of the exhibit. She used her hand to tent her eyes from the sun as she visually searched the man-made plains, then interjected; "Samantha Marie, get off of there right now."

I looked over to see that Samantha had stepped up onto the smooth, metal barrier railing to get a better look. With characteristic childhood defiance, she ignored her mother and took another step up the metal rungs; seemingly not giving a thought to the hard, unforgiving pavement that lay below her. I felt like I should admonish her as well but, being new to fatherhood, I wasn't sure how to go about it without being either too mean or too delicate.

"Sa-man-th-a, I said *down right now*," Sara annunciated every word to let the child know she was serious and then began to walk over to her.

As if she hadn't heard her mother at all, Samantha said, "Ooool! I think I see one."

She absentmindedly lifted her foot to take another step up. Thankfully, I saw her start to slip before she actually began to fall.

Without even thinking, I ran as quick and straight as a well-thrown dart to where she was and snatched her backwards falling body into my arms in midair. Holding her all-but-weightless and helpless body, I felt as protective of her as the unseen lions in the pen next to us did of their cubs. Even though I had only saved her from a nasty bump, an hour's worth of tears and a week's worth of cuts and scrapes, I knew now that I was her father, I wouldn't hesitate to attack if any danger were to approach.

"Thank God!" Sara panted, having sprinted to where we were. She clutched her hand over her heart.

"You're correct, God had *everything* to do with it," I replied wild-eyed as the adrenaline of the moment pumped through my body.

"Since when did you start giving credit to God?" Sara asked, peering at me oddly out of the corner of her eye as she transitioned Samantha firmly back on the ground.

I shrugged my shoulders nonchalantly. I wasn't sure if Sara's opinion of God was favorable and I didn't want to start a philosophical debate that might ruin the mood of the day. So instead, I tried to change the subject.

"Déjà vu," I said.

"How do you mean?" Sara asked, hugging Samantha close to her.

"Remember when *you* slipped climbing that huge rock and I scurried down to help?"

"Slipped climbing a rock?" she paused as if she were sorting through her memory bank until something clicked. "You don't mean when we were at the chasm do you?"

I nodded, thrilled that she remembered.

"Wow, I can't believe that you remember that. It was so long ago," she said.

"Seems like yesterday to me," I replied.

"I do remember that you carried me through the woods but if I recall correctly it wasn't you that got to me first after I fell. It was Sam."

I perked up at the mention of my real name. She was finally speaking about me and not about the person whose body I temporarily inhabited. The thrill I got at hearing her speak the name Sam in context made me want to tell her that I was here, in Christian's body; that some fantastic charade was taking place and she could talk to me, right now, in the flesh. But I didn't know how to explain it, especially in front of Samantha. The poor child would be confused beyond belief, wondering what happened to her real father. As much as I wanted Sara to know that I was with her, I couldn't be selfish. I had to play along.

"Are you sure Sam got to you before me?" I asked, secretly hoping to hear some praise for what I had done all those years ago.

"Yeah, I'm sure. You were just slacking off, doing your own thing as usual," she said, rolling her eyes.

By the sarcastic tone in her voice I could sense that her relationship with Christian wasn't all she hoped it would be. I was uncomfortable with this glimpse of intimate knowledge regarding their relationship, but since I was already in the thick of the conversation I figured I might as well keep going. After all, I was finally able to talk to her directly and might be able to get answers to some long-standing questions of mine.

"Are you saying that you think Sam is better than me? Would you have rather married him?" I asked. I couldn't resist knowing the answer, even if it wasn't the one I wanted to hear.

Sara appeared momentarily startled but quickly wiped any emotion from her face.

"It doesn't matter anyway. It's irrelevant. Sam's gone," she replied matter-of-factly.

The words, *Sam's gone*, stung my heart like a second-death. They reaffirmed the fact that no matter what game I was playing at here, the Sam she knew *was* gone. Not wanting to cry, I turned away from her.

"And why do you suddenly care so much about all of this?" she added in an exasperated tone.

I remained silent, lost in thoughts of my semi-existence.

"No, seriously. I mean it," she said, grabbing my shoulder to make me face her as she spoke. "You've been acting weird today."

Her sudden physical contact jolted me back to the reality that was in front of me and I decided to put off metaphysical contemplation until a later date.

"Weird? How am I acting weird?" I asked, raising my left eyebrow in curiosity, signaling that I wanted a detailed answer.

"I don't know, like, weird meaning *better* I guess," she said. The way she slipped the word, better, into the sentence, you would have thought it was a secret she was letting spill out.

"Bet..t..e..r," I said slowly, deliberately letting the syllables hang in the air. "I like better. Better *how?*"

"I don't know, I guess, better as in wanting to do something with your family instead of your friends and acting like a little kid with Samantha and being more appreciative of me."

I smiled openly, proud of myself for being the husband to her that I always knew I could be.

"Hey, don't let it get to your head. It's only one day. And one day certainly isn't going to make up for being a jerk the rest of the time," she said, picking up a few kernels of stray feed off the ground and tossing it at me playfully.

"Ok, ok, I get it," I laughed, pretending to shield my face from the deer corn as it harmlessly bounced off my body.

I loved being here with her like this, spending time together, talking about our relationship, laughing; I wished I could ease her mind and tell her that, from here on out, every day would be better. But I couldn't. This future was not mine to promise her; it belonged to someone else. When I spoke, I chose my words carefully.

"Sara, I can't make any promises for tomorrow or the next day because I simply don't know what the future will bring, but what I *can* promise is that I will make this the best day that you've ever had with me."

She shifted her eyes and crinkled her mouth sideways in thought. She stood there for a lingering moment, clutching the sweater she had forced Samantha to bring with her in case the weather turned chilly. Her face reflected the puzzle that her brain was sorting through and I couldn't help but wonder if her thoughts were on deeper things than the promise of this day being great. She looked at me as if she were seeing right through the man that was her husband to someone entirely different, yet familiar. She began to slowly move her head up and down until she was looking straight at me with a full nod as if she were satisfied with whatever conclusion she came to.

"Next one, please," Samantha said, breaking my concentration by tugging on my pants.

She gestured her arm toward the rhino field a few yards away. She was looking fidgety so I obliged her desire to keep moving.

"Alright little one, let's go see," I said, following closer behind her now than I had before.

Sara gave the go-ahead with her hand and stayed to gather up our belongings. As I caught up to Samantha and took her hand in mine, I vaguely heard Sara say something. I turned around to see who she was talking to, but no one was there; she just smiled, watching Samantha and I as we walked.

"Did you say something?" I asked.

She shook her head, no, but when I turned back around again I distinctly heard her speak this time. She uttered a single word: "Better."

CHAPTER 19

The air was getting cooler as the afternoon began the slow fade into evening. This had always been my favorite time of day. There was a sense that the rush of work and school was done as the whole Earth seemed to be unwinding to welcome the nighttime. I was thankful to be experiencing the peacefulness of twilight again, especially with Sara. Samantha dangled between us, swinging from our clasped hands.

"Lions, and tigers, and bears, oh my," we sang as we approached the walkway up to our house.

She ran to be first to the door, stopping only briefly to wave at a misty grey cat who squinted down at us from its post in the front window. She bounced on her tip-toes while Sara found the key and unlocked the bolt. Before I had made it through the door, Samantha was already in the kitchen, onto the next task.

"What are we having for dinner Mommy?"

"Hmm, I don't know. What do you want?"

"Pizza and Cookies!" Samantha shouted.

"Pizza and cookies, huh? That doesn't sound very healthy. Are there any fruits and vegetables in that meal Miss Samantha?" Sara asked.

"Uh-huh." The child nodded her head emphatically.

"And what would those be?"

"Well, Daddy gets pineapple on his sometimes and you get the little green trees."

"Broccoli. The little green trees are called broccoli sweetie," Sara said, plopping her purse on the table.

"Bwoccoli. Uh-huh, you get bwoccoli."

"Broccoli. B-R-o-c-c-o-l-i. With an, R. Not a, W," Sara corrected.

"Oh, yeah, broccoli. Those are good for you, aren't they?" Samantha asked.

"Yes, pineapple and broccoli are healthy but *you* don't get those on your pizza, you only get cheese. And all you've had to eat today was chocolate, cotton candy and french fries. Or as I like to call it, *junk*," Sara said, tapping her finger against the end of Samantha's nose.

"Don't you think this is a day for exceptions?" I asked, looking to Sara for approval.

"If you want me to eat something healthy Mommy, I can eat a salad first, and then I can have pizza!" Samantha proclaimed.

I had to smile at the child's ingenuity.

"I can see I am being ganged up on here and I don't like it one bit. Even though I hate to admit it, Daddy's right, today has been full of exceptions and I guess dinner can be too. Besides, pizza and cookies are my weakness."

"Yay!!" Samantha yelled in victory. "I spread the sauce and you roll the dough Mommy."

Before she had even finished her sentence, she began rummaging through the fridge. I watched as she pulled out the cheese and dough and set them on the table. I hadn't expected we would be making the pizza ourselves. I couldn't recall when, if ever, I'd had a homemade pizza. But, I guessed it was more fun and cost effective to make one from scratch rather than ordering out from the local pizza joint like I had done so many times as a bachelor. I was interested to see how the flavor would compare to takeout.

"So, I guess that's the plan. If you wanna go watch T.V. I can call you when it's done," Sara said.

Her casual words were directed at me.

"Aren't I gonna help?" I asked. Sara looked taken aback. "That is, if you don't mind me hanging around your kitchen," I added.

I could tell by her reaction that having her husband help out with the cooking wasn't the norm. She flashed me a bright, clear smile and, as if a switch had been flipped, her face lit up from within. In that moment, she looked so happy, I couldn't resist holding her. Grabbing her gently by the waist, I pulled her close to me. Her smile widened until it seemed to be the only feature on her face.

"This is more of the better part of me," I said softly to her.

"Are you dancing Mommy and Daddy? Because you're standing like the people on the show who dance slow together," Samantha said.

I forgot that she was watching us, and momentarily I felt self-conscious.

"No, we are not dancing. Daddy was just giving me a hug," Sara said chuckling, and then added, "Daddy doesn't know how to dance."

"What?! I most certainly do know how to dance," I said with fake indignation.

"Oh, really? Well, this is the first that *I* am hearing of it. Prove me wrong then," she said and leaned over, turning on the kitchen radio.

The uplifting sounds of Mozart floated through the air, inviting all in listening range to be swept up with the melody. I took her dare. Guiding her body towards me, I placed my left hand gently at her waist and slid my fingers down her arm until I found hers and intertwined them tightly. I lifted her hand effortlessly into the air with mine, creating a waltz-stance. We danced formally around the linoleum squares, making box steps with our feet.

"One, two, three. One, two, three," I repeated rhythmically, as if giving a dancing lesson.

Samantha giggled wildly at the sight of her parents acting in a way she probably had never seen before. She swung her arms in the air like a conductor instructing our movements. "Faster, faster, faster," she demanded.

Sara and I indulged her and shuffled our feet quickly side to side to keep up with her demanding pace. As the music began to wind down, I dipped Sara backwards, gesturing that our performance had come to an end.

"Hooray!" Samantha yelled and applauded.
Sara smiled and curtsied in an old fashioned manner.

"Thank you very much sir, to my surprise, you were a marvelous dance partner," she said.
I gave an over-exaggerated bow in response.

"...next up, a well-known piece by Beethoven, the classic 'Moonlight Sonata', as performed by the Boston Symphony Orchestra," the male monotone voice of the radio host announced.

The momentary silence in the room was cut into by the ivory keys of a piano masterfully plinking out the hauntingly romantic introduction to what I knew to be one of Sara's favorite compositions. She lingered for a moment in front of me, mesmerized by the melody. Seizing the moment, I wrapped my left arm tightly around her waist and pulled her towards me again, cradling her right hand in mine at chin level against our bodies. Sara's smooth cheek fell lightly against my own. I led her in a soft sway with the rhythm. Back and forth. Back and forth. She allowed all the weight of her head to rest against me, nestling her face deeply into my neck. The unbridled movement of our bodies tossed her hair around causing the strands to tickle my neck like stray down feathers floating on a pillow. The low, continuous refrain echoed in my ears, hypnotizing me into a dancing trance where we seemed to melt together into a single energy which flowed across the floor. Eventually, the piano notes slowed until they came to a stop. Our feet went still but we remained together in an embrace.

"Mommy, I'm hungry."

The words rang loudly through the silent kitchen. Sara blushed slightly and pulled back as if she suddenly remembered, as I had, that our intimate moment was being shared by a bored child.

"I guess I should be getting back to dinner," Sara sighed, looking up at me with the disappointment of obligation.

She turned to walk away, sliding her hand down my arm before letting go. I gave her warm palm an affectionate squeeze before it slipped off my fingers. I watched as she walked to the counter and began rolling out the dough. Her arms looked strong as she kneaded the thick crust into shape. Samantha kept busy, gathering more ingredients from the refrigerator. I thought of myself at that age and how my own mother would have snapped at me by now to close the door and stop letting the cold air out. But Sara just let the little girl be, obviously trying to encourage her helpfulness in the kitchen.

"Mommy, I got all the stuff that we need!"

"Wow, good job. Thank you sweetie," Sara said, surveying the items on the counter. "Now we just need the sauce and we'll be able to put this thing together."

"But I can't reach the sauce. It's on the top shelf."

"I bet you could reach the sauce if you were on my shoulders, couldn't you?" I said, quickly hoisting the tiny girl in the air.

"Weeee!" Samantha squealed in delight and surprise.
I opened the cabinet and positioned her towards it so that grabbing the glass jar would be an easy acquisition.

"Got it!" Samantha gloated.

"Now *that* would be a cute picture," Sara commented, looking affectionately at the father and daughter totem I had created.

"Cheeeese!" Samantha said through a toothy grin.
Sara mimicked a snapshot of the moment with an invisible camera. I whirled Samantha around the kitchen in a final circle before putting her safely back on the ground.

"Sweetie, could you please go wash up and change your clothes? You were touching all sorts of animals today and I want you clean before you start adding ingredients," Sara said.

"Ok and I'll make sure I wear something special for dinner since it's a special day," she said, running off in the direction of the bathroom.

"Goodness only knows what she'll come out wearing," Sara chuckled as she turned around to preheat the oven.

"I see a lot of you in her," I pointedly remarked.

"Really?" Sara asked, turning her lips up curiously. "People usually say she looks a lot like you."

"It wasn't really looks that I was talking about. It's more her...big spirit."

"How so?" Sara asked with interest.

"Well, the way she bounces around when she walks, and how she looks at everything with such curiosity, and how she giggles and sings little tunes all day to herself. That's the kind of stuff that reminds me of you."

"Hmmm," Sara said before pausing. "That *is* the way I used to be, *isn't it?*"

"That's the way you *still* are," I corrected.

"No. Not really," Sara said introspectively and softly retorted; "I haven't been like that in a long time. Life kinda just took the spark outta me. You know?"

The spark...hearing that word immediately brought visions to my mind of what I had seen in heaven: two sparks falling to Earth away from one another. We were now in separate realms and everything in our existence was askew.

"Yes, I do know what you mean," I said after a pause. "There's emptiness where there used to be a whole."

I walked to where she stood, facing the oven with her back to me; tenderly I slid my arms around her waist, wrapping her thin body entirely in my arms. I felt the usual rigidity in her body give way to relaxation and she rested her head on my shoulder.

"Most of the time I feel like you don't understand me. But it's weird, right now I feel like you do. Totally and completely. I feel like you really get me," Sara said.

Unwilling to fight the magnetic pull between our bodies any longer, I leaned in for a gentle but passionate kiss. At first her lips were stiff but I greeted them in a soft manner and soon they loosened. She reciprocated. Our lips locked for a moment and then parted smoothly.

"I should have done that a long time ago," I whispered in her ear.

I knew that the full meaning of the statement was lost to her, still a smile of excitement crept over her face in a way that made her eyes sparkle. She got up on tiptoe, wrapped her arms around my neck and squeezed tightly.

"You've made me happy today in a way that I forgot was possible. I miss feeling like this. Promise me, promise me, *promise* me," she pleaded, still clutching me; "promise me that we won't be unhappy anymore. That we can have good times together and be a real family, like we were today."

The words "I promise" almost escaped my lips before I realized the impact of what I would be saying. If this life that I was living today were truly mine, I would have promised her all of that, freely and honestly. But I knew I couldn't. I understood, somewhere inside of me, that this was a one and only day, a life which was on loan to me. To promise a happy tomorrow to the woman that I loved wasn't my promise to make. I had no more tomorrows in this life with her. I pulled her an arm's length away, grasping both her shoulders so that I could look her in the eyes, face to face. Even if I couldn't promise her what she wanted me to, I could promise her something else.

"I promise that I will never stop loving you," I said. I spoke the next words slowly and deliberately to create significance with my voice; "Sara, no matter where I go, no matter what I do, I will come back to you."

She shook her head in understanding and buried her tear-streaked face in my chest. I enveloped her tightly with my arms and held her still, like a statue, while she cried gently. There was no need for me to ask why she was crying, I already knew, though I doubted that her logical mind did. An innate part of her recognized the hidden piece of me. Her soul was weeping for the loss of our love on Earth. I didn't want to ever let her go. If only I had more time in this physical form, I was sure that eventually she would consciously recognize the soul within. Slowly she pulled back from me, wiping her cheeks dry and blinking her eyes.

"I'm sorry. I got away from myself there. I just couldn't help it. It all came rushing forward like a flood. I guess I needed a good cry," she said.

I thought it odd that she was apologizing for expressing her emotions since I had always known her as a heart-on-the-sleeve type. If what she said earlier about life changing her was true, then this was one of the parts of her personality that *had* changed. Perhaps her way of dealing with emotion now was to internalize it. I wondered if my death played a part in that.

Though I was the one who died, I think that night had actually been harder on her. I remember hearing psychics telling grieving loved ones that the person they were trying to communicate with on the other side was fine, even happy, and that the real burden of death was not placed on the dead but on the loved ones that they left behind. The yoke of despair fell heavy on the survivors. Seeing Sara standing before me now, a victim of the tragic events of her life, I saw the despair they spoke of. All these years since my accident, she had been trying to build a new life and a new happiness without me. She had stuffed her hurt down, deep within, but couldn't fully erase the scars of brokenness that my passing had left behind. Now my presence here had reopened the wound.

"Good thing I don't wear makeup or I'd look like a raccoon," she said half-laughing, still wiping wetness from under her lower lids.

I smiled sweetly at her gesture to break the gloom.

"Sam, what are you doing here?" Sara said in surprise.

I took a step back and looked at her quizzically, wondering if perhaps I had transformed before her eyes back into the old body I used to inhabit. Maybe our exchange just now had been so intense it opened her eyes to see into the soul of me and she had a revelation of who I really was.

"Do you know who I am?" I asked timidly.

"What do you mean? Of course I know who you are. What kind of question is that?" Sara asked. "Sweetheart, why are you just standing there?"

I saw now that her attention was focused not at me, but behind me to where Samantha stood in the doorway. I had been so wrapped up in my own thoughts that I forgot I was not the only Sam in the house. Sara walked over and bent down on one knee to look her in the eyes.

"I was just watching you and Daddy hug. I like it when you guys hug," she said.

"Oh, baby, you startled me. Come here," Sara said pulling her daughter close to her heart.

"Mommy, do you like my special outfit?"

I turned around to see what she was wearing and had to stifle a laugh. She had on a pink bathing suit with a purple tutu and tall cowboy boots that covered her legs.

"It definitely is *special*," I said. Sara nodded in agreement trying to suppress a smile. "Did you make plans to ride a dancing unicorn at the beach and not tell us?" I joked.

Sara burst out laughing.

"Hey! It's not funny! It's my special outfit for the special day!" Samantha declared.

"Sweetie, I wasn't laughing at you. I was laughing at what Daddy said. Wasn't it funny?" Sara asked, hugging Samantha with one arm.

Samantha nodded her head, giving a little ballet twirl as she did, and giggled.

"Ok, guys," Sara said trying to catch her breath as the laughter began winding down. "Let's get this supper going so that we can eat before midnight."

Mother and daughter resumed preparations and gave me the task of setting the table. I made quick work of placing the plates and napkins on the dark wood rustic table. Once I saw that their attention was focused away from me, I took my chance and snuck out the door. This certainly was an extraordinary day and there was something I wanted to do to make it just a little more special.

CHAPTER 20

The limbs on the tall oak trees in the front yard stretched over the well-kept grass like a parasol. The powerful sun that earlier had broken through the leaves and consumed the yard was now replaced by a creeping shadow of shade signaling the end of the afternoon and the start of the evening. I felt as if the day was running away from me faster than I could catch up to it.

I had first noticed the large pillow-like pink blossoms of the peonies reaching up from the garden when we returned home from the zoo. Other than a rose or a tulip I hadn't been one to easily place a flower with its name but I remembered this one because they were Sara's favorite flower. Here in her garden, they grew in abundance. She must have planted ten or more clusters of them. The sight of so many gigantic, yet delicate petals lining the side of the house was breathtaking. I recalled Sara lamenting every year when the bud and bloom time of the peonies had passed. "I only get to see them for such a short time every spring," she would say.

Because the day had been hot, I erroneously judged the season to be summer. But the peony petals were bursting open now for the world to view signaling that it was spring. Similar to me in this unfamiliar body, everything around was newly formed. The grass, the leaves, and the flowers had been buds only weeks ago. The robins who were poking around at the ground for a meal were probably returning to their nests to care for their newly hatched young. The miracle of rebirth was in the air.

I walked up to an unopened bud and breathed in the aroma: it smelled green. Logically of course on Earth, a scent does not have a color. But in Heaven, colors and smells had flooded my senses and they were all associated with one another. Green had been one of them and this was definitely its smell. Being up close to the plants I noticed the small black and yellow bees busy at their work of collecting pollen from the bounty for the queen. Before I died the fear of these little insects with their stingers would have driven me away from the flowers and back into the house. But now pain had become so insignificant in the scheme of my existence that the thought of it was not enough to miss out on this precious moment with nature. I remained motionless next to the flowers for a few more minutes, watching them bend in the slight wind. I let my body absorb the feeling of the air on my skin as my eyes focused in and out on the light which still filtered in through the clouds. I felt almost as close to God here as I had in Heaven.

I scooped together five stalks in one hand and snapped them off at the middle, leaving the top flower and some greenery for length. I said a silent *thank you*, to the plants for their sacrifice and promised them they'd be as loved by their new owner as they were here with their roots in the ground. Bending down to feel the grass one last time with my free hand, I made my way back to the house to deliver my gift.

Samantha waved and smiled as she saw me walk through the door. She was sitting at the table, kicking her feet back and forth for amusement while she waited for the pizza to cook. I bent down and spoke quietly to her. Sara was nowhere in sight, probably changing her clothes after the day's activities, so there was no need to whisper but I wanted to emphasize to Samantha that she was being let in on a secret.

"I have a small surprise for Mommy. Do you think you could get me a big glass with a little bit of water in it for these?" I said, motioning to the flowers behind my back.
Her eyes widened as she shook her head in acknowledgment. She scurried off, burrowing under the sink cabinet until she found something she deemed suitable to hold the flowers.

"Is this a good one Daddy?"

She was barely able to contain her excitement as she ran over to the table. I looked at the glass; it was tall with an hourglass shape and had a thick, sturdy base. There was a German-looking logo on the side. She carefully lowered it down in the center of the place settings. A smile curled my lips up as the familiar logo came into focus.

"Your beer cup!" she squealed.

I hadn't expected her to know what the drink-ware was used for and I speculated that Christian must consume a fair amount of beer in front of his daughter for her to be able to identify the glass so readily. I hoped I was wrong about that.

Beer cup or not, I slipped the flowers into it adding the water to the heavy container myself so as to avoid any spills by Samantha's small hands. The make-shift vase proved to be the perfect container for the fragrant blooms as it held them steadily in place. The flecks of white against pink, and the deep buried centers of the flowers fell perfectly into place and no arrangement on my part was required. I stepped back, proud of the centerpiece I had created for our special dinner.

As if on cue, Sara entered the room, confirming my notion about her whereabouts. She was wearing a clean white, loose blouse and casual pedal pusher jeans which accented her newly bare feet. Her hair had been removed from its ponytail and fell loose and wavy, ending just above her shoulders. Though she was years older than when we were together in body, she still had pinkness in her cheeks that made her look youthful. Older age agreed with her and I silently lamented her coming years of silver streaked hair and wrinkles that I would never get to experience.

"Is the pizza done?" she asked, wiping her hands dry on her pants.

"The pizza. Shoot, I forgot," I said.

I rushed over to the oven, and the centerpiece which had been obscured on the table behind me became exposed for her to see.

"My peonies!" Sara gasped.

I snapped my head back to see her expression. I wasn't sure if her tone indicated delight at the sight of them in her house or if she was upset that they had been cut out of her garden. I hadn't thought that might bother her until now.

"They look absolutely gorgeous in here. How thoughtful!" She bent down, grabbed the underside of a bloom, and drank in its scent. Samantha clapped satisfactorily in triumph.

"Thank you, sweetie," Sara said, herding her daughter in her arms to give her a hug.

"It was Daddy's idea not mine, Mommy. He should get the huggies."

"*Daddy's* idea? Since when does Daddy get such great ideas?" Sara asked.

Samantha shrugged.

"If it is his idea then he *does* deserve a hug, doesn't he?" Sara said. She walked over and earnestly wrapped her arms around me in a bear hug. "Thank you," she whispered into my ear.

I felt weakness take over my limbs as her soft voice reverberated in my eardrum.

"They still won't be the prettiest thing at the table," I said, trying to flatter her.

Smiling like an awkward schoolboy, I retrieved the pizza from the oven.

"I think you've been eating too much candy because you're becoming very sweet," she remarked with a good-humored wink and a wiggle of her finger.

"No, that's not it," I said speaking more seriously than the moment warranted. "It's just that I've realized today I have everything I've always wanted."

"What took you so long?" she asked.

"I always knew, I just never got the chance to experience it until now," I said.

She paused, probably trying to make sense of my statement, then said, "Well, maybe we should all take days off together more often."

I nodded my head half-heartedly in agreement, knowing it was futile to explain the deeper meaning of what I was saying to her. "Please, sit and let me serve you. Both of you," I said, pulling out two chairs and motioning for Samantha and Sara to take a seat. As if they were diners at a fancy restaurant, I pulled their chairs out and placed napkins on their laps.

Turning my attention back to the pizza, I took it from the oven and placed it on the counter. The cheese was golden brown and luckily it hadn't burnt at all underneath either. I searched the area for something to cut it with. A pizza wheel was amongst the utensils in the top drawer and I rolled it slowly through the cheese, slicing each piece into identical portions. The impeccable, shiny surface of a flower patterned serving dish caught my eye as it gleamed through the glass-paneled cabinet in front of me. I took it out and carefully slid each piece of the cheesy pizza onto it, creating a fanciful zigzag design on the platter. I looked down at my presentation and was proud to have plated the meal in a manner so pleasing to the eye.

"Dinner is served madams," I announced and confidently set the dish down before them.

"Cool!" Samantha exclaimed.

"Cute," said Sara.

"Thank you ladies. Time to eat. Youth before beauty," I said putting the first slice on Samantha's plate, then serving Sara.

"Luckily that went right over her head," Sara remarked.

"I knew it would," I said, watching the child devour her first slice.

"Whoa, someone was hungry. I know we don't usually eat this late but slow down a little Sam or you'll get a tummy ache," Sara instructed.

I flinched at the mention of my name but quickly realized that I wasn't the Sam being addressed and went back to nibbling my slice. Samantha nodded her head in acknowledgment at what her mother said but still continued to eat ravenously. Her cheeks were stuffed like a chipmunk.

"Take a sip of water to wash it down please," Sara said.

"Oh, water, that's what I forgot." I wiped my mouth and got up to fetch some from the tap.

"Bottled please Chris, the city water's been awful lately," Sara called over her shoulder.
I doubled back to the fridge to grab a bottle when suddenly, I heard choking.

"Hands up honey. Relax," Sara said calmly.
She was standing behind Samantha tapping her back to try and help move the food along smoothly.

"ACK...ACK..." Samantha coughed violently.

"Water, now!" Sara's voice had urgency as she held out her hand backwards to grab for a bottle from me.

I could hear muffled breathy sounds coming faster now from Samantha. I thrust the water into Sara's hand and she managed to get a little liquid into the girl's mouth but it immediately dribbled right back out. Samantha's swallowing reflex wasn't cooperating.

"Oh God, I think she's got something stuck in there," Sara said.

Without a second thought, I swooped in behind the child, placed my fist on her belly button, rolled my hand up a notch to just below her sternum, covered that hand with my other and began thrusting an appropriate amount of upward force. Sara stood watching in helplessness as the scene unfolded before her. I pushed once…nothing. Twice…a gag. Three times…*HUFF*. A wonderful release of air puffed from her throat, followed by a hard piece of crust which went flying out of her mouth, landing at her feet.

"Huuuuu…..huuuuu….huuuu…huuu…hu…" she gasped. The breaths started pouring out fast. Eventually they became steady and even. Soon, tears began rolling down her face.

"Are you ok?! Can you talk?" Sara asked with desperation.

Samantha nodded her head at first then whimpered, "Yes, Mommy."

"Thank God," Sara said, breathing a sigh a relief.

She clung to Samantha, gripping her for dear life with one arm and stroking her hair with the other, assuring the little girl that everything was alright. I stood back, amazed at what I had just accomplished. I'd never learned the Heimlich maneuver, yet, on instinct, I had just executed it flawlessly. I didn't understand how that could be possible, until I remembered that I was in Christian's body. My spirit had taken the place of his but every other physical part belonged to him, including his brain which contained all his memories and knowledge. Of course being a river guide, he would be required to learn CPR and first aid. His muscle-memory must have kicked in and carried out the lifesaving maneuver without any help from me.

"We are so lucky that your daddy was here," Sara said.

She looked over at me gratefully. I returned a bitter-sweet smile, knowing that without Christian, I would have been nothing in this situation.

"Mommy, I'm not hungry anymore," a teary Samantha said.

"I don't blame you sweetie. I think some quiet time would be good right now, don't you?"

Samantha nodded slowly. "Could you put in Mary Poppins for me?"

"Of course I can," Sara said stroking her back.

Without a word, Samantha wiped the leftover tears from her eyes and walked towards the living room. Sara started to follow her but I held up my hand in protest. The ordeal had obviously drained every bit of energy from her body. Her face was pale and I saw a slight tremor coming from her legs. She looked as if she had been spun around in circles to the point of nausea.

"Let me," I offered.

She started to make an objection but instead conceded and nodded her head for me to take the reins. I wandered after Samantha into the living room and found her sitting on the floor, movie in hand, staring trance-like at the blank television screen. Her tutu and boots lay sloppily next to her on the floor. Obviously the cute accessories now felt constricting.

This was the first time I had stepped in this room all day and, looking around, I was reminded of Sara's father's living room the first day I met her. The latest, and I'm guessing the top-of-the-line, stereo and video equipment was proudly on display in the entertainment center. Under different circumstances, I would have loved to explore the unfamiliar gadgets and handheld glowing screens that surrounded me but feeling that time was not on my side, I ignored them and continued on to the task at hand.

A lot of years had passed on Earth while I was in Heaven and this new technology was totally unfamiliar to me. The television was so thin that I avoided touching it for fear that it might tip over. I fumbled around for a few minutes, trying to figure out how to get the movie into the player, I had never seen one on a disc before and I honestly didn't know what to do with it. I scoured the button captions and eventually found the one that opened the tray to place the movie in. Thankfully, an auto-play feature took over from there.

"Thanks Daddy," Samantha said as she snuggled in to what appeared to be her regular spot on the couch.

"No problem. Do you think you will be ok in here by yourself for a little bit while I go talk to Mommy?"

"Mmm hmm," she replied nodding, but never taking her eyes off the bright, clear, flat screen in front of her.

I had to admit, the clear picture and the large display were mesmerizing; it was like being at a movie theater. Previews for upcoming children's movies and television shows began to play and I peeled myself away quietly, walking back to the kitchen. I found Sara slumped at the table, head on one arm, the other hand extended towards the flowers, rubbing a petal between her thumb and forefingers. She appeared to be coming down from the adrenaline rush she had just experienced and was physically crashing hard. I put my hands on her shoulders and began massaging them gently.

"Is she alright?" she asked.

"She's fine, mellowing out watching Julie Andrews sing. My question is, are *you* alright, because you certainly don't look it?"

"Oh, I'm fine," she replied with a dismissive wave of her hand.

I took my hands off her shoulders and gave her a doubting look. I figured she'd want to sit and hash out the experience with someone and now I was confused as to why she was shutting down. Perhaps Christian was the type of husband who didn't like discussing his feelings and she had gotten used to that type of avoidance. Or maybe, she didn't like the feedback she received when she did talk about deep matters with him. Either way, I wasn't going to let her close herself off from me.

"I don't know about you, but I'm pretty shaken up by the whole thing," I said.
I was being honest but also using my feelings as bait to lure her into starting a conversation with me.

"Really? You seemed calm when it was happening. I mean, you sprung right into action and basically saved her from choking to death," Sara said, sitting up and turning around to face me.

"I did what I had to because I knew how to, that's different from feeling calm," I explained.

"I just wish *I* knew how to do that, because if you weren't here, God only knows what would have happened to her," she said. She spoke quickly and with such force that she almost tripped over the words.

"Maybe you could take a CPR class. They teach all that kind of stuff. We could go together, I could always use a brush up on what I know," I said, not thinking beforehand that I couldn't actually make good on that offer.

"I would really like that," she said. She turned away from me and back to the table and I heard her speak under her breath, "I couldn't take it if another person I loved died in front of me."

"What was that?" I asked, more for an elaboration than a reverberation.

"Nothing."

"I heard what you said Sara. I just want to know why you said it."

"Forget about it, it's nothing," she said as she began busying herself with clearing the dishes from the table.

"If it's nothing, then why did you say it?"

"Because it's what I was thinking," she replied still avoiding eye contact as she shuffled the dishes around.

"Sara, please, stop for a minute."

"I've gotta get this done."

"No, you don't," I said, placing the tips of my fingers on her upper arm gently to bring her focus back to me.

She dropped the napkins in her hand and plunked down sloppily into the nearest chair. I pulled out the one in front of me and took a seat too, so as not to appear like an authority figure that was looming over her.

"It's just that...she went so quickly from laughing to gasping for air, there was no time to think. I felt helpless and I wanted to make it all better, but I couldn't. Her face turned red, and for a second, I thought I might lose her right in front of me...like I lost Sam."

I went utterly silent. So many years had passed since my death that it stunned me to hear her bring it up now in everyday conversation. I was shocked in a wonderful way and I couldn't speak. She continued.

"Watching him take his last breath was the most awful thing I've ever witnessed. I will never forget that," she said.
I remained silent.

"Sorry to be talking about this now, it's just that earlier today you brought up that story about Sam in the woods, and now this happened, and I was reminded about that night," she explained, fumbling her words a bit.

"No, no, I don't mind talking about him. It's just surprising to hear, that's all. I knew it was traumatic for you but I didn't know you still thought about it."

"Every day," she confessed.

"Yeah, me too" I said.

I didn't suppose that Christian really thought of me every day like Sara did, but I figured that if she thought he did it might open up the dialogue further.

"You do?" she said with relief. "We never really talked in depth about it after he passed, so I wasn't sure how you felt. There was so much going on at the time."

"Well, let's talk now."

"Ok."

"I have a question, don't take it the wrong way, but I've always wanted to know why were you alone with Sam that night?"

Although I already knew the answer, I had ulterior motives for asking. Firstly, considering there had been a secret meeting between his best friend and fiancée the night before their wedding, I logically assumed this was a question that Christian would ask. Secondly, I knew if she gave me an honest answer to this question that I could trust her to give me truthful responses to the questions I didn't have the answers to.

"Ok. I get why you would ask that," she said. "Sam called and asked to come see me before the wedding…" She paused. "…only he wasn't coming over to wish me good luck like I originally told you. He came over to tell me that he had feelings for me. Strong feelings. He told me that he loved me and had for a long time." Her voice shook with trepidation.

"And what did you say when he told you that?"

"I was shocked, of course, because we had been friends for a long time. But I didn't really get a chance to respond because the accident happened right after that."

"What were you going to say to him?"

There was a long silence and I could almost see Sara's mind wrestling for the right response.

She maintained steady eye contact and then blurted out, "I was going to tell him that I had feelings for him too. Chris, I loved him."

She had answered the test question I had given her truthfully, now I leaned in to ask the real one. The one whose answer meant something to me. Actually, not just something, the answer to this question meant *everything* to me. I plowed ahead without so much as a wince at her last answer, which surely would have been out of character for Christian, but at this point, I wasn't thinking about the charade.

"So, if Sam hadn't died that night, given the choice between him and me, who would you had picked?"

I stared at her with a passion that pleaded for a candid answer.

"Wow, what a question." She straightened her body, obviously taken aback. "If I answer this totally and truthfully then you have to answer a question for me the same way."

I nodded in agreement, feeling that it should be easy enough to give an answer to a question that I wouldn't be around to suffer the consequences for tomorrow.

"Alright then, here it goes. Honestly and truthfully...*back then*, I would have chosen Sam."

My heart jumped with elation and I tried desperately to suppress a huge grin which was pushing at the corners of my mouth; considering the body I inhabited, that gesture would be inappropriate to the point that she might think her husband was insane. These were the words that I had wanted so desperately to hear. I knew she loved me a long time ago when we were young, but that night of my death I really wasn't sure if she would have chosen me over Christian. Now I knew. In this lifetime, under different circumstances, we would have been together. To be telling this to Christian, her husband, all these years later, when she had nothing to gain and everything to lose, made me realize that if I hadn't died that night, the life of my dreams would have become reality. The thought was bittersweet but I wasn't going to let the sting of loss ruin this moment for me.

"Christian, you promised," Sara said, seemingly repeating herself although I hadn't heard her say anything.

"Huh?" I asked, puzzled.

"My question. Answer it," she demanded.

I had been so lost in sublime emotion that I must have completely blocked out whatever she had said after her confession of choosing me. I felt stupid having to do so, but I asked her to repeat herself.

"Ugh," she sighed in annoyance, "I feel like you are just dodging the question."

"No, I'm not. I promise."

"I asked you: would you make the same decision all over again to marry me and have this life?" she said, turning her hands up to gesture their home around her.

I pondered for a moment, as I did every time a serious answer was required of me. What I said right now would likely make or break their relationship. A lot had been confessed tonight and I could tell that she was looking for a reason to stay or a reason to leave. At this point in my existence, I had nothing to gain by answering in a way that would defame Christian and tear them apart. Deciding not to over-think my answer, I opened my mouth and let my life-long good sense do the speaking.

"At times, I thought my life would turn out differently but when it's just you and me and Samantha hanging out and enjoying each other's company, I know I wouldn't want my life to be any other way."

I could tell by the grin on her face that what I said was what she had hoped to hear. She leaned in and gave me a heartfelt hug.

"Thank you. I've been wondering that for a long time."

"I'm glad I got some things cleared up tonight too," I replied.

"How do you feel about that stuff anyway?" she asked, pulling back from the hug and looking at me face to face.

"Well," I chose my words carefully so that they would be believable coming from Christian; "it was quite a shock."

Sara pursed her lips and nodded her head.

"But, I think I'm at peace with what you told me." My words were genuine and seemed to resolve the conversation satisfactorily for Sara.

"If you ever need to talk about it again, I am up for it," she offered.

I reached for her hand and entwined it with mine.

"I may take you up on that someday," I said.

It was surreal to think that years down the road she might be having a continuation of this conversation with the real Christian; hopefully what I said would be stored in his memory bank.

"I'm gonna go check on Samantha. She's been in there alone for a while and it's awfully quiet," Sara said, giving my hand a squeeze as she headed out of the room.

"I'll be right there."

Before I followed her out of the kitchen, I made good on my earlier promise to clear the table. Carefully, I placed the glasses on the top rack of the dishwasher, wiped down the pizza stone, and disposed of the paper goods in the trash. I hadn't really had a chance to eat anything because dinner had been cut short so I nibbled the leftovers as I worked. The pizza tasted delicious; the dough was infused with a zesty Italian flavoring and the crust had a delightful crisp to it. Sara obviously had a knack for cooking. I lamented over the many delicious meals she cooked that I would never be able to taste.

I finished sweeping up the last of the crumbs and took a seat. The eyes of the peonies stared back at me from their bountiful covering. A few of the stalks had bent from the pressure of holding up the heavy blooms, but even that didn't affect their loveliness. I couldn't help but thinking that they would be lonely in here all night without anyone to admire them. So, I picked up the vase and walked them into the bedroom. I peeked at Samantha and Sara as I slipped by the living room. Both were cuddled on the couch, Samantha's head in her mommy's lap. They didn't notice me. I walked across the bedroom floor where laundry lay strewn from this morning's confusion. I cleared a spot on Sara's nightstand and carefully placed the flowers there, picking up the laundry as I passed, throwing it into the wicker basket in the corner. Having completed my mission, I walked back into the living room. Samantha was rubbing her eyes are Sara stroked her hair.

"Bedtime soon," Sara whispered to me, gesturing down at Samantha.

I nodded.

"But, I can watch the rest of my movie, right?" Samantha questioned, looking up at her mother for approval. Obviously the whispering had been in vain.

"Yes, you can," Sara confirmed. "You don't have to though if you are too tired."

"I'm not too tired."

"I can see that," Sara said with a grin.

"Do you mind if I cuddle up too?" I asked, flicking off the overhead light and taking a seat on the couch.

Samantha's eyes stayed glued to the screen as she shook her head left to right to indicate that she didn't mind if I joined them. From her lack of verbal response, I could tell that she didn't want any more interruptions to her movie.

I took a spot on the end of the couch, opposite Sara, squishing Samantha between us. The cushion gave way comfortably underneath me which provided ample space for my broad legs. Draped behind me was a soft, navy-blue blanket. Though none of us appeared to be the least bit chilly, I pulled it down and spread the fuzzy fabric across our legs. I enjoyed the sense of security that the weight of a blanket provided, especially at night. Samantha immediately pulled it up to her chin and Sara smoothed the trim out around her, tucking an end up under one arm as she settled deeper into the couch.

Staring at the pair next to me on the couch and hearing the familiar dialogue of the children's musical in the background, I felt a wave of complete serenity wash over me. Any thoughts of the past and future left my mind; I was totally engrossed in the moment. In fact, I never wanted the movie to end, but eventually the final refrain of "Let's Go Fly a Kite" was over and we were faced with a blank screen.

"Bedtime," Sara said to a yawning Samantha.

"I'll take you," I said, reaching out my hands for her to climb into my arms.

She complied, and I carried her into the bedroom that I had seen her exit from this morning. The walls were cotton candy pink and a Pegasus poster hung on one wall. I was surprised to see a bunk bed standing in the corner of the room. Usually they were reserved for households with two children, I figured Samantha must have broken her parents down with an ample amount of begging to get this one. I lifted her sleeping body onto the top bunk with barely any effort; it was most likely many years of paddling canoes and kayaks that had developed these arm muscles I now possessed into exquisite shape.

"Good night sweet girl, it has been my wonderful pleasure to know you, even if it was only for a day," I whispered into the sleeping child's ear.

Kissing her forehead, I carefully pulled the covers up over her body. I slipped out of the room, closing the door behind me. Sara was standing in the hall waiting for a report, obviously used to being the one in control of the bedtime routine.

"Is she asleep?"

"She was out before I even put her down."

"So, I guess she's sleeping in her leotard then," Sara said.

"I guess so, I didn't want to wake her to change it."

"No, of course not. I just hope she's comfortable enough to sleep through the night," Sara said, with a hint of worry.

"I'm sure she'll be fine, she was already in a deep sleep," I assured.

Sara nodded in agreement.

"Plus, she got plenty of fresh air today," I added.

"That's for sure," Sara said. "To tell you the truth, I'm just as exhausted as she was; I think I'm going to bed early. Don't stay up too late hon, ok?" she said, giving me a quick kiss on the lips.

"Stay up late doing what? I'm going to bed with you," I said. I wanted every moment with Sara, even if that meant just lying in bed next to her for my final hours on Earth.

"You never come to bed this early. I figured you'd be up for at least another three hours," Sara said surprised.

"I guess the day wore me out too," I replied, though I didn't have a fatigued bone in my body.

"Can you lock up then while I clear the dishes?" she asked.

"Dishes are already done."

"They are?"

"Yup," I said, shaking my head affirmatively. "Remember I told you I would take care of it?"

"I know you *said* you would but I didn't know you were really gonna do it."

"The table is cleaned up too and everything is put away nice and neat," I bragged. "There's nothing left for you to do but go to bed."

"Well, well, look who's the superstar today. You certainly have turned a new leaf."

"Just don't expect it all the time," I said.

"Ah! I knew it was too good to be true," she said, snapping her fingers. "But, I guess I can't complain; one day of bliss is better than none."

She turned and walked into the bedroom. I let out a heavy sigh.

"I suppose it is," I said to myself.

CHAPTER 21

The house already felt familiar, and I walked alone through the rooms with ease, securing the locks on the doors and windows. As I neared the back of the house, I came upon a room I hadn't seen before. I peeked in and noticed puzzles, books, and games stacked neatly around the room. I figured this must be a sitting room, used mostly for reading. I took a few steps in and scanned the walls which were decorated with reproduction prints and amateur paintings. The wallpaper was a feminine floral print and jar candles were scattered along the shelves which told me that Sara probably used this room the most. In the corner a straight-backed chair with well-worn padding sat next to the bookcase. I was about to leave, when a black-framed photograph on the side table next to the chair caught my eye.

Peering up at me from within the frame were the three most familiar people in the world: Christian, Sara, and me. Christian was in his high school cap and gown, I was in a button down shirt and Sara stood between us. Someone must have snapped the picture unexpectedly because the scene looked clumsily thrown together. Our arms hung haphazardly around each other's shoulders; Christian was caught in a half-smile; Sara had an over-exaggerated, wide, toothy grin; and there I was: staring at Sara. Even now, seeing the evidence in front of me, I couldn't remember the moment this photo was taken or even *who* had taken it. I wondered why Sara had chosen this sloppily posed photo to prominently display all these years later.

I sat down in the chair and picked up the photo to examine it more closely. The glass on the frame was smudged by fingerprints; a clue that suggested someone looked at it often. I imagined Sara sitting here in the chair, reaching for the photo, examining our expressions, and perhaps pondering what might have been.

The four-paned window behind me reflected the last bits of color that were leaving the sky as the sun dipped below the horizon and the moon took control of the hemisphere. I became aware that time was continuing to pass while I sat here. I set the picture back in its place and glanced one more time at the smiling faces captured in time before I left the room.

Sara was sitting up in bed when I returned. In an odd sense, I was glad that she was already changed and in her pajamas. That's not to say that I didn't want to be with her intimately, but considering the circumstances, I felt like watching her undress would be an invasion of privacy. After all, she was under the assumption that her husband was in the room with her, not a man who had never seen her naked before.

"Whatchya watching?" I asked motioning my head at the small television set across from us.

"Just flicking through the channels. You can have it if you want," she said, offering the remote to me.

"No thanks."

"Come on in, the bed feels extra comfy tonight," she said, patting the blanket next to her. "And by the way, don't think I didn't notice that all the clothes are picked up and my beautiful flowers mysteriously followed me into the bedroom."

"Must have been the fairies," I said, smiling as I took a seat on the edge of the bed.

The night was warm and my body felt unusually burdened by the clothes I wore. Everything about having a body again felt constricting. I removed my shirt first, then my shorts. My modesty wouldn't allow me to remove my boxers. I settled in next to Sara, pulling the sheet up over my exposed body parts.

"You know, there's nothing sexier than a man who does housework," she said, smirking. Her eyes were seductive, trying to lure me in.

My face felt like it was on fire as an internal heat wave rushed over me. I grabbed the back of my neck, pinching up the skin where sweat had begun to form. The magnetic pull was trying to draw my body close to hers. Like Jesus being tempted in the desert, I had an unquenchable thirst of desire and she was offering me the proverbial water.

I squeezed my eyes closed, trying to push back my thoughts and allow myself to succumb to the desires of this masculine body. But closing my eyes didn't make my conscience disappear. I knew that if I went through with this, I would always feel like I had taken advantage of her. I couldn't get past the fact that she thought I was her husband; she thought I was Christian. My head slumped in defeat. I looked up at her with a regretful grimace.

"As amazing as you look and as much as I love you, I'm gonna have to take a rain check tonight. My body is seriously beat." I gulped hard, trying not to choke on the words as I said them.

She stopped her advance abruptly and looked taken aback. I'm sure having offered herself to me and then being refused was a stab at her pride. A man refusing a woman sex didn't happen very often and was probably confusing and hurtful to any female.

"Oh," she said. "Anyway, it doesn't matter to me one way or the other, I just figured you'd be wanting it since it's been a while."

"I do. *Want it*, I mean. More than anything." I scrambled to find an excuse that wouldn't offend her. "It's just that, ya know, my back's been bothering me and I don't want to pull it."

"You don't have to explain. It's alright. It's not like I haven't turned *you* down before," she said, shuffling back to her side of the bed.

I was prepared to go into a lengthy explanation about my back and the delicacy of pulled muscles, but I decided not to press the issue any further. Besides, the more I thought on it the more frustrated I was becoming.

She turned back to the television, and after several seconds of clicking, settled on what appeared to be a rerun of a situational comedy. I kept glancing at her out of the corner of my eye, not sure if she was harboring sour grapes about the refusal. When she chuckled lightly along with the canned audience laughter of the television program, I sighed in relief and let my body relax into the bed. I kept one eye on her, paying no attention to the plot of the show, more interested in watching her laugh and fidget during commercials. After about thirty minutes, the show was over. She turned to me, and I expected her to say goodnight and turn off the light. What she said instead surprised me.

"Wanna talk?" she asked.

"I'd love to. What about?" I said, trying to contain my excitement.

"Nothing in particular." She clicked the television off. "I just thought it would be nice to catch up on life. With Samantha around we don't get to talk much about that stuff anymore."

"That's for sure," I said.

I had no point of reference on which to base that statement but I figured that having a small child at home and both parents working must create a strain on a romantic relationship. That was just one of the many things that I didn't know about the adult Sara and Christian. I wasn't sure how I was going to navigate through this conversation, but I figured as long as I directed the questions and nodded my head appropriately, I could get by.

"So, how's work?" I asked.

"Kinda slow, but then again, it's always slow this time of year. Not many people buying pellet stoves in this weather," she said, motioning outside.

That's what she does for work? "Sounds like fun," I lied.

"Ugh, yea, tons of fun. You want me to be honest?" I nodded my head.

"I can't stand it there anymore. The office politics are out of control. This one said this, and that one said that. 'Are the sales reports done yet? Where's my coffee? Don't open the window too much Sara, you know I get a chill'," she said, mimicking a bossy tone.

"Sounds awful."
I hoped that she knew I was being sincere and not mocking her.

"Tell me about it," she replied, much to my relief. "It's not exactly what I thought I'd be doing with my life, pushing papers and taking coffee orders."

"Then why do it? Why waste your time and effort on something that you don't want to do?"

"Uh, because it helps pay the bills and gives this family health insurance," she explained in a redundant tone. Then added, "Not everyone can do what they love for a living like you."

I guessed by the mood in her voice that she and Christian had probably talked about this before and that their previous conversation had frustrated her.

"Hey, no matter what I said in the past, I want you to know that I will back you up with whatever you want to do in life. Even if that means changing careers and being without health insurance for a little while. I want you to be as happy in your work as I am."

"You really mean that?" she asked after a short pause.

Thankfully, she appeared to be less irritated at me than she was a second ago.

"Yes, I really mean that. I don't think your time or talent should be wasted, especially the kind of talent that you have. If you don't like it there, I think you should just quit. Give them your notice this week and take some time to figure out what you want to do next."

A flush of exhilaration brushed over her face, but after a moment it changed to consternation.

"But how will we afford it? We'll have to use all of our savings just to survive," she said.

"Then we'll drain our savings. Oh well. Isn't that money there to use in case one of us is out of work? We'll just pretend you got laid off if that'll make you feel better about using it."

"Chris, if you are really, really serious about this I would love to start looking for something else. Maybe someplace where I can actually use my degree and work flexible hours so that I can be home with Samantha after school. Now *that* would be ideal."

"I most certainly am serious," I said looking her straight in the eyes.

I knew the real Christian may not agree tomorrow with what I was telling her tonight, but right now *I* was her husband and more than anything, I wanted her to live life to the fullest and be happy; even if it was without me.

"Ok. I'm gonna do it. I'm gonna do it! I'm really gonna do it!" She was giddy with excitement, almost hopping off bed. "Thank you for supporting me," she said.

I blushed as she wrapped her arms around me, giving me a tight, quick hug before bouncing back to her side of the bed.

"I think I'll wear my Nancy Sinatra boots to work tomorrow as I walk out the door."

"See, she *was* in there all this time after all."

"Who was in where?" Sara asked, looking around.

"My carefree, lighthearted Sara. She's still in there. She just needed a little prodding to come out."

She smiled; "I do feel like a weight has been lifted off my shoulders, that's for sure. Maybe you'll see more of that Sara now that I don't have to be a glorified secretary for a male chauvinist pig Monday through Friday."

"I'm just happy that you're happy."

"And what about you, are *you* happy?" she asked, poking me playfully in the chest.

"Right now, today, I am very happy." The answer passed my lips quickly and easily.

"I think from here on out we will *all* be a little happier," she said smiling.

"I hope so," I said, picking her hand up and gently cradling it in mine. "If there is ever a time when you are unhappy, please, tell me, so that we can work it out. Don't shut down on me."

"I guess that's something I tend to do isn't it?" she asked.

"It is, but then again, I haven't encouraged the sharing of emotions either."

"Well, you've got a point there," she said.

"I'm not one to deny my mistakes."

"Oh, yes, you are!" she said laughing as she spoke.

"Am not!" I whined.

"See there you go, denying again!"

She was rolling back and forth in laughter now, holding her stomach with one hand and pointing her finger at me with the other.

"Huh? OH! Crap! Ok, ok, so I'm a denier; if that is even a word."

"Oh honey, don't be so hard on yourself. At least you are a cute denier," she said, pinching my cheek.

As her laughter subsided, she pushed herself backward against the headboard, resting her head on the mauve tufted upholstery.

"I think I've made my point," she said, crossing her arms satisfactorily.

"I have a funny feeling there's more points about me you could make."

"Per-haps," she said. "But those points can be made a different day. I am much too tired to get into all *that* right now."

"You mean years of pent up aggression can't be solved at eleven o'clock at night?" I asked.

"Eleven? Oh God, is it that time already? I don't think we've talked this long since we were dating. I've got to get to bed, Samantha will be up early and that's means *I* will be up early."

My first instinct was to offer to get up in the morning so that Sara could sleep in, but then I remembered that I wouldn't be here to follow through with that. Suddenly I felt an impending doom. The night seemed to be ending just as quickly as the day had begun. I wasn't one hundred percent sure if this gift of a day would end at midnight or when I laid my head on the pillow and closed my eyes. All I knew was that I was still here and I wanted every minute with her that I could possibly have.

"Aw, let's stay up until midnight like we used to, *p.k.*," I coaxed.

"P.K.?"

"Pre-Kid."

"Of course, what else could it have been," she said as if it were a revelation. "Aren't you tired yet though?"

Truthfully, I sensed a heaviness pressing on my eyelids, but my mind was so electrified by being here with her that it overrode all my other bodily senses.

"Nah, not me. So, you gonna do it with me? Stay up I mean," I said, clarifying the question.

"Hmm, what's in it for me?" she asked.

I had to think quickly on my toes to persuade her.

"You can take another sick day tomorrow and have the whole day to yourself to relax," I said, pleased with my answer.

"Done," she replied without hesitation.

She held out her hand to seal the deal with a handshake, I returned it with a firm, business-like grasp and we shook to make it official.

"So, what now? You'd better keep me entertained or I'm gonna fall asleep sitting here," she said.

My eyes scanned the horizon above Sara's head while I searched my memory, both mine *and* Christian's, trying to recall a game that might keep her engaged.

"Ok, truth or dare?" I asked, falling back on an old standby.

"*Truth or dare?* Oh God, I haven't played this since my sleepover days in high school," she sighed nostalgically. "Since we've already had a lot of truth today, I will go with, dare."

I hadn't expected that response, in all the times I remembered playing this game, only a small percent of people had chosen dare, presumably because they were more willing to risk physical than emotional humiliation.

"Ok," I said. "I dare you to kiss me with your eyes closed the entire time from start to finish."

Since our first kiss earlier in the day, I had been trying to get another, but this time I didn't want her to be looking at the face of Christian while she did so, and closing her eyes was the only way I could think of for her to have the experience fully with only me.

"How will I know where your lips are?"

"You'll just have to feel your way around," I said, leaning in her direction.

"You can't just stare at me like that! I'll feel weird."

"I'll close mine too," I said, squeezing my eyes shut.

"Alright, here I come," she said.

Even though I couldn't see her, I could sense her face approaching.

"A little closer," I encouraged.

Her lips smashed clumsily into mine. I flicked my eyes open, thinking that she was going to pull away, but she continued to press harder into the kiss. I could feel every crevice of her soft, naked lips as they opened slowly and exhaled a breath of hot air into my mouth. She moved her body in closer, fumbling her hands along the comforter as she went. The weight of her body fell against my chest as she sank further into the bed, kissing me sloppily while she got her bearings. I leaned in too, feeling the passion rising as our bodies drew near to one another. I could feel the intensity of the kiss escalating and I didn't know if I had the will power to refuse a physical encounter with her a second time.

We rolled around a bit and landed, lips still locked, near the end of the bed. I felt her break contact for a brief second as she fumbled with something. I peeked, opening one eye, to find her peeling off her top and tossing it to the side. She returned to kissing, harder and faster now, grabbing at the hair on the back of my head. Contrary to my best intentions, I lifted my hands and began caressing the soft skin of her back from top to bottom. I noticed the contrast of the calloused, rough skin of my hands against the satiny smoothness of her torso. Opening my eyes fully, I gently guided her backwards, laying her down atop the strewn sheets and comforter.

My body was now positioned directly over hers. I dropped down on my elbows and pushed aside the hair that was covering her face. With eyes still closed, she smiled sweetly in appreciation and gave the slightest nod which seemed to indicate I had permission to proceed as I wished. My veins pumped hard and heavy, filled with a surge of adrenaline. I reached down to slide off her pants and as I did, my eye caught a glimpse of the full length mirror standing in the corner. She must have flipped it back over when she came in to change for the night.

In the reflection I saw an amorous, attractive husband and wife about to make love. My heart sank, dropping to my stomach, as I realized that I was not part of the reflection in the mirror: Sara and Christian were. I sighed and diverted my head, trying to block out the image I had just seen.

"Damn it," I said, first silently, then out loud.

"What is it?!" Sara said with bewilderment as she sat up. My frustration at my conscience was at a boiling point and I clenched my teeth hard until the pressure in my head made me wince.

"My back. I think it just went out," I grudgingly lied.

"Are you ok?" she asked concerned.

I could feel my anger choking me to the point that the reply got stuck in my throat. I could only bring myself to shake my head.

"No? Can you move?" she asked with added concern.

I shrugged my shoulders tersely.

"You'd better lay down then."

She helped lower me to my back, grabbing pillows and fluffing them to support my neck.

"Here, I'll put this one at your legs. Does that feel comfortable under your knees?" she asked.

I nodded.

"Are you gonna be alright? You look miserable. I knew I shouldn't have pushed you. You already told me that your back hurt. I can get you an ibuprofen," she offered.

"I'm just frustrated."

"Let me tell ya, you're not the only one," she said with a slight laugh. "And this," she swirled her pointer finger between our bodies, "is to be continued when you feel better. Hopefully a good night's rest will do the trick. If not, I give you permission to call out tomorrow too," she said smiling.

To be continued alright, but I'll miss the ending, I thought.

"Love you," she said, patting me on the arm.

"I love you too."

I reached up and cupped her face in my hands before giving her a soft, sweet kiss on the mouth.

"I must say that when I woke up today I had no idea I would be married to the person I always hoped to be," she said with more irony than she knew.

I felt my eyes fill to the brim with tears and they pushed against my lashes. I strained to see her through my watery lenses. I didn't want the last image of her angelic face to be blurred, so I let the tears spill out. I wiped them away quickly before they were noticed.

"Sara, I'm glad you had a good day because honestly, it was the best day of my entire life. I wish it didn't have to end."

"Me too, but unfortunately I am so beyond tired that I don't think I can stay awake another minute," she said through a yawn as she crawled back to her side of the bed.

She sunk her head heavily into the pillow and pulled the covers up until her face was half-covered.

"Goodnight," she mumbled.

"Goodnight," I whispered.

I felt time running out. I knew there was more I wanted to tell her, but I was so overwhelmed with the circumstance of being with her and having to leave again, that I couldn't think of a single thing to say. Rolling onto my side, I propped up on one elbow so that I could catch a few last glimpses of her as she slept. A wave of physical exhaustion swept over me as I watched her peaceful slumber. Gravity began tugging heavily at my lids. I bulged my eyes to keep them open and my face twitched in defiance. My chest rose and fell heavily with each long, methodic breath I took. I realized this was the end. I could feel my impending second-death creeping into this body and every cell fought the finality of what I knew would be upon me any minute when my eyes closed.

"Sara?" I tried to wake her with my gentle voice but got no response. "This is probably my last chance to tell you, so I hope you can hear this. I'm not sure yet what purpose this past life served us, all I know is that I wasted the time I had here trying to make everyone else happy and I made myself miserable. But this isn't our only chance. Since the beginning of time, we were meant to be together, a pair, incomplete without the other. We can have happiness again. Just please, don't forget me, think of me every day. Remember me so that you can come back to me."

I slipped my arm beneath me and lay face to face with her. I heard her rustling slowly as if she were about to wake up but my eyes defied me. They drew closed like the curtains on the final act of an extended play, until only darkness stared back at me.

"SAM?!" I heard her shriek.

But I couldn't respond. Once again, it was too late. I had slipped into another space away from her. I was gone and this time I wasn't coming back.

CHAPTER 22

I glared blankly into the all-encompassing blackness until a soft, white light appeared in my field of vision. The orb moved toward me, multiplying into hundreds of tiny balls of brightness, until the darkness had completely vanished, swallowed up by the pixels of light.

"She said my name."

"Yes, she did," said a voice in a resounding boom.

"How is that possible?"

"It is like *Namaste*. The soul in me recognizes the soul in you. Sara was beginning to sleep and enter the dream realm, where all people are closer to Me and spirit," the Creator explained.

"Closer to You how?"

"During sleep, the body's physical needs and all external stimuli are diminished, therefore making it easier for your brain to tap into the bits of Me that flow through the Universe creating energy. This is why you are able to produce elaborate mini-movies or dreams as you call them, in your mind every night. What she had known subconsciously all day: that you were in Christian's body, she dismissed as foolishness, but this thought became plausible to her when she crossed over into the ethereal state of sleep."

"So, this day *was* real, every minute of it, and she did recognize me."

"Yes," the Creator confirmed.

"I want to go back."

"As we mentioned before, there is a random selection to the reincarnation process and it may not play to your advantage."

"No, not like that. I want to go back exactly like I was, in Christian's body."

"My dear Sam, that is impossible."

"I thought nothing was impossible with God," I pointed out.

"One thing is, and that is to take away the free will of an intelligent Being whom I created. There is an iron lock around each individual man's autonomy to which I never made a key. What you are asking me to do would require essentially ending Christian's human experience."

"But, didn't you already manipulate Christian's free will by allowing me inside his body?"

"No. I had permission from Christian to do what I did."

"How?" I asked in wonder.

"The night you entered Christian's body, I approached him while he was in the dream realm. I explained that you were here with Me on this side of reality, and that, with his help, I would like to give you a gift; that all he would have to do is remain in the dream realm with Me a little longer than usual. He agreed immediately. He was actually quite sad about all the suffering you had endured in the body and was eager to help."

"He was?"

The Creator nodded happily.

"What did you do? Erase his memory when he woke up?"

"No," the Creator replied with a chuckle; "that too would interfere with free will. Christian doesn't remember his dreams once he is awake, but even if he did, in the physical he would most likely dismiss it as the musings of sleep. What happens is, his brain will have the memories of your day with his family but he will simply take them on as his own experiences."

"Please tell me, is there any way, any way *at all*, for me to be with her like I just was?" I implored.

"None that would allow you to be together in the way that you wish - no."

"Then what do I do now?" I asked, heavy with the weight of disappointment.

"Come with Me and wait."

The light orbs came together in the form of a luminescent woman with mesmerizing features whose glossy blue wings seemed an extension of her arms.

"You're beautiful, like a virtuous butterfly," I said in awe.

"What you are seeing Me as is just another reflection of Love. Now come, unburden yourself, and rest in my presence a while."

"But, I can't rest. I feel as though there's nothing good for me here without her."

"On the contrary, if you try, you will find that waiting for her *here* is infinitely easier than going back and searching for her on Earth."

The Creator turned her wing and the landscape before us changed into a green, lush, rolling hillside. Dotting the hills were undersized but sturdy looking wooden doors carved into the rocky ledges. I could see every detail of the speckled dirt perfectly; not a spot of grass was bare, and the color rising from the ground was so vivid that it appeared to be lit by its own unique tint. I felt my life source ignite in me once again, as I had only felt when I was a child. The Creator smiled as she watched me absorb every element of the panorama before me.

"Why don't you explore what *this* realm has to offer? I promise, no sorrow lurks behind those doors, only enlightenment awaits you."

I gave in to the majesty and closed my eyes; rolling my head backward, I inhaled the freshness of the air. There were no pollutants to block the crisp smell of grass from pervading my senses. I felt an infusion of oxygen rush into my pores and settle in my Being which reinvigorated and calmed my mind. A slight breeze blew past, beckoning me toward the meadow.

"Is this another place I've created?" I asked.

"The places which you journey to here will always be a reflection of the way you imagine them to be. What you are seeing is the container you have created to hold My loving space. Beyond those doors are the places of your wildest imaginings that I have saturated with My life force which is healing, light, and love. Stay a while in there and all woes will disappear. It is a place of transition, shown to those who are having difficulty leaving the previous life behind."

"Why are there so many doors? How do I know which one goes to the place of transition?"

"They all go to the same transitional space. You imagined multiple doors to give yourself a choice. You'd rather choose your own way than be told where to go."

I stared for a long time at the Supreme Being in front of me who I now totally and implicitly understood to be God. I contemplated on space, time and existence without the limitations that I once had in body. I suddenly had a deep understanding that anything *was* possible. Being in the presence of the Divine had convinced me of that. I felt the sensation that in an instant, I could travel to any world I wished and experience anything I wanted to just by thinking it.

"You understand. You are ready," She said.
Suddenly, an invisible wind lifted the Creator's wings and She was floating above me.

"You see, without speaking, you have spoken. It is time for Me to fly away so that you can begin your next journey," She said.

I felt the delicate flutter of Her wing at my cheek and then She flittered away, disappearing into the fertile landscape ahead, as if She had always belonged there.

I fixated my gaze on the knotted door which was situated in the mid-line of my vision. I took four large steps in its direction then stopped briefly. I glanced back at what I was leaving behind. Back there was a vast emptiness of space which I knew would change into anything I wanted as soon as I imagined it. I noticed a woman standing at the far edge of the darkness, motionless, watching me.

"Hello?" I called out.

"Hello," her voice echoed.

"*Sara?*"

"Sara," she parroted back.

As I got closer, I could see the shape and features taking form into the woman I loved. She was just as she was the last time I saw her, before I had closed my eyes forever. I ran and embraced her.

"You're here?!" I exclaimed.

"You're here!" she said in reply.

I grabbed her waist, holding her at arm's length. She smiled back at me, not saying a word.

"I can't believe you are already here. You didn't die young, did you?" I asked sympathetically.

"Didn't die," she said.

"Didn't die? But how are you here?"

"How am I here?" she asked.

I stepped back in confusion and searched her eyes for an answer. For the first time, I saw that they were devoid of any emotion.

"You're not really her."

"Not really her," she said, without feeling.

"I'm just seeing you in my mind right now, like I did before. I'm imagining the way you are but I can't recreate your spark. I want you to be her, but you're not. It's not the same. I'm sorry. There's nothing to do but wait. I have to wait for you," I said and she faded into the darkness.

With renewed resolve, I turned to face the decision doors. I peeled off my imagined shoes and abandoned them on the edge of the grass, walking barefoot through the plush, thick blades. When I reached the nearest door, I placed my hand on the knob; it was squishy and molded easily to my grip. Exhaling a purposeful, deep breath, I felt the frustration, disappointment, sadness, and longing from the past leave my Being all at once. I swung the solid, wooden door open without resistance. Stepping forward over the threshold, I left the darkness behind and began my journey into the next unknown.

CHAPTER 23

The change in the atmosphere around me was the first sense I had about this new place. The exquisite blend of coolness and warmth, reminiscent of the mid-summer nights I spent camping sitting beside the fish pond, caressed my skin as I entered. The whole place was illuminated with a muted glow which didn't seem to originate from a sun or any identifiable source. The white flecks in the azure sky flickered like flames in a bonfire. I was able to look above, directly at them, without squinting.

As I continued walking, the red-trunk trees, which towered over me, bowed themselves inward to create an archway for my path. Their leaves were constantly changing colors from raincoat yellows, to blood reds, to ocean aqua, and many more exotic hues which I did not recognize as a part of Earth's color palette. A cascading wave of foliage followed me as I walked along.

The soft moss beneath my feet felt cushiony and cool. I paused to scrunch up my feet and feel the squishiness that the texture created. Something furry, which had the ears and tail of a bunny, and the height and face of a bear, lumbered slowly in front of me as I squeezed the dew between my toes. The adorable creature turned in my direction and visually examined me. The mouth opened into a smile and the bear-bunny continued on to the other side of the path where it met up with a small family of like-featured animals. I followed them a short distance off the path and through the dense woods.

My ears became attuned to the soft meanderings of a babbling brook. Almost as soon as I heard the moving water, I saw the sparkle from its gleam in a clearing past the woods. I ran to drink from the untouched waters, wanting to experience the refreshing feeling of the liquid on my tongue. When I got closer, I noticed that the water was translucent and seemingly had no bottom; it was so transparent that staring at it was like looking through spotless glass.

I knelt in the short, wet grass by the stream and scooped the crystal clear water into my cupped hands. I was surprised to find that it was tangible; it appeared to be made of silk. The temperature was slightly cool and I smiled as I drank it slowly. Every molecule of the water invigorated me with a wonderful tingling sensation as it passed through my Being. After consuming it I felt healthy and energized, more than I ever thought was possible.

Dangling my feet playfully in the brook, I watched as the water glided gracefully by me over rocks and around twigs. The occasional bubble broke the surface of the water, followed by the jump of a brightly colored orange and yellow fin-less fish; I marveled at the way it suspended in the air before returning to the water.

Off to my right, the bunny-bear animal had also found the stream and was lapping the water up daintily while intermittently removing berries from a fiercely red and perfectly round bush as if they were a delicacy. The steady lapping of the brook and the lovely melody of a miniature blackbird who sat perched on a nearby fallen log, were the only sounds I heard.

Everything moved in, around and through each other gracefully like trained dancers in a ballet. Not an inch of space was lifeless. The grass beneath me, the sky above me, the energy inside me, were all in a constant state of harmonized motion. I leaned back on my hands, closed my eyes and craned my neck backwards to bask in the warm glow of the atmosphere. I sat there for a long moment, frozen in time, feeling as though I were a part of everything.

"Has there ever been anything other this?" I wondered aloud, completely immersed in my surroundings.

"Yes." A voice answered me. The sweetest, softest, most familiar voice I had ever known to exist, had answered me.

"Sara?"

I looked around but saw no one. I wondered how, in this perfect place, I could let myself imagine her, knowing that it would only bring me sorrow. Suddenly, a gentle hand touched my shoulder. I turned around. Her twinkling eyes were the first thing I saw. She was here, seemingly unchanged from the Earthly appearance I knew, yet somehow infused with more brilliance, beauty and life than ever.

"It's you," I said in awe. "It's really *you*. You're here. You're real."

She nodded her head excitedly and smiled.

"I remembered," she said.

I pulled her close and held her tightly against me. She buried her face in my shoulder and rested it there. I rocked back and forth with her in my arms, until we both felt satisfied that neither was leaving again. I was thankful that measured space did not exist here. Time could not limit us in this microcosm of the universe.

"Let's sit a while. The grass looks so inviting," she said, patting the ground.

"As long as I'm next to you, I'll sit anywhere," I replied.

She snuggled her body against my chest and dipped her feet in the water as we looked up at the changing sky.

"How long have I've been here?" I asked.

"I'm not sure. Time feels fuzzy to me already. All I know is that I passed when I was eighty six years old."

"Wow, it felt like only a few moments since I last saw you," I said.

I contemplated this phenomenon, but even here, I still couldn't make sense of it.

"I tried everything I could to get back to you. I was lonely, even after I passed and I was afraid that you were too. Was it hard living all those years on Earth?" I asked.

"Yes. There was a looming sadness in my heart after you were gone that I was never able to shake. I think that's why I couldn't stay with Christian. He reminded me too much of you," she said.

"You left Christian? When? What became of him after you left?"

"Oh, he was a happy bachelor, living life his way until the very end, which came only a few years before me. Our separation was mutual, I think we both knew early on in life we weren't right for each other. The only real connection we had was you and then our daughter, until she passed too, then there was nothing left between us."

"Samantha passed before you? She must have been so young."

"She was. Mid-twenties. Joined the Peace Corps and never made it back from a foreign mission. A hurricane leveled the town she was in. After I lost my mom, I was confused. After I lost you, I was heartbroken. After I lost Samantha, I became numb. She was my third big sadness and incredibly, not my last."

"Sara, I'm so sorry. I wish I was there for you."

"Oh, I know none of that was in your control. It's funny, I remember the pain of those losses, but I don't feel it anymore. I think that is the beauty of this place, isn't it? No sadness," she said. "Don't you love that?"

"I do," I said, smiling.

"You haven't asked me about your parents or your brother."

"*My parents*, wow, I'm almost ashamed to say that I hadn't thought about them until now. And *my brother*, how could I have forgotten about him? I guess I was so wrapped up in getting you back to me that everyone else seemed un-important. What happened to them? Did you stay in touch?"

"I did. Here and there over the years I would run into them or hear things from Chris's mom about them. I actually became good friends with your brother. He started a scholarship in your honor. After you passed, your parents wanted details from me about your death. One of the hardest things I had to do was sit down with them and describe what happened that night. They were devastated. Your father had a lot of regrets. Actually, I don't think your mother ever really got over it. She refused to look at any pictures of you until the day she died; she said it hurt too much."

"I can understand that. Even though we didn't have the best relationship when I was growing up, I think I might have appreciated them more if I had been given the chance to be an adult and have my own family. I'm surprised I haven't seen them yet on this side. They must have died a while ago."

"Oh, you will when you're ready, or when they're ready, whichever comes first and we'll both see Christian too. I'm sure I'll see Samantha soon as well."

"You haven't seen Samantha yet?"

"How could I when I hadn't seen you? Without you, I am incomplete, I can do nothing. Don't you feel it now? Things are different. Things are right again."

"I do. For a while I wondered if I'd ever feel that again."

"Sam?"

"Yes."

"I have to ask you something."

"Anything," I replied.

"Did you ever really believe that I could forget you?"

I answered her with certainty; "No, I don't think I ever really did."

She smiled contentedly and rested deeper into my arms. I inhaled the scent of her hair which smelled like spring rain. Having her with me made this place feel like home. I felt a sudden compulsion to explain everything I had ever felt for her, but something inside told me that words weren't necessary anymore: she already knew. And I knew something too. I knew that she was the missing part of me. I knew that for the rest of eternity, no matter what we did; no matter where we went; no matter who we were; no matter how much space was between us - we would always come back to each other.

ABOUT THE AUTHOR

Rebecca Carenzo has had a love of reading and writing since a young age and can vaguely remember turning pages in the womb. Her favorite books are those that take you inside the mind of a character and make you forget who you are. She especially enjoys the Anne of Green Gables Series by Lucy Maud Montgomery and can often be heard talking to a tree or a flower as if it were a kindred spirit. She resides in Worcester, Massachusetts with her husband Nick, son Ryan, and a bipolar cat named Misty. This is her first novel.

Made in the USA
Charleston, SC
25 November 2013